CONQUERED BY THE BEAST

By

Desiree Acuna

Dark Fantasy Erotica

New Concepts   Georgia

Be sure to check out our website for the very best in fiction at fantastic prices!

When you visit our webpage, you can:
* Read excerpts of currently available books
* View cover art of upcoming books and current releases
* Find out more about the talented artists who capture the magic of the writer's imagination on the covers
* Order books from our backlist
* Find out the latest NCP and author news--including any upcoming book signings by your favorite NCP author
* Read author bios and reviews of our books
* Get NCP submission guidelines
* And so much more!

We offer a 20% discount on all new Trade Paperback releases ordered from our website!

Be sure to visit our webpage to find the best deals in e-books and paperbacks! To find out about our new releases as soon as they are available, please be sure to sign up for our newsletter (http://www.newconceptspublishing.com/newsletter.htm) or join our reader group (http://groups.yahoo.com/group/new_concepts_pub/join)!

The newsletter is available by double opt in only and our customer information is *never* shared!

Visit our webpage at:
www.newconceptspublishing.com

New Concepts Publishing, Inc.
5202 Humphreys Rd.
Lake Park, GA 31636

ISBN 1-58608-845-9
© 2006 Kimberly Zant
Cover art (c) copyright 2006 Jenny Dixon

NCP books are available at special quantity discounts for bulk purchases for sales promotions, premiums, fund raising, or educational use. For details, write, email, or phone New Concepts Publishing, Inc., 5202 Humphreys Rd., Lake Park, GA 31636; Ph. 229-257-0367, Fax 229-219-1097; orders@newconceptspublishing.com.

First NCP Trade Paperback Printing: September 2006

DEMON SEED

Chapter One

Brigit cried out as the carriage hit a particularly deep rut.

"What is it, sweetheart?" Lady Beauchamp asked anxiously.

"Probably yet another cramp," Colette said dryly without bothering to look up from the book that lay open on her lap.

Both women turned to give her censorious glances.

"I can not help it if I'm too delicate for such a frightful road," Brigit complained petulantly. "I am bruised and battered until I don't know how I will be able even to go to my coming out ball. How I would love to have your constitution."

"No you wouldn't," her elder sister disputed, "for then everyone would go about saying you were as healthy as a horse--and you far prefer to be likened to a delicate blossom--and you would not have mother cosseting you each time you moaned."

"I do not cosset her," Lady Beauchamp rebuked her eldest daughter. "You know how delicate and sickly she is. I am often amazed that she outlived her childhood."

"Me also. If I had physicked myself half so much I expect I would not have outlived *my* childhood."

Brigit's chin wobbled. "You are hateful, Colette! I did not even complain."

Colette rolled her eyes. "You have done nothing *but* complain since we left home. One would think to hear you that this disagreeable trip weren't entirely your idea. I have not complained, and I am just as miserable and have nothing to show for the misery I've endured other than a bruised posterior and a headache from listening to your incessant moans and groans."

"That will be quite enough!" Lady Beauchamp snapped. "If you are ill tempered that your own coming out went so poorly you have no one to blame but yourself. I saw no reason to buy you any new gowns when you have no interest in catching a husband, and none in attending any of the social functions I slave to put on to provide you girls with the opportunity to meet acceptable young men."

Marking her place in her book, Colette closed it and looked out the window of the coach at the forest. She supposed she should be ashamed for snapping at her younger sister. Brigit *was* fragile--mostly in her mind--but she at least looked delicate in face and form, as well, so she supposed her mother could be pardoned for her perception that Brigit needed to be assiduously pampered else she would fail to prosper.

She still resented the fact that her mother was always so swift to defend Brigit in every way. "We could take the forest road and carve a half a days ride from our journey. It is not so well traveled, either, and its bound to be in better shape."

"Absolutely not!" Lady Beauchamp exclaimed with a shudder. "The Vile Forest is a place of evil."

Colette glanced at her mother in surprise. "Surely you do not believe that? That is only old superstition. Besides, it is full daylight. We could cross through in no time at all and be well out of the wood before nightfall--and nearly home."

"Oh! I will be so grateful to be home again where I may sleep in my own bed!" Brigit exclaimed, looking at her mother hopefully.

Lady Beauchamp sent Colette an angry glance and patted Brigit. "I know, dear, and I am anxious, as well, but it would not be at all wise to take the road through the wood. It is far too dangerous."

"But--we have the outriders," Brigit complained. "And they are armed in case of brigands. Couldn't we please, Mother? I am so ill from riding in the carriage."

"You will be fine. We will be home before you know it."

Brigit's chin wobbled. Tears filled her lovely, pansy blue eyes. She sniffed, threatening the fit of hysterics she generally had when she didn't get her way. Lady

Beauchamp soothed her a little more frantically. "Now Brigit, you mustn't cry, dear. You know it makes your lovely face swell and redden and we are so very close to home now. You don't want to chance meeting up with any of your beaus with a red nose and swollen eyes, do you?"

"I don't care!" Brigit exclaimed petulantly, but the tears she'd called forth rolled down her cheeks and no more welled in her eyes.

Sighing, Lady Beauchamp rapped on the panel. The coachman slid it back. "Yes, my lady?"

"How near are we to the turn off through the Vile Forest?"

"About a mile, I'm thinking, my lady."

"Do you think we could make it through before dusk?"

"We can if I spring 'em, my lady."

Lady Beauchamp considered it for several moments and finally nodded. "Then do so, for I am heartily sick of the journey myself--just don't drive too fast."

"Very good, my lady," the coachman responded and closed the panel once more.

Brigit giggled and clapped her hands excitedly like a child that had been offered a special treat. "Oh thank you, Mother! I can not wait to get home and try on all the new gowns you bought for me. Which one do you think I should wear for my coming out?"

Rolling her eyes, Colette opened her book once more and began to read as her mother and younger sister began to discuss the merits of each and every dress. Her input was not necessary and probably would not be welcome even if she felt inclined to give it regarding which dress most set Brigit's delicate coloring to advantage, which was most flattering to her blue eyes, and which brought out the golden highlights of her hair.

To her mind, Brigit set all the dresses off to advantage, a subject that had already been thoroughly hashed when the style and fabric of the gowns had been ordered, agonized over when Brigit had taken her first fittings and cooed over by Brigit, her mother, and the seamstresses when they had done the final fittings.

She was fond of her younger sister. She truly was. It was only that she often felt as if some evil fairy had taken her from the home where she belonged and left her in Lady

Beauchamp's keeping instead of her own child. She was short, which her mother referred to as squat, sturdily built, which her mother called common, her skin was freckled in spite of everything her mother could do to remove the 'ugly spots', and her hair was red, which her mother called low. How she had ended up in a home with beautiful blonds, she hadn't a clue, but the difference was more than skin deep. She was bookish and retiring. She didn't especially care for social gatherings because she always felt like everyone was comparing her unfavorably to her younger, far more beautiful sister, and she always managed to say something her mother found 'unforgivably rude'.

And the worst of it was that she had not managed to capture the interest of even one potential suitor when she'd had her come out the year before and she would probably remain a spinster in her mother's home for the rest of her natural life.

She found that prospect deeply depressing. The only thing more disturbing was the idea of marrying only to escape being a spinster and at her mother's mercy, for she had not met a single man whom she had more than a mild interest in.

Secretly, she had always dreamed of falling desperately, passionately in love. She did not know from whence the dream had sprung, for she knew of no one in their circle who felt passion for their spouse at all. Most could barely tolerate one another. They saved their passion for their lovers--and their love for themselves.

Her mother would have fainted if she had ever had the nerve to voice that wish, however, and so she kept it to herself, pretending she had no real interest in marrying at all.

Sighing, she closed her book again as the carriage slowed for the turn into the Vile Forest, feeling a welling of anticipation. Not that she believed the silly superstition that kept most folk from traveling the forest road, but she was anxious to get home to her books, her needle work, and the garden she loved--and equally anxious to escape the confinement of the coach, her mother, and her younger sister.

Oddly enough since she didn't consider herself the least bit superstitious, she felt a cool chill wash over her as the coachman turned upon the road that led through the Vile Forest and began to pick up speed again as he straightened the coach upon the road's hard, cracked surface. She dismissed it, certain that it was only the tales themselves that made the hair creep along her neck, or possibly the fact that the road was instantly cast in shadow by the tall trees that seemed to loom over the road, their branches interlocking overhead to form a dense canopy that blocked out the much of the sunlight.

It occurred to Colette to wonder how the tales about the Vile Forest had come about when supposedly those who had encountered the Demon Lord of Sinister Abbey were never seen or heard from again. Had they simply vanished, the victims of wild beasts, or robbers, and the tales grew out of their disappearance?

It seemed possible. The forest lent itself to frightening tales. Beyond the road one could see nothing but twisted, gnarled trees and tangles of thick underbrush and vines. One could easily imagine all sorts of things peering from that tangle, watching. If one happened to be caught upon the road after dark, or in the gloom of a storm ....

She shivered at the thought, watching as the daylight dimmed and a fat droplet of water splattered against the window embrasure. Almost simultaneously, something close at hand shattered with a sharp crack, the coach lurched, tilting and bouncing to a stop so suddenly that Colette was thrown from her seat, landing almost on top of Lady Beauchamp, who had been thrown across Brigit.

Brigit screamed like a banshee, ear splittingly. The sound was cut off abruptly as first Lady Beauchamp and then Colette were pitched on top of her. Colette struggled for a moment and finally managed to lever herself off of Lady Beauchamp. The coach was still tilted, however, and dipping toward the ground at the rear. With an effort, Colette grasped the window embrasure on that side of the coach and hauled herself toward it.

Outside, mayhem reigned. The coachman lay in the road groaning. The horses, screaming and rearing, were fighting the outriders, who were trying to calm them and untangle the traces.

Both Lady Beauchamp and Brigit had yielded to hysterics. After glancing at them and seeing they were more shaken than hurt, Colette fought the door latch and finally managed to get it open, half falling, half climbing from the tilted coach. Once she had picked herself up and dusted herself off, she saw immediately that it was just as she'd suspected. One of the rear wheels had come off.

The coachman was still groaning. When Colette knelt to examine him, she saw that he had injured both an arm and a leg when he'd been pitched from his perch. She knew nothing about medicine, but it seemed very probable that both were broken. He needed a physician. She was certain of that much.

Seeing that the two outriders had finally managed to calm the team of horses down, she summoned one to have a look at the wheel. It began to rain hard as they trudged back along the road to examine it. Despite the thick canopy overhead Colette was drenched to the skin within a very few minutes. Her soaked hair, already straggling from its pins from the accident, fell around her. Her skirts quickly became so heavy with water that it was a struggle to move.

The wheel, they found, was not broken, but the outrider was still doubtful that they could reattach it to the coach and travel in safety if they could do it at all with only two men to lift the coach and position the wheel.

Nodding, Colette went back to the coach to discuss the situation with her mother.

Lady Beauchamp had collected herself sufficiently to realize that hysterics were useless when there was no one around to play to. The same could not be said for Brigit, unfortunately, though she'd quieted somewhat.

"The wheel has broken off," Colette told her mother. "And John Coachman is badly injured. He needs a doctor. William says he doesn't think that he and Robert can fix the wheel by themselves."

Lady Beauchamp merely blinked at Colette blankly.

"Oh! What are we to do?" Brigit wailed. "We can't stay here. Mother, tell her we can't stay here! I'll be dark soon and the demon will come after us! It's all her fault! If she hadn't insisted we come this way, we wouldn't be in this mess now!"

Colette glared at her sister, before she could think of anything to say in her defense, her mother seconded her sister's accusation. "Just look at the fix you've gotten us in to! What are we to do now? For I tell you, I will not be in this evil place come nightfall!"

Colette gaped at her mother, stunned. It sank in slowly that her mother was going to be as useless as her sister for neither of them could think of anything beyond flinging accusations and recriminations. Her jaw set. "Get out of the coach, both of you."

This time it was Brigit and Lady Beauchamp who gaped at her. "Are you out of your mind? It's raining. We'll be soaked to the skin and I will catch my death of cold. I know it," Brigit shrieked.

"How dare you speak to me in that tone, young lady!" Lady Beauchamp snapped at almost the same time.

Colette blushed at her mother's rebuke, but stood her ground. "We have only two choices that I can see. We can unhitch the team and ride them out of the forest. Or we can stay here and send someone for help. If we stay, it could be well into the night before help returns. If we ride the horses, we can send someone back to take care of John Coachman."

Brigit and Lady Beauchamp looked at each other in silent communication. Abruptly, Lady Beauchamp began to struggle toward the door.

"Mother!" Brigit complained. "I will be ill if I must travel through this rain and there are no saddles for the horses. How are we to stay on them?"

"Come, Brigit," Lady Beauchamp said sharply. "We will get you home and into bed in a thrice and you will be perfectly fine. We can not linger here."

Brigit's chin wobbled threateningly.

Seeing they meant to comply with her suggestion, Colette left Brigit to her mother's care and called William over to unhitch the team from the carriage. When they had done so and had led the horses off to the edge of the road and tied them, William and Robert lifted John Coachman and helped him into the tilted carriage to get him out of the rain.

Lady Beauchamp was not happy about it, standing over the men and directing them to place him on the floor of the coach so that he wouldn't ruin the seats with blood and mud. As embarrassed as she was by her mother's callous behavior, Colette couldn't think the coachman would be a good deal more comfortable on the narrow seats. Instead, she directed them to take the pillows from the seats and tuck them under the man's head and his injuries to make him as comfortable as possible.

"You must stay with him, William, and look after him the best you can until we can send help."

"He must certainly will *not!*" Lady Beauchamp snapped in outrage. "We will have need of him for protection."

"We will have Robert," Colette pointed out. "He is armed. He should be able to protect us well enough if we need protection--which I can not think that we will. Someone needs to stay with John. He is too hurt to be left alone."

"If we go now we should have help for him in no time," Lady Beauchamp said dismissively. "I won't hear another word about it."

Colette stared at her mother in dismay. "I will stay with him then."

"You'll do no such thing! He will be in no danger--without you. Suppose someone came along? They are far more likely to take an interest in you than a mere coachman. If you stay, he will be obliged to try and protect you."

Colette still didn't like it and she couldn't see that there was any great possibility that anyone would come along. They had seen no one on the road since they had turned upon it because most folk avoided the road through the wood. She didn't quite dare to defy her mother, however, and since there seemed no hope for it, she thought it best not to waste time arguing a battle she wasn't likely to win. While Robert helped her mother and sister to mount the carriage horses, she and William rounded up what they could to see to John's comfort, placing food and water near enough he could reach them.

She wasn't certain he even attended her promise to send help back for him as quickly as possible, for he was in too much pain to do much more than moan piteously, but she did her best to offer what comfort she could.

The rain, which had eased somewhat as they struggled back and forth between the carriage and the horses, became a deluge as they at last got underway.

Chapter Two

A gloom settled beneath the canopy of forest with the advent of the storm that leached the light from the day and made the mid-afternoon seem more like dusk. They had been riding for perhaps an hour when the rain finally slackened from a downpour to a light sprinkling rain. Almost the moment it did so, a mist began to rise up from the road and forest that curled and twisted sinuously as the mounted riders stirred it in their passing.

Colette, bringing up the rear, could barely see Robert, who had taken the lead, although she knew he was barely a full length in front of her mother. The mist seemed to collect around him as he cut a swath through it, so that he faded in and out of view. She had just urged her mount forward, trying to come alongside her sister, when Brigit's horse abruptly veered to her right. Thinking at first that the horse had merely swerved to the side for her own mount, it was several moments before Colette realized with surprise and a touch of alarm that the horse had cut off the main road onto a narrow trail leading into the deep woods.

"Hold up! Brigit, turn your horse. You're going the wrong way!"

Her voice seemed to be swallowed and muffled by the thick bank of fog. Brigit's voice came back to her, but it was indistinct and Colette didn't catch the words. She saw though that Brigit didn't slow or turn the horse.

A moment later, Lady Beauchamp's mount veered sharply, almost unseating her as it whirled to follow the horse Brigit was riding. Despite the poor visibility, Colette was close enough that she could see her mother was struggling with the horse.

"Robert! William! Help!" Colette called, pulling back on her make-shift reins to follow her mother and sister and then urging the horse to move faster to catch up to them.

The fog was far thicker along the narrow two rut lane they had turned upon and within moments both Lady Beauchamp and Brigit had completely disappeared from sight. Colette's surprise and mild concern gave way to anxiety that deepened rapidly when she realized she wasn't gaining on either of the other riders.

"Mother! Brigit! Stop!" she called out, ignoring the limited visibility and urging her horse faster.

Somewhere ahead of her, she heard the scream of horses. Brigit's terrified high pitched screams cut across the mingling sounds of her mother's cries and the horses' whinnies of alarm and distress.

The sounds cut through Colette like knives, driving her own anxiety into full fledged terror. Instinctively, she pulled back on the reins, trying to slow her horse, her first thought that the two horses had slammed into each other in the fog and her mother and sister had been thrown. The horse ignored her, barreling into the thick fog in mindless panic.

Abruptly, something huge and back against the dark fog parted the mist before them as it landed in the middle of the road. Colette screamed almost simultaneously with the horse as the horse came to a sudden, skidding, rearing halt. The horse's antics tore the reins from Colette's grasp and she felt herself tumbling backwards. The ground seemed to rise up to meet her, slamming into her so hard it punched the breath from her lungs. Stunned, she curled into a ball instinctively to protect herself from the horse, covering her head. Even as she did so, large fingers curled into her upper arm, jerking her to her feet.

"I am Nuri, lord of these lands," he said in a low growl that seemed to vibrate from deep in his massive chest like the ominous rumbling of distant thunder. "And those who trespass upon my domain are violated."

Still too stunned and shaken from her fall to allow room for any sort of emotions, Colette tried to pierce the gloom and the tangle of hair straggling over her face to look up at the man who held her. A hazy impression of sharp, angular features filtered into her dazed mind, but one glimpse at the curling horns that grew out of his head and the leathery, spiked wings behind him wiped everything else from her mind.

An internal darkness gathered around her mind. She struggled against it, trying to keep her feet under her as he hauled her through the disorienting fog. A monstrous black

horse appeared before them. Catching her around the waist,
he swung her onto the beast's back as if she weighed no
more than a feather and then leapt up behind her, curling an
arm tightly around her. Weak and dizzy, still fighting the
blackness that threatened to claim her, Colette slumped
limply against the hard wall of chest behind her, looking
around vaguely for her mother and sister. The writhing,
restless mist unveiled two other horses much like the one
she was mounted upon. Her mother was upon one, Brigit
upon the other, both limp, both captive of misshapen
creatures that barely bore resemblance to anything human
beyond two arms, two legs and a massive, grotesquely
malformed head.

Like the drifting mist, darkness wove in and around her as
the beast who held her kneed his mount, commanding the
steed into a gallop that might have unnerved her if she
hadn't been too dazed to consider the possibility of the
horse losing its way in the fog and crashing into a tree.

Awareness surfaced after a time as Colette lifted her head
and saw the towers and twisted spires of Sinister Abbey
through the mist before them. Darkness lay upon most of
the sprawling structure so that the windows looked like
eyeless sockets staring down at them. Flickering red and
gold light poured through the cavernous door in the center
of the great hulk, like the yawning maw of hell, but even
that failed to penetrate Colette's shock enough to rouse her
from her semi-stupor.

Drawing his mount to a halt before the wide entrance, the
demon dismounted. Deprived abruptly of her support,
Colette struggled to rouse herself and failed, sliding into
darkness even as she felt herself slipping from the horse.

With awareness came the sound of weeping, though
Colette didn't instantly recognize what seemed distant,
distorted voices. Light flickering against her closed lids
roused her awareness further and Colette struggled to open
her eyes. She stared blankly at the man's face that was
scarcely a foot from her own as her eyes slowly focused
and memory flooded back.

The flickering light of the torch he held in one fist,
whipped by a chill draft, bathed his features in a golden
glow, limning his sharp features eerily and picking out blue
lights in the long, virtually straight midnight hair that fell

around his face and shoulders. Colette's belly clenched, but fear was not amongst the emotions that rolled through her, tangling in a hard knot in her belly. As hard and angular as his face was, it was fascinating in a wholly pleasing way that went beyond beauty, or handsomeness. Beyond the pleasing regularity of his facial structure and hard, finely chiseled lips, his eyes were truly beautiful, surrounded by thick, long black lashes that formed a perfect, exotically almond setting for his gem colored eyes.

Colette blinked slowly, breaking the spell that had held her entranced. "Why have you brought us here?"

Something flickered in his emerald green gaze. His lips hardened. His eyes narrowed. Until she spoke, she hadn't realized that he was examining her face with equally intense scrutiny. "No one trespasses upon my domain with impunity, mortal."

Fear at last awakened, but anger, as well. Colette pushed herself upright and glanced finally toward the weeping pair, seeing the dim shape of her mother and sister huddled in one corner little more than an arm's length from where she sat.

Her gaze focused on the rough stone, weeping moisture, behind them. She could tell little else about the windowless room beyond the fact that the torchlight flickered upon walls close around on every side, but she knew instantly that they were in a dungeon cell. Scooting away from him abruptly, she sought comfort in the nearness of her mother and sister. Neither looked up, for they were clutching each other desperately, their faces hidden by their wet, straggling hair. "We didn't come willingly. You brought us here," she said accusingly. "What did you do to Robert and William?"

Something flickered in his emerald green gaze. His lips hardened. His eyes narrowed. "The yellow bellied mortals that kicked their horses faster and sped away even as you cried out for help?"

Distrust settled uncomfortably among the dregs of fear and anger. Would they have done such a thing? Left them? Or was the demon lying? Were they dead? Had they fled for help? But that last thought brought no comfort. Even if they had, her and her sister and mother would not be found unless the demon allowed it.

It occurred to her after a moment that she had cried out
for help when they had left the main road, confirming her
suspicion that the demon had orchestrated their 'trespass'.
"Most likely, Robert and William went for help," Colette
said, as much in defense of the men as to reassure herself
that there was a possibility that help might come.

His face hardened. "This Robert--he is your lover?"

Colette's jaw dropped in stunned surprise and
embarrassment. "He most certainly is not! He is a servant
in my father's house, sent along to protect us on our
journey."

"William?"

"No!"

"They have done a remarkable job of protecting," the
demon growled sardonically.

The anxiety in Colette's belly tightened a notch. "What do
you mean to do with us?" she demanded a little weakly.

He tilted his head speculatively. "I've need of an offering
to appease my overlord. Two pure maidens may please him
enough to end my exile."

Any doubt that Colette had nursed that her sister was too
wrapped up in her misery to attend the conversation fled.
Brigit let out a scream of terror, clawing at her mother as if
she would crawl inside and hide herself. The demon winced
as the sound sliced through him. Colette felt her belly
clench painfully, not just from the scream, but from the
demon's calm pronouncement of their fate.

"Bully!" she snapped, fear and despair fueling her anger.
"Foul, craven monster! How dare you speak of Robert and
William as cowards when you prey upon women half your
size and strength! Nay, not even that, for we are mortal
women and you a demon beast!"

"For godsake, Colette!" Lady Beauchamp cried out.
"Have you lost your wit? Leash your tongue. He will slay
us all!"

Colette's heart cramped painfully, but she barely glanced
at her mother. "He has already said he meant to. He can not
kill us more than once!"

The demon rose to his full height, slamming the torch he
held into a bracket on the wall. Before Colette grasped his
intent, he leaned down, his hands clamping painfully
around her upper arms. Effortlessly, the demon dragged her

to him until they were nearly nose to nose and her feet were dangling in the air. "There are other things that are not at all pleasant that I could do to you," he snarled.

"Then we will not die slowly here," Colette snarled back at him. "My sister and mother are weak and chilled to the bone. How long do you think they will last in this foul dungeon?"

Surprise flickered in his eyes. Her blast of temper, instead of fueling his, seemed to deflate it. He studied her curiously for several moments and set her on her feet, turning to consider the two women still huddled together on the floor. "This is true?"

"Of course it's true. We are all soaking wet. This place is freezing. We will grow ill and die. Look! Brigit already shivers with a chill."

His eyes narrowed suspiciously. "You can not escape," he said slowly.

The thought hadn't entered Colette's mind until he put it there, but the moment he did she realized that there was at least some possibility of it if they were not locked in the dungeon.

"The imps will take you to a warmer room and allow you to see to their needs."

"It would be far better if you simply sent us along our way," Colette suggested boldly.

"No."

She'd expected as much and was still deeply disappointed. "My mother and sister then?" she said on sudden inspiration. "My father will gladly send you a dozen virgins if you will only free us--and I would be willing to stay as surety of his word," she lied, for she could not believe her father would even consider such a horrible thing. If her mother and sister were freed, however, she felt her own chances of escaping would be tremendously better. She certainly could not consider escaping and leaving them behind and she had a very bad feeling that even if the three of them could manage to escape the Abbey, they would not get far before the demon caught up to them for Brigit would do nothing but weep and ring her hands and would have to be dragged every step of the way.

His gaze flickered speculatively from Colette, to Lady Beauchamp, lingered there for several moments and then moved on to Brigit, who cowered in white faced terror. "No."

Before Colette could try to convince him, he vanished in a whirl of smoke. The door to their cell creaked open. Brigit shrieked as a gnome like creature that was little taller than Colette entered the room. The misshapen creature grinned, exposing a mouthful of pointy teeth and then cackling delightedly at Brigit's scream of horror. "I am Jala. My master summoned me to take the prisoners to a tower room."

Brigit balked. Resisting the urge to slap her, Colette helped Lady Beauchamp carry her from the room. Before they were halfway up the steep stairs that led up from the dungeon, Colette's shoulders and arms were burning and aching from the strain. "Stand up and walk," she hissed at her younger sister, "or I swear I will let you roll to the bottom!"

"Colette!" Lady Beauchamp gasped, outraged. "She does not mean it, sweety."

"She does!" Colette snapped, losing patience. "And she will!"

Brigit, apparently convinced, straightened her spine and thrust Colette's hand from her, leaning on her mother instead.

"Take care, else you and mother will be at the bottom together."

Brigit sniffed, but she ceased to hang upon Lady Beauchamp so heavily. Without pausing, the imp, Jala, led them down a long corridor once they had reached the upper level, across the great hall where a whole tree trunk burned in a fireplace as wide as their coach and then up a spiraling set of stone stairs. Colette glanced around curiously as they passed through the great hall.

The demon, she discovered, was standing before the hearth, his legs braced slightly apart. She sensed that his gaze was focused upon her, though she couldn't be certain at such a distance and knew he could simply be watching the procession as a whole.

Awe and fear cut through her like a knife--and disbelief that she'd had the temerity to speak so challengingly to him.

He stood head and shoulders above any man she knew and there was no softness about him. The knee breeches he wore conformed faithfully to rock hard muscles along his thighs and that part of his calves not encased in high, black leather boots. The white shirt he wore hung open to the waist, exposing a chest and belly equally well defined with bulging muscle. The loose fitting sleeves were deceptive, for she recalled vividly the feel of those arms and knew they were as large and muscular as every other part of him.

Shock had turned her mind to mush and she had had nothing to fall back upon but the instinct to battle for her life with an ill advised ferocity. Her mother was right. She was fortunate he had not taken her viper tongue to heart else she would not have lived long enough to consider escape for he could've crushed her with no more effort than killing an insect.

Weak kneed from the memory of what she'd said and done, she had to brace her palm along the wall as they began to climb the steep stairs upward. By the time they had reached the top she felt both ill and faint with dread. It took an effort of will to steady herself and follow the imp to the room he indicated at the top of the tower stairs.

Once inside, she discovered the room was nearly thrice the size of the one they had so lately occupied. Tall, narrow windows covered in scraped hides ringed the circular room. A narrow cot, barely wide enough for one, stood against one wall, a tall armoire against another and a washstand that contained a pitcher and bowl.

In the center of the room a tub had been set up. Two imps, each of which looked a little uglier than the last, were busily filling it with buckets of steaming water.

There was no fireplace, but the room was far warmer than the dungeon cell, warm currents of air flowing upward from the great hall below.

"Oh!" Brigit cried, clapping her hands in delight. "A hot bath! How divine!"

Colette sent her sister a curious look. Even for Brigit the behavior was empty headed to the point of bizarre, but she supposed Brigit had had enough to scare her witless.

Jala, they discovered at that point, was not only female, but she assumed she would attend them in their bath, which Colette very much feared they were expected to share.

Brigit began to struggle from her wet clothing the moment the door closed behind Enis and Pell, the imps who'd been filling the tub. Since she wouldn't allow Jala within three feet of her, Lady Beauchamp helped her out of her wet clothing then handed them to Jala, ordering her to remove them and have them cleaned.

Jala took exception, screaming obscenities at Lady Beauchamp and pelting her with the soaked clothing, one soggy, muddy piece at the time as Lady Beauchamp raced around the room trying to escape her and dodge the muddy missiles.

Colette was too stunned to react at once. Brigit, after gaping at the quarreling pair for several stunned moments, merely climbed into the tub and ignored them.

"Colette! Do something!" Lady Beauchamp screamed as she made another circuit of the room.

Thus adjured, Colette leapt into the creature's path. The collision sent both of them crashing to the floor, Colette on bottom. Nevertheless, Colette recovered first, bucking the screaming imp off and rolling on top of her.

She hadn't had the time or the presence of mind to formulate a plan, however. She had merely reacted to her mother's tearful plea and once she'd gained the upper hand, had no notion of what to do with the creature.

Before she could decide, two great hands caught her beneath her arms and lifted her off of Jala.

and trapping them between his knees and the arms of the chair.

Cool air caressed the sensitive flesh of her nether lips.

Embarrassed, feeling a strange tension enter her that she couldn't quite decipher, she stared down at herself in horror and then glanced quickly at the demon. His gaze was on her body, specifically the apex of her thighs. Swallowing with an effort, unable to refrain from watching, she turned to look as he lifted his free hand and settled it on her full breasts, massaging each in turn, plucking at her nipples with his fingers as they responded to his touch, hardening, standing erect in tight little buds that absorbed the pleasure his fingers gave her, channeling it downward through her body until her belly began to clench and unclench rhythmically and heated moisture gathered inside of her. She sensed the movement of his head, felt his heated breath and then his mouth closed over her ear, his tongue teasing, sending waves of dizzying sensation through her as he explored the swirls. His fingers curled in the thatch of hair on her mound, stinging as he tugged slightly at the sensitive flesh the hair was embedded in.

"Maidens cringe," he whispered softly against her ear. The heat of his breath sent a fresh tingling along her flesh, lifting the fine down along her neck, her arm, the entire side of her body. Before his words could sink in, she felt his fingers parting the soft nether lips between her thighs, felt his finger delve her cleft.

She tensed all over then, trying to pull away. His arm around her waist tightened like a vise. In a leisurely manner, he probed her. Finding her body's opening, he pushed his finger inside of her. Colette gasped, struggling harder, fighting uselessly as he pressed deeper and deeper until he encountered her maidenhead. She sucked in a sharp breath, squeezing her eyes tightly closed as he pressed against it until pain took the upper hand, driving pleasure back.

"You are full of surprises," he murmured. "Still, I am tempted to breech this tiny barrier and mount my spirited little mare."

Fear and anger filled her abruptly and Colette began to fight him in earnest. To her surprise, he released her almost at once. She sprawled in the floor at the foot of his chair, glaring up at him. "You tried to trick me!" she said accusingly.

His eyes were heavy lidded as he gazed down at her, tumultuous with desire. "I am the demon Nuri. I am not bound by the beliefs or behavior of mortals. I do as I please."

As he placed his palms against the chair arms to rise, Colette scrambled to her feet and fled. He caught her. Lifting her effortlessly, he tossed her onto the bed, following her down and pinning her to the mattress with his weight before she could recover and try to scramble away. She shoved at his shoulders, wiggled, bucked, trying to crawl out from under him. He caught her wrists, pinning them to the bed on either side of her head and levering himself over her until her breasts were flattened against his chest.

"You said you wanted a sacrifice," she gasped a little desperately.

"I have one," he growled, his voice deep, rumbling from his chest. "I would rather ride my little mare."

"I don't want to be ridden!" Colette snarled at him.

"Liar. I saw your desire for me in your eyes, smelled it, felt your creamy juices of need as I explored your body."

Shameful as it was, she had felt desire, but she could hardly be faulted that her body had betrayed her. Denying it was useless, however, when he obviously knew better.

"I could not want a man determined to take the lives of my mother and sister," she spat at him.

"I am not a man."

She glared at him. "That only makes it less likely, not more so."

"Another lie--one that I could prove," he murmured after studying her for a long moment.

"You can not make me want you," Colette whispered angrily, turning her face away.

He leaned his head closely to hers, nibbling and teasing her ear as before. The results were the same despite all that she could do to try to focus her thoughts elsewhere. Liquid pleasure poured through her, making her flesh prickle with awareness of every brush of his skin against hers, the hard muscles of his chest and belly, his hard thigh lying across hers. "What makes you think that that is of any importance to me?" he murmured against the side of her neck as he made his way downward.

It took Colette several moments to collect her wits even to understand his question, and many more to delve her disordered thoughts to find an answer. "Because everyone wants to be desired by the one they desire," she whispered shakily.

She saw anger in his eyes and in his taut expression when he lifted his head to look at her. "I am a demon," he reminded her.

Her gaze flickered over his face. "You are still a man."

Something flickered in his eyes. Abruptly, he rolled off of her and strode to hearth where he had discarded the toweling. Bending, he snatched it up. He tossed it at her as she sat up. Catching it, Colette stared at him in confusion and dread and finally wrapped it around herself.

One of the imps scurried through the door and prostrated itself at his feet. "Take her back to her beloved mother and sister," Nuri growled without glancing in her direction, his gaze focused on the dancing flames in the fireplace.

Lady Beauchamp and Brigit were huddled together in the narrow cot when Colette was pushed roughly into the room and the door closed and bolted behind her.

Both sat up, staring at Colette in horror.

"It is only I," she said tiredly.

"You're--naked!" Brigit exclaimed, making it apparent that her dismay had had nothing to do with her fear that the demon had returned.

"What have done?" Lady Beauchamp demanded sharply.

Stunned, feeling guilt and shame well inside of her when she resented feeling either, Colette's anger surfaced. "I have done nothing, mother!"

"Then where are your clothes? That vile, despicable creature violated you, didn't he?"

There was no place to sit Colette discovered after she'd glanced hopefully around the room, unless she piled on the narrow cot with her mother and sister, and she didn't particularly want to at the moment, not when both of them were looking at her so accusingly. Tiredly, she moved to the wall and sat down with her back against it, wrapping the cloth around herself protectively. "He did not."

That was not strictly true, of course--not in the sense that her mother meant anyway. He had not taken her maidenhead, but he had done things she had never even imagined before.

And she had enjoyed it.

She thought that was probably the worst of it.

She had always thought that she was different from everyone else, but she had not doubted that she had strong morals and principles. She felt no shame for trying to bargain with the demon for their lives. No one else would have thought that was acceptable, she knew, but she would not have been conscience stricken over it. She would have thought that it was worth it.

She had envisioned it more in the nature of martyrdom, however.

There had to be something seriously wrong with her to find the beast attractive, fascinating, to find pleasure in his touch--to feel anything at all for him beyond fear, contempt, and revulsion.

It occurred to her after a bit to wonder if he had used his powers against her. Briefly, she felt a surge of relief at that thought. It did not last. For as she carefully resurrected the memories and examined them, she not only could not recall anything that she could positively identify as possession of her will, but the same thrill of excitement flushed her once more, as if he were touching her at that moment.

Finally, she crossed her arms on her knees, dropped her forehead to rest on her arms and fell asleep.

She dreamed. In her dream she felt the presence of the beast as he knelt before her, felt his brooding gaze upon her. He scooped an arm beneath her knees and one behind her back, lifting her up and holding her against his chest.

An awareness of movement roused her, but she could not manage to open her eyes. She could not seem to throw off the binding threads of slumber completely, for it trapped her mind in a peaceful haze still. She had only the vague sense of being carried, imagined she could feel the silkiness of some fine fabric against her cheek, warmth from the flesh beneath it and hear the comforting tattoo of a heartbeat against her ear.

The next thing she was aware of was firmness beneath her that was yielding like a fine mattress. Coolness washed over her as the warm flesh moved away. She stretched, enjoying the relief from cramped muscles from having slept so long with her arms and legs drawn up closely to her body.

More movement. This time the surface beneath her dipped as something heavy settled beside her. A touch. A rough palm settled on one breast, massaging it gently. Warmed invaded her senses, curling tentatively in her belly. She felt her nipples tighten almost painfully as blood engorged them.

Something hot and moist settled over the tender tip of her other breast. As it closed tightly around the sensitive bud, drawing upon it, sensation sharpened and instead of a gentle invasion of warmth, heat scoured her. Still, she lay passively beneath that caress, curious, enthralled with the feelings it evoked within her.

It did not cease or subside. The sensations built, steadily growing stronger with each tug on her nipple until she could no longer hold still, could no longer contain the pleasure. She moaned, uncertain of whether she wanted to escape the sensations or feel more, absorb all of the heat into herself.

"You want me. You find pleasure in my touch."

The voice was soft, but husky with some emotion that pulled at her as surely as the teasing mouth, making the warmth flow like hot wax through her woman's place.

She needed to resist that lure, she knew, and turned her face away, biting her lower lip to keep him from knowing she found pleasure in his caresses. For a time, she succeeded, but he would not have it. Moving his hand to the breast he had teased with his mouth and tongue, he massaged it, opening his mouth over her other nipple, sucking it hard and dragging a sharp gasp from her.

A restlessness invaded her. She began to feel almost feverish with some need, dismayed that he did not hold her tightly enough to prevent her from moving.

"Say that you want me and I will give you what you hunger for," he whispered near her ear.

"I don't," she lied, knowing she had to or she would be lost.

Chapter Four

Colette was aware of dread before full consciousness lifted her into awareness. She could not entirely grasp the anxiety or the discomfort, but she could not shake the sensations either.

Finally, she groaned and forced her eyelids open.

Daylight streamed through the narrow windows that lined the wall on either side of the bed. Her dread deepening, Colette pushed herself upright and looked around.

She had not a stitch of clothing on and she was lying in a great four posted bed.

Confusion filled her when she recognized the room. It was the demon, Nuri's, bed chamber.

He had sent her back to the tower room, hadn't he?

She found her mind was still too clouded and sluggish to remember anything very clearly. After glancing around and discovering that there was nothing nearby to cover herself with except the bed linens, Colette struggled to drag the sheet loose. Freeing it after a determined battle, she scooted to the edge of the bed and got out, wrapping herself in the sheet.

A washstand stood along one wall. She moved to the pitcher, lifted it and filled the basin. The water was warm, she discovered with a touch of surprise, realizing that someone had left it only a short time ago. Perhaps it was that that had wakened her?

When she had washed her face and teeth, she felt a little more alert, but still puzzled and uneasy. How had she gotten here? She was certain she remembered being led back to the tower room. Her mother and Brigit had accused her ....

She *had* gone back! As tired as she had been, she knew she hadn't dreamed that. And she had fallen asleep huddled on the floor.

The dream about the beast hadn't been a dream at all. He'd returned for her, placed some sort of spell on her and brought her here. This time, she was in no doubt that he had placed a spell on her. It had been dreamlike--she hadn't been able to fully awaken--but not a dream at all.

He'd tried to trick her again!

She frowned at that thought. Why? He had said it did not matter to him whether she was willing or not, and she had had no trouble believing that. He was a demon, after all. Perhaps there was some sort of limitations, however, that he could not overcome? Perhaps he could not ravish her?

She didn't think that she believed that, but what other reason could there be?

She jumped when the door opened, only slightly relieved when she saw that it was the imp, Jala. Carrying a tray into the room, Jala slammed it onto a table so hard that the dishes on it rattled. "Food," she snarled irritably, then turned and stalked out once more.

Colette realized that she was hungry, but she was reluctant to take the offering.

Trying to ignore the appetizing smells wafting from the dishes, she looked around the room instead. There were four windows in the outer wall, all very narrow, but not so narrow she could not climb through them.

And she was alone.

The temptation washed over her to attempt escape. If she could make her way home she could bring her father and many men back and rescue her mother and sister.

But what if she couldn't? What if the demon simply placed a spell upon the abbey and they never found it?

She felt almost ill at the war waging inside of her. She wanted to run, to save herself, but she didn't think she could live with herself if she left them to die. And even if her own conscience didn't weigh her down, everyone else would condemn her for being such a coward.

Turning away from the temptation the windows offered with an effort, Colette surveyed the rest of the room. It was a very large room, but not richly appointed. The huge four poster bed and the massive fireplace with its ornately carved surround were the most luxurious appointments in it. Aside from the bed, there was very little furniture. The floor was stone, as were the walls. One large rug covered a rectangle of space between the bed and the small table with two straight chairs on one side. Beyond the bed hangings, there were no drapes around the windows to cut drafts, and no hangings upon the walls. A tall armoire stood along one wall, a chest at the foot of the bed, and the washstand along another wall. One high back, overstuffed chair stood near the hearth--the same chair the beast had sat in when he had fondled her.

Warming at the memory, Colette looked away at once and spied a chest near the door that she hadn't noticed before. It looked familiar. Frowning, she gathered the linens around her to keep from tripping over the fabric and moved closer.

It was *her* traveling chest!

A wave of dizziness washed over her as shock jolted through her system.

The chest had been left with the broken down carriage.

Certain she must be mistaken, Colette moved to the chest and knelt beside it, pushing the lid up. It was filled with her belongings as she'd suspected and she merely stared at the familiar things, wondering about poor John Coachman.

The beast had gone for the chest or sent the imps. What had happened to the poor man?

Abruptly, Colette sensed a presence behind her. She whirled on her heels, sprawling in the floor beside the chest when she discovered it was Nuri and gaping up at him fearfully.

He frowned at her expression, gesturing toward the trunk. "I have brought your belongings."

Colette swallowed with an effort. "What happened to John?"

Puzzlement and suspicion drew his brows more tightly together. "Who is John?"

"Our coachman. He was hurt when the wheel came off the coach. We were going to send back help." It hit her then that the poor man was very likely dead from his injuries.

The demon knelt, catching her upper arms and drawing her to her feet. Without a word, he turned her so that her back was to him and placed his palms on either side of her head. Uncomfortable with his nearness, she immediately tried to move away.

"Be still and I will show you what you want to know."

She did not trust him, but the offer was too much temptation to resist.

He leaned down until his face was near her ear. "Close your eyes."

A shiver skated down her length, but she did as she was told. Again, he placed his palms on either side of her head. Almost at once an image began to form in her mind. Through a veil of fog, she saw the broken coach. Men surrounded it, among them William and Robert. At a short distance from the others, she saw her father, mounted on his favorite stallion. His face was drawn with worry as the men with him dismounted and pulled John from the carriage. Another man, one she recognized as their physician, knelt in the road beside the injured man, examining him and binding his broken limbs.

Colette shifted uncomfortably, wanting to pull away, disbelief tightening inside her.

This wasn't true vision. He was showing her what she wanted to see.

"Be still."

She subsided, but this time only because of the harshness of his voice that told her he was impatient with her efforts to move away.

After a moment, she saw her father lift his head. The worried look on his face became an expression of surprise and then gladness. The mist parted and she saw Brigit and her mother stumble from the woods wearing nothing but their under clothes and those torn to shreds. Both bore expressions of fear and bewilderment until they saw her father.

Colette's eyes flew open. She jerked away from the demon, putting some distance between them. "That's not real. You made me see what you knew I wanted to see!" she said accusingly.

His face grew taut. "It is real. You know that in your heart."

She shook her head. "You're just trying to trick me again."

His lips tightened. Without a word, he caught her arm in an unyielding grip and dragged her from the room. She had to scurry to keep up with his long stride, tripping on the linen she was still wrapped in. When they reached the tower room, he flung the door wide, releasing her arm at last.

Fearful, Colette moved into the doorway and looked around. There was no sign of either her mother or Brigit.

Their muddy gowns still lay on the floor where Jala had left them, but there was no other evidence that they had even occupied the room.

"They're not here," she said bewilderedly. "What have you done with them?"

"You saw," he said tightly.

She whirled on him angrily. "I don't believe! I don't trust you. You deceived me twice already, tried to trick me. Why would I believe you?"

"I gave you what you asked for," he growled angrily. "Now you will give me what you offered."

"I'll do not such thing, for I do not believe for one moment that you have kept the bargain at all. You have put them in the dungeon--or slain them!"

His eyes narrowed. "Search then. You will not find them for I have freed them."

She found herself staring at nothing more than a swirl of dark smoke as he vanished. Swallowing, afraid to hope that what he had shown her was true, she left the tower room and began to search for her mother and sister, calling out to them as she moved down one dark hallway after another, peering into room after room until she lost count of the number.

The place was a maze. For hours she wandered, down narrow stairs, up another set, down into the dungeons where she searched every cell, and then up again. She searched the room in every tower, weary from searching but too anxious to stop and rest.

There was no sign of them, no sign that they had ever been anywhere in the abbey other than the tower room. Finally, exhausted but still worried, Colette climbed the stairs again. She found herself in Nuri's room before she had even considered where she was going.

She was so tired she almost felt like weeping when she saw a tub filled with steaming water sat before the hearth. The tray that Jala had brought earlier was gone, but the small table had been set with two place settings.

Nuri was sprawled in the chair before the hearth, his gaze brooding as he studied her.

She was not comfortable with the idea of bathing in front of him. Having done so the night before had not cured her of her embarrassment over her nakedness or the strangeness of bathing beneath the gaze of a stranger.

She was too tired and too miserable to ignore the temptation of the heated bath, however. Finally, she moved to the tub, discarded the now filthy linen sheeting and climbed into the hot water.

"You did not eat."

She didn't bother to open her eyes. She felt ill from not eating and from the exhausting search. "No."

"You will grow weak."

Wryly, she thought she already had grown very weak. She had barely had the strength to climb the stairs and none to resist the temptation he had left for her. She wondered if she cared. Her mother and sister were gone, and she had no idea of whether she could trust that they were safe or not. Could she flee to save herself without that certainty? What if it was only another trick and she discovered when she had found her way back that she had left them behind to suffer alone and afraid?

With an effort, she sat up in the tub and bathed the filth she'd gathered along the way in her search, dust, cobwebs, muck from the damp, earthen floors of the dungeon. She was so listless when she had finally cleaned herself, all she could think about was climbing into bed and sleeping.

Nuri would have none of that. When he saw that she had finished, he pulled her to her feet and wrapped her in a fresh length of toweling, drying her as he had the night before. "I'm too tired to eat," she complained as he drew her toward the table.

"But you will eat."

Clutching the linens around her, she eyed him resentfully as he settled across from her. "I should dress."

"Why? I mean to bed you when I have fed you," he said matter-of-factly.

Colette blushed to the roots of her hair. What little appetite she'd had vanished.

Completely illogically, her body tensed with the heat she'd felt before when he'd caressed her.

Jala appeared with food.

"I will dress before I eat," Colette said stubbornly.

He studied her in tightlipped silence. "You will eat-- willingly, or not."

Colette subsided, deciding it wasn't worth a battle of wills. She was hungry, and she could not defend herself if she was weak from hunger.

The food was surprisingly good. Colette found her appetite returning the moment she took her first bite. She ate far more than she should have and not nearly as much as she wanted.

"More."

It was an order, not a question. "I can not. I have eaten my fill."

"Then it is no wonder that you are so puny," he growled irritably. "Or perhaps you are too anxious for desert to eat more?"

Colette immediately felt ill with nerves. "I am too full for desert," she said a little breathlessly, willfully misinterpreting his comment.

"You will be fuller."

She felt her cheeks flame. Deciding that pretended ignorance would get her no where, she sent him an angry glare. "I do not make or keep bargains with demons--who have no honor, and are not above using their magic to trick the unwary."

"Then I will take what I want," he growled, surging out of the chair.

Her heart nearly failed her as he rose above her, towering, making it impossible for her to ignore the fact that she was no match for him at all. "You will *have* to take," she said shakily. "Amuse yourself if you must. I can not stop you, as you well know. But I will not yield gladly or willingly. You can not make me believe the lies you placed in my mind. For all I know you have slain my mother and sister and it revolts every feeling to even consider laying with...."

Furious, he grasped her arms, hauling her from her chair.

Colette swallowed with an effort, but she met his gaze unflinchingly.

He studied her face for several moments and released her arms, placing his hands on either side of her head as he had before.

Colette struggled, fearful at first of what he meant to do. The images began to form inside her mind, however, and she closed her eyes as a wave of dizziness washed over her. Almost at once the mists cleared and she saw her mother and sister in the sun room of their home. Brigit was weeping noisily in her mother's arms. "I can't believe it. I simply can not!"

"Hush now, dearest. You will make yourself ill! Your father will surely find her."

Brigit sniffed. "But my party will be ruined anyway!" she cried out.

"Brigit! You do not mean that!"

Brigit looked up at their father guiltily. "What did I say? Oh! I am so distraught I don't know what I'm saying. I didn't mean that the way it sounded. Truly I didn't!"

Colette broke free of the demon's grasp and backed away several steps. Hurt formed a painful knot in her chest as she stared up at him.

"Do you still think I lie? Was that not the home you know?"

In her heart, she knew it was true. Yet, she still wanted to deny it, not only because it obligated her to keep the bargain she had struck, but because she was unwilling to think that Brigit cared no more than that for her.

She was spoiled, willful, and thoughtless. No doubt Brigit truly hadn't meant the words the way they had sounded, Colette told herself. Naturally she was upset about her coming out party. It had been planned for nigh a year.

It was not as if she had not thought of herself. She loved her mother and sister, and she had been worried about them, but she had known her own chances of survival were better without them.

It wasn't as if Brigit could actually help her.

Or that it would do any of them any good to mourn her loss.

She realized then that the main reason she was hurt had nothing to do with Brigit at all. Brigit was being Brigit. She had expected no better of her.

Her mother was still focused upon Brigit, however. She had not seemed distraught at all that her eldest daughter was still captive of the dreaded demon lord, Nuri, only concerned that Brigit would fall into hysterics and make herself ill. Her father had seemed appalled by Brigit's remark, and yet he had not appeared to be particularly distressed either.

Did they not love her at all? Was her absence more of an inconvenience than a matter for distress?

She tried to shake the sense of abandonment she felt, told herself she was being far too sensitive when she had no more than glimpsed their expressions, but she could not. Doubt had entered her heart and would not be quieted.

She did not even object when Nuri lifted her into his arms and carried her to the bed ... but for the first time since she had been a small child, she wept.

Nuri's hands stirred warmth to life as he stroked his palms over her body, but that only made the tears flow faster, for there was no love in his touch, no wish to offer the comfort she needed, only carnal desire.

He hesitated when he lifted his head at last to look into her eyes. His brows drew together in a frown that was part puzzlement, part irritation. "Why do you cry?" he demanded gruffly.

Colette stared at him in surprise. "I feel ... lost," she said finally.

He was silent as he absorbed that and considered it. Abruptly, he pushed away from her. "Mortals and their maudlin sentiments! Bah!" he growled angrily as he surged up from the bed, stalked across the room, and vanished in a swirl of dark smoke.

Chapter Five

For many moments after the demon had vanished, Colette wavered between the desire to yield to a luxurious bout of self pity and anger at his insensitivity. Amusement squelched both emotions as it dawned on her that she had dampened his ardor and sent him packing without even trying.

Why would he care if she wept while he had his way with her anyway? It could hardly be worse that screaming and fighting him.

But then he hadn't wanted that either. How odd!

Evil demon indeed!

Of course, it did appear that he had evil designs upon her, or why else would he have freed her mother and sister?

That thought brought her to a realization that she had been too emotional to consider before. She was free to escape!

Scooting off of the bed abruptly, she rushed to her chest and opened it, digging out clothing and dragging them on quickly if a little haphazardly.

Out the window? Or down the stairs?

He would be in the great hall. She knew that.

Moving to the windows, she pulled the hide loose and looked down at the ground. The soil below was hard and strewn with pebbles--and it looked like an awful long drop even though she knew it could not be such a great distance. She was only on the second floor, after all.

After a little thought, she went to the door and tested it. To her surprise, the door opened. Anxiety tightened in her chest. Was he so certain she could not escape? Or had it been left unbolted because he was testing her?

She eased the door closed again, trying to bring her thundering pulse to a more comfortable level, chastising herself for her cowardice. Her mother and sister were safe. She had only to implement the remainder of her plan--to save herself.

When she had calmed her racing heart the best she could, she opened the door and peered up and down the corridor.

Nuri would be in the great room. Very likely the imps would be somewhere close by their lord, if not in the great room itself. She had no confidence that she could slip down the main stair unnoticed, but she had found several narrow secondary stairs when she had been searching for her family.

Stepping from the room, she closed the door carefully and began to move as quickly and quietly as she could to the stairs she remembered in the north wing. She had been greatly distressed the day she had searched the abbey, though, wandering round and around and she discovered a flaw in her memory.

The stair was not where she had thought it would be.

She stopped, trying to think how much time had passed since the demon had left her, wondering if she should continue to search or go back before he returned and found her gone. She wasn't certain she could gather the nerve to try again, though, and more importantly, she was still untouched. If she stayed the demon would ravish her and then she would be ruined even if she managed to escape. Perhaps her family would not even allow her to return if she was a fallen woman, tainted by the touch of a demon.

Galvanized by those thoughts, she continued her search with less concern for quiet and more for the passing time. At last she found the stairs that she had been searching for and hurriedly descended to the first floor.

The wing she found herself in was as dark as a cave even in the daylight, for it had been unoccupied for many years. Hurrying along the corridor, she checked each room for some egress from the abbey. Each had a window, but glass covered them and they could not be opened. She could break the glass, of course, but she didn't want to make enough noise to attract attention. She found a door at last, but that, too, was sealed and she could not open it.

Much time had passed. She knew that that was not anxiety or imagination, for she had been wandering around the great cave of the abbey down long corridors, searching rooms.

Nuri would almost certainly have found her gone by now and he would be furious that she had broken his trust and fled the fulfillment of the bargain she had begged him to make with her.

She could not bring herself to return to the room and face his wrath.

With no other option than to break a window, or return to Nuri's bed chamber, or try to escape through the great hall, she opted for the window. It was not as easy to break as she'd anticipated. She had beat upon it with the metal candlestick repeatedly before the glass finally shattered.

The noise was horrendous. In her frantic haste to escape, she cut her palms on the glass still clinging to the now empty sill and landed in more broken glass when she leapt from the window to the ground. Ignoring the pain, she glanced around quickly and headed for the woods.

She had not really considered what she would do if she managed to make it out of the abbey beyond the thought that she would hide herself in the woods as quickly as she could reach the covering of vegetation. She had not been conscious when Nuri had brought her to the abbey and had no idea in which direction the road lay.

She could scarcely believe her good fortune when she reached the woods without an outcry behind her. Pausing to catch her breath, she searched through the thicket of limbs above her for the position of the sun. Dismay filled her when she could not see it. She finally decided that she had pinpointed the brightest area of the sky and began to struggle through the brush.

It was thick and tore at her clothing, shredding it as the day wore on. By her estimation, she had been fighting her way through the thick tangle for hours when she finally stopped to rest and catch her breath. Puzzlement settled over her as she sat on the fallen long.

She had heard no pursuit at all. Why?

She did not believe Nuri had simply allowed her to leave. He must know by now that she was not in the abbey, however.

Shaking that worrisome thought off when she'd caught her breath, she got up and began again, hoping that she would find the road--any road, a trail animals had worn through the wood. She found nothing but more of the same. Each time she found a patch of sky, she searched for the sun and not once did she spot so much as a sliver of actual sunlight.

The forest had begun to dim around her when she stumbled upon an area that looked vaguely familiar to her. Stopping again to catch her breath, fighting the hope that had surged inside of her, she looked more carefully, searching for something else that looked familiar.

Her heart seemed to stand still when she found it.

Through the trees she could just glimpse the stones of the abbey.

She'd done nothing but walk in a circle and ended up in the same spot where she had originally entered the woods.

Consternation filled her but she was so weary from fighting the thicket of vegetation all day that she couldn't even find the strength to run. Her legs simply gave out and she sprawled in the brush, staring in dismay at the abbey and trying to think what to do.

Nuri appeared before her. His face was a mask of pure fury. "This is how you repay my trust? Are you satisfied now that I did not lie when I told you that you could not escape?"

Colette stared up at him mutely, too tired even to feel more than a tiny flicker of fear.

Reaching for her, he hauled her to her feet and escorted her from the forest and into the abbey once more. He did not take her up the stairs, however. Instead, he took her to the stairs to the dungeon.

She resisted then, trying to break his hold for all the good it did.

The two imps, Enis and Pell, appeared at the foot of the stairs and seized her as Nuri gave her a push in their direction. Whatever thoughts flickered through her mind that she might succeed in fighting them where she could not fight Nuri vanished within moments. They were small, but far stronger than she. Dragging her into a cell, they stripped what remained of her clothing away in spite of all she could do to fight them off and then placed a manacle around her ankle.

When they had left, she scurried into one corner and huddled in a tight ball, shivering as the fear her weariness had held at bay began to take hold of her.

She should have simply accepted her fate, she realized belatedly. He would have amused himself with her, but in time he might have grown bored and released her. He might also have grown bored with her and killed her, but she would never know now.

Now, he would punish her.

She didn't want to think about that, but all sorts of horrible images filled her mind, each more frightening than the last. In time, even those images faded, however, and weariness once again produced apathy. She saw then that a hard crust of bread and a pail of water sat in one corner.

When she'd ate the bread and drunk her fill of the water, she curled into a ball again and fell into an exhausted sleep.

She had no notion of how long she had slept, but she was still drunk with exhaustion when she was roused, too disoriented to struggle. A cloth was bound tightly about her head, blinding her. Hands tightened around her arms, pulling her to her feet and the manacle was removed.

She knew it must be the imps once more even though she couldn't see them. She also knew her punishment for defying the demon was at hand. Despite her fear, she had little strength to fight them. The contest was lost even before they had dragged her from the cell.

She stumbled and nearly fell as they led her into the corridor and turned down it, but they merely gripped her more tightly, holding her up and carrying her. She had no idea where they took her beyond the fact that they climbed no stairs. The room, therefore, was in the dungeon.

Her skin pebbled with the chill of the air. She was forced down upon something cold and hard that bit into her stomach. Wrenching her arms upward, she felt the cold stone on the inside of her arms and then the cold of metal as they manacled her wrists.

Fear and puzzlement filled her. Her face and arms, and her belly lay against stone, but the stone didn't bite into her breasts. Before she had had time to consider what she must have been bound to, her ankles were seized and her legs pulled too far apart to support her. Manacles were clamped around her ankles as had been clamped around her wrists.

Cool air caressed her cleft and her breasts.

She struggled to rise and found that she couldn't, could do nothing more than lift her head away from the stone. Subsiding after a few moments, she lay panting with her cheek against the cold surface, tense, certain that any moment she would feel the bite of a whip on the bare flesh of her back.

She gasped sharply when she felt something hot, wet and faintly rough glide over first one nipple and then the other. Of their own accord, her nipples stood erect, filling with blood until they pounded with each hard pulse beat.

Something hot closed over her nipples, sucking hard. A flash of heat went through her. Gasping, horrified, Colette struggled again to move, to pull away. As before, she found it useless. The only effect it had was to cause her sharp needles of pain, for the mouths--and she knew it was mouths--sucked harder still.

The imps?

Revulsion filled her, but she had heard them move away from her. She had heard them leave the room and close the door. Once her ankles had been secured, she had listened to their retreating footsteps, for she had been listening fearfully for Nuri's approach.

Who, or what, was suckling her?

She had no idea, but she could not ignore it. She tried to distance her mind from the sensation flowing through her. She tried to hold onto the surprise and revulsion she'd felt when it had begun. She tugged, ignoring the pain it caused her to try to pull away, but she could not move far enough away and as soon as she wilted helplessly against the stone again, the pain eased and heated pleasure surged into her from the tugging and teasing, the heat and suction.

She bit her lip when she discovered that her breath was coming in short pants. Dizziness washed over her. Heat and tension coiled in her belly, grew tighter. She had expected pain. She thought she could have fought that and she would not have felt any shame if she hadn't been able to. Pleasure was not something she could fight. Her body had a will of its own. It awakened to it, flowered, absorbed the sensations hungrily.

The muscles low in her belly quivered, began to flex and relax. Moisture gathered inside of her, flowed. She felt the tender petals of her sex grow damp.

Almost the moment her awareness of her femininity became impossible to ignore, she felt the touch of fingers, spreading her wide. A tongue, hot, moist and faintly rough like those she felt tugging and lapping at her nipples, glided along her cleft. She jerked all over, but she found she could no more evade that intrusive touch than the mouths that still suckled her breasts and she could not close her mind to the sensation that made her belly clench more tightly.

The tongue lapped her sensitive flesh, sucked her. Finding a tiny nub of flesh more tender than any other, a mouth closed upon it, sucking. A moan escaped her, the sound loud in the silence of the cell. Yet she was hardly aware of it, aware of nothing but the unceasing stroke of tongue, the suction of mouth as she was licked and sucked hungrily.

Something built inside of her, a tension she would doubtless not have been able to identify even if she could have kept her wits about her, which she couldn't, for she had never felt anything like it before. It grew harder, stronger. Without warning, it ruptured, sending hard convulsions of pleasure through her.

To her consternation, the teasing did not cease and then she felt the ultimate torture, pleasure that rocked her ceaselessly until she was gasping hoarsely, frantic to escape it, certain she could bear no more.

Instead, when she had fallen into nearly a stupor, the tension began to build again.

Sated, barely conscious with the release, she groaned as she felt her body begin to respond, felt pleasure invade her. Her body responded slowly, but with determination against her will. The tongue suckling the tiny nub between her legs ceased. Torn between relief and disappointment, she waited for the maddening mouth to return and toy more with the nub of pleasure. Instead, it raked along her cleft and pushed inside of her.

She shivered, but quickly discovered that it brought her far more pleasure that she would have believed possible. The muscles inside of her passage flexing and relaxing, clutched at it and she realized at last what it was that her body craved--something there, something to wrap themselves around.

The hot tongue delved deeper, until she felt it probing against her maidenhead.

It teased her. She ached to be filled completely. She knew it would hurt if her maidenhead was breached and yet she began to yearn for it with an illogical desperation.

She felt like weeping when the tongue was withdrawn and she was left with a craving unfulfilled.

The suckling upon her breasts built the tension in her belly again, hotter and more tightly than before. The other mouth closed upon the bud once more, teasing it, sending jolts of pleasurable tension to join with the other in her belly. Pleasure poured through her like warm honey.

This time, she knew what to expect. This time, she knew the moment her body reached the point where it could no longer contain the pleasure. Even so, when it exploded, the force rocked her. She groaned as the shockwaves rolled over her, her belly cramping with the force of the convulsions.

At long last the waves gentled and her muscles relaxed. She lay spent, panting for breath as the stimulation was withdrawn.

Her mind drifted lazily, random thoughts flickering through her but vanishing as she tried to grasp them.

She jerked all over at the rough rake of a tongue over one nipple. Instantly, it responded, pebbling in a hard, tender knot. A mouth covered it, sucked. Her other nipple was covered also and then she felt the tongue along her cleft. Dread filled her, but it slipped her grasp as her body responded and the tension began coiling once again.

Again, she was taken to the heights of pleasure and before she had even caught her breath, yet again. She lost count of the number of times she was taken to the peak of the most excruciating pleasure she had ever felt, but each time they began again, her body responded no matter how weak she was.

After a time, she was less conscious than aware, and still they tortured her endlessly with pleasure until she finally reached a point of exhaustion that prevented her from feeling anything at all.

She was released then, but too weak even to lift her head. Someone lifted her. She felt a broad chest and knew it must be Nuri, but she was too weary feel anything but relief that it was over.

She wasn't even aware of being lain down upon the cold cell floor. She wasn't aware of anything until she was roused once more by two hands that seized her and lifted her to her feet. She tried harder to fight this time, knowing what was coming. In the end, it made no more difference than it had the first time.

She was still blindfolded, but she was certain it was the same room as before. Instead of being forced over the stone table as she was the first time, however, she was set on her feet. Manacles were attached to her wrists and her arms pulled out to her sides.

Two hands caught at her legs, fitting something around her tights just above her knees. She gasped sharply as her legs were drawn upward and to either side of her until she could feel the strain on her arms, could feel her fleshy nether lips part and stand wide, exposing her tender inner lips.

Tongues began to lath her, finding every tender spot on her body--there was more than one, she knew, though she was dizzy with the drug of euphoria long before those mouths and tongues found her most sensitive flesh and began to tease it. Despite the number of times her body had responded before, or perhaps because of it, her body leapt almost instantly into rapturous delight as her nipples and clit were suckled and licked.

As before, she was brought to completion over and over until she was too exhausted even to respond anymore. Then she was unbound and returned to the cell.

She lost all track of time, for days, or perhaps weeks, each time she woke she was dragged willingly, or unwillingly, and tortured endlessly with pleasure. She was allowed to rest, relieve herself, eat, drink, bathe, but the sessions continued until she hardly knew where she was.

The day came, though, when she woke upon a bed. She stared up at the canopy overhead blankly, too weary even to identify it for many moments. She might not have identified it then except that Nuri leaned over her, planting a fist on either side of her head and staring down at her.

Chapter Six

He moved away after a few moments and Colette struggled to push herself upright.

A tub of steaming water awaited her before the hearth. As she looked around the room, she saw the table was set for two.

Weak kneed, she slipped from the bed and moved to the tub without a word and climbed in. When she had bathed herself, Nuri held up a length of warmed linen to dry her. To her surprise, he released it the moment she'd grasped it, allowing her to dry herself. When she had finished, she looked around and discovered her chest had vanished.

"My chest is gone," she murmured in surprise.

"Yes. I brought it here for you, but like every kindness I offered, you spurned it in favor of defying me and breaking your word to me."

She turned at the sound of his voice and saw that he had seated himself at the table. After a moment, she wrapped the linen more tightly around her and crossed the room to settle in the chair left for her use.

"Did you enjoy punishing me?" she demanded sullenly.

His eyes narrowed. "Almost as much as you enjoyed it."

Colette reddened, but she could hardly deny that she had enjoyed it when she had moaned and screamed with pleasure. "Then it *was* you," she said faintly, wondering how he could have done those things to her.

"I am a demon," he said, almost as if he could read her mind. "In time, perhaps I will show you all the things that I can do."

Colette swallowed with an effort as her body responded to his voice, and the images he'd conjured, growing heated with remembered pleasure. It occurred to her abruptly, and with a decided dampening of her ardor, that she was a virgin still. Despite everything he had done, he had left that intact and that meant that he could still sacrifice her to his overlord if the whim struck him.

Silence settled around them as they ate. Colette found she had little appetite, but she was weak from eating so little for so many days, and she could not allow herself to continue to grow weaker.

When they had finished and the imp, Jala, had come into the room and removed the remains of their meal, Nuri rose from his chair and went to stand before the hearth.

After a few minutes, since she didn't know what else to do, Colette rose and followed him. She stood uncomfortably for some time and finally settled on the floor at his feet, staring into the flames. "Am I forgiven?" she asked after a time, irked that she had to ask, but nevertheless hoping that he was no longer angry with her.

"No."

She glanced at him sharply, feeling her belly clench with a strange combination of fear, hope, and desire. "Why?"

He tilted his head slightly. "You gave me nothing."

Blood flooded Colette's cheeks again as the realization filled her mind that he spoke nothing but the truth. He had pleasured her unmercifully, beyond what she'd felt like she could possibly endure, but she had not gone to him willingly, and she had given him no pleasure beyond what he might, or might not, have experienced from giving pleasure to her.

With that realization, it dawned on her that she had not been 'punished'. He had been teaching her body to respond to his touch. He had given her the knowledge of what her body was capable of.

Or, perhaps in part, he had done it to make it impossible for her to lie to him or herself that she desired him.

She still had a chance to survive, she realized after a moment. If she kept her word and gave herself to him, he would accept it--she thought--and then the only use he would have for her would be for pleasure. He could not hope to curry favor with his overlord by sacrificing her once she had given him her maidenhead.

It still took more courage than she would ever have thought necessary to get to her feet and approach him. There was no welcome in his face when she stopped in front him and dropped the linen to the floor. "Teach me and I will give you pleasure,' she said with an effort.

His expression hardened, but when she moved to the bed and lay down upon the mattress, he stood watching her. After a moment, he sat in his chair and pushed his boots off, then stood up, peeling his shirt from his shoulders. When he had dropped it to the floor, he unfastened his breeches and pushed them from his hips.

Colette's eyes widened as she watched him. She had never seen a man naked before, and certainly not *his* man root. It looked impossibly huge for her body, almost painfully engorged.

Contrarily, her belly clenched at the sight, her femininity growing moist and heated with want. That, she knew, was what she had wanted so badly before, what she wanted inside of her so much she ached for it.

When he had settled on the mattress on his side, he placed his palm on her mid section, slipping it upward and capturing one breast. Kneading it, he plucked at one erect nipple with his fingers and lowered his mouth to capture the other peak between his lips.

Instantly, pleasure jolted through her. Any doubts that had lingered that it was he who had caressed her vanished. His touch was like fire, sending a raging storm through her to collide in a whirlpool of need in the pit of her stomach.

She gasped, moaned, holding still with an effort as he teased her with his mouth and tongue, but she found as he moved from one breast to the other that she couldn't continue to remain still. A fever gripped her. She began to move restlessly beneath his caresses.

It was almost disappointing when he moved away and began to caress her belly with his hands, his mouth and tease her with his tongue. Shifting, he settled between her thighs, pushing her legs wide. Her breath caught in her chest as he dipped his head toward her sex and she felt the rough caress of his tongue along her cleft. Releasing the breath she'd held on a gasp, she arched to meet his questing mouth as he settled it over the tender, aching bud, sucking it into his mouth.

Tension coiled rapidly inside of her. Her skin burned. Her body clenched, seeking the fulfillment that he had denied her each time he had brought her to release. She knew what she needed--him, his turgid flesh.

She was stunned when he stopped and rolled away. With an effort, she opened her eyes and turned to look at him.

She saw that he lay on his back, his arms beneath his head. His eyes were glazed with his own desire, tumultuous with need. She sensed a breathless waiting.

Rolling onto her side, she caressed him as he had her. With her hands, she explored his body, testing the strength of his hard, bulging muscles, the smoothness of his skin. With her tongue and mouth, she tasted his flesh, marveling at the thrill of excitement that went through her as she felt him move restlessly beneath her touch, heard his heart thundering in his chest, his short gasps each time she touched a particularly sensitive patch of flesh.

When she lifted her head to look up at him, she saw that his eyes were tightly closed, his face drawn almost as if he were in pain. A sense of power washed over her, and with it excitement.

He was as helpless in the face of the pleasure she gave him as she was in the pleasure he gave her.

Dragging in a shuddering breath, she moved lower, dipping her tongue into his naval, nibbling kisses along his lower belly. He jerked when she wrapped her hand tightly around his turgid man root, startling her, but she saw in his face that it was from pleasure akin to pain. Feeling more certain, she massaged him experimentally and then kissed the tip as he had kissed the sensitive bud of her femininity.

He groaned, digging his fingers into the mattress.

Drunk with passion and power, she opened her mouth over him and sucked him. He caught her shoulders, digging his fingers into her almost painfully and she looked up at him questioningly. "You don't like it?" she asked, her voice husky with her own desire.

Passion blazed in his eyes as he opened them to look at her. "Yes," he said hoarsely and then swallowed audibly. "I don't think I can stand it without exploding."

His words washed over her like an intimate caress, making her belly quake with her own need. After a hesitant moment, she took him into her mouth again, hungry now with the need to find fulfillment, to be filled with him.

He began to shake and thrash beneath her ministrations, groaning hoarsely. She felt her own body tensing toward that pinnacle she had come to covet and moved over him more feverishly still.

He caught her once more, dragging her up his body. Spearing his fingers in her hair, he dragged her face close and opened his mouth over hers. A rush went through her as he made love to her mouth with the fervor of his need.

She broke the kiss after only a few moments, sliding down his belly, trying to align her own body with his.

He rolled, flipping her onto her back and covering her body with his. "You want me?" he asked harshly.

"Yes," she said on a gasping voice. "Please."

She thought that he would split her in two when he pushed the head of his cock into her. She relished the pleasure/pain, arching upward, forcing her body to accept him as he drove a little deeper with each thrust until she felt him pierce her maidenhead and move deeper still. The sensation was maddening, a warring of pleasure and pain that only made her yearn for more. "Nuri! I need," she gasped, uncertain what more she needed, but certain that he could give it to her.

She heard him grinding his teeth. Slowly, he withdrew and almost as slowly thrust deeply once more. She dug her fingernails into his shoulders, mindlessly urging him on, bucking against him when he paused. He let out a low groan and began to thrust more smoothly, retreating and thrusting again. Each stroke took her higher, made the tension coil harder and tighter inside her until she was sobbing with the need to find release. She learned the rhythm, arching up to meet him each time he drove his hard flesh to her depths, and with each stroke, he withdrew and returned harder and faster than before until bliss caught her, exploding around her in a white hot flash of ecstasy.

Groaning hoarsely as her flesh began to convulse around his, he plunged harder and faster and then abruptly went still as his cock jerked inside of her. Slipping his arms beneath her, he clutched her tightly, his body shuddering as he pumped his seed deeply inside of her.

For many moments, he simply lay still when his body had ceased to convulse in pleasure, breathing harshly next to her ear. Finally, as if he could not bear to withdraw his flesh from hers, he slipped a hand beneath her buttocks and held her tightly to him as he rolled onto his back.

Colette didn't even think to object. Despite the pain from the loss of her maidenhead, despite the fact that he was so big she'd felt as if he would split her in two, the pleasure had by far outweighed the pain and her culmination was better even than all the times before when he had given her pleasure without embedding his flesh in her.

She found it nearly as pleasurable, though in a different way, to feel his big body beneath hers, to feel her breasts flattened against the hard muscles of his massive chest.

Passion. She had dreamed of it, but she had never truly grasped what it was.

She desired nothing at the moment other than to do it again, and again.

Lifting her head finally, she kissed his chest, licked him with her tongue.

She liked his taste.

He roused slightly. Lifting an arm, he dropped it heavily onto her back. Colette grunted at the blow, but as he began stroking her back almost lazily she relaxed again, realizing he simply had no clear idea of how monstrous big and heavy he was--and all his parts.

Colette was drifting lethargically when he slipped a hand down along her thigh and dragged her leg around his waist. Rolling again until she was beneath him, he nuzzled her neck, sucking a string of love bites along her collar bone and then downward. She felt his member swell tightly inside of her again.

"I enjoy fucking you far more than I had even thought that I would," he murmured, nipping languidly at her nipples as they puckered and stood up for his attention.

The comment pierced the glowing warmth of Colette's euphoria, bringing her abruptly back to reality. What had she been thinking, she wondered, to feel even a pinprick of hurt at such a remark? She was not prone to fanciful daydreaming, despite the one she had nursed to herself for years. She considered herself intelligent and practical.

She had offered up herself because it had been the only logical thing to do to try to save herself. She was not being wooed by some suitor. She was being ravished by a demon beast.

She should be glad he had brought her to her senses.

As much as she enjoyed being fucked by him, this was no solution for her. She had to keep her wits about her or she was lost.

On the other hand, she *did* enjoy it and, however bad of her it was, she was glad she did. She would not have to pretend and fear that he would realize it and be angry.

He could not use her to appease his overlord now. She was safe from that fate, at least.

The problem now was that she had no idea what he would do when he tired of her. Would he allow her to go home? Continue to hold her prisoner? Or--something she didn't want to think about?

She finally decided as she felt her body respond to his touch that she would worry about it later. Later, when she could think clearly, perhaps she would figure out a way to escape him.

He took her to the peak of rapture again and as she lay sated and weak, he began again to build the fire until she was feverish with need and he brought her to culmination once more.

Finally, exhausted, she fell into a deep slumber.

She had no idea how long slept, but she was awakened rudely when her wrists were seized. Still weak from having been sated over and over, and disoriented from sleep, she struggled half heartedly, trying to pry her eyelids open when they felt as if they had been glued shut.

She saw as she was dragged from the bed and forced to kneel on the floor, that it was the two imps Enis and Pell who had awakened her. When they had forced her to her knees on the floor, her hands were dragged behind her back.

"His lust for you has weakened the Halfling Nuri," said a voice in a deep, rumbling growl that sent a shaft of fear through Colette. Of its own accord, her head jerked in the direction of the sound.

A demon stood before the hearth. He was veiled in shadows that prevented more than a glimpse of his face, but his voice alone was enough to assure Colette that it was not Nuri. He did not wear the clothing of a human as Nuri usually did, but stood before her naked. He was built much like Nuri--with hard bulging muscles all over his body, but bigger, perhaps twice as big as Nuri, taller by nearly half a foot, broader. His cock was enormous, red, swollen, standing out from the nest of hair at the apex of his thighs in obscene threat.

"You are both in need of a lesson. Bring her," he ordered the two imps, vanishing abruptly in a swirling cloud of darkness.

Fear and not logic ruled Colette as the imps dragged her from Nuri's chamber and down the corridor to the stairs. She struggled mindlessly, uselessly against their hold, succeeding in doing nothing more than expending the little strength she had left and bruising herself. She was too weak to struggle further long before they reached the dungeon of the abbey and the imps dragged her into a cell, manacling her wrists and ankles before they left her.

She sat shivering in one corner when they had left her, too frightened still even to think. Two things slowly became clear in her mind, however. She could not escape. She had tried before when she was not even bound and Nuri had caught her effortlessly.

And it was not Nuri she needed to worry about now, but a demon without Nuri's 'weakness', mercy.

* * * *

Nuri had ceased to fear his overlord long ago. Pain had been his constant companion for so long that he had little dread of it, and he had long since lost any concern over his existence or lack of it, for it gave him no pleasure. He obeyed because his overlord was far more powerful than he was and he had no choice. Refusing meant banishment, or pain, or both, but in the end his overlord simply exerted his superior powers and Nuri was compelled to do what his overlord wished.

It was disconcerting and debilitating to discover that he felt both rage and fear as he was chained to the wall in the sacrificial chamber.

It did not take long to understand the source of both.

Colette.

Terror brought a cold sweat to his body as in sank in upon him that she was at Milak's mercy and he could do nothing to protect her from his overlord. Mindless, impotent rage quickly followed it and he strained uselessly against his bonds, ignoring the pain and succeeding in doing nothing more than arousing Milak's amusement and inciting him.

When it finally sank in upon him that he had given away his desperation to protect her, Nuri felt a surge of fear and impotent fury at himself. He ceased to struggle, however, holding his rage and fear inside.

Too little, too late, he realized, knowing that his behavior was enough to encourage Milak to do his worst.

He felt almost ill with the hate that welled up in him then, but he began a hard battle against his hate, his rage, and his sense of hopelessness. He could not break the bonds that chained him. He could not bear to simply watch as Milak destroyed his delicate little Colette, however. He needed his wits about him to find a way to save her before it was too late.

The answer did not come to him swiftly, but when he saw that Jala had come into the chamber, he used his control of her and drew her near. "Go to Colette and tell her this: She must be strong and endure. I will find a way to save her."

* * * *

Colette had no idea of how long she sat alone in the cell. It seemed many hours, but fear had a way of lengthening the minutes. When the door opened, she gasped in sharply on a breath of fear, relaxing only fractionally when she saw that it was Jala.

Jala knelt on the floor in front of her. After glancing around uneasily, she leaned near and spoke low next to Colette's ear. "My master bade me say this to you--endure without struggle. If you fight him, you will only give him strength over you, and incite him to worse. Master will find a way to free you."

If it was meant to comfort her, it failed. The opposite was true, for her fear had been leavened with weariness in the time that she'd been in the cell and the words sharpened it once more to terror.

"Release me and I will flee and save myself," she whispered back, her voice shaky with nerves.

"I can not," Jala snarled fearfully.

Snatching up a length of fabric, she wound it about Colette's head, covering her eyes and tying the thing snugly.

Colette fought the blindfold mindlessly, but it was secured in spite of her efforts and she heard Jala leave once more.

It occurred to her that the blindfold might be a blessing as well as curse. She could not see the things that frightened her, but her imagination might scare her worse.

The words Jala had spoken tumbled around in her mind, but like the blindfold itself, it had two blades. A spark of hopefulness flickered to life at the promise to rescue her, but doubtfulness followed quickly on its heels, extinguishing it.

The demon who had seized her was undoubtedly his overlord, and far more powerful even that Nuri. What hope was there that Nuri could free her? And what must she endure?

Chapter Seven

Colette was not left to dwell on the possibilities long. The imps returned. She knew it must be them even though she couldn't see them, for she felt the presence of two and the hands of two as her manacles were unfastened and then her arms were seized and she was half carried from the cell and led along what she knew must be a long corridor from the way the sounds echoed off the walls.

They entered a great chamber. This she knew from the way the sounds echoed hollowly. The place was chill and damp as the cell had been, but she felt the warmth of bodies around her, heard the whisper of breaths. How many were there she couldn't begin to guess, but she felt the presence of many, felt the gaze of many.

'Endure', she thought as she was pushed against something hard and felt it bite into her belly as the two hands that held her captive and guided her forced her to bend over the thing until she was bent almost double.

Manacles were attached to her wrists and her arms positioned out to her sides. She tugged on them experimentally when she was released and discovered she could not move her arms in any direction. Giving up the effort after a moment, she lay panting fearfully, tensed against what would happen next.

Her ankles were seized and her legs drawn apart until the muscles between her thighs began to strain. Finally, when she'd begun to think she would be split in two, the coldness of manacles clamped around her ankles. She heard the rattle of chains and knew even before she tried that she would not be able to move her legs either.

Hands caught the cheeks of her buttocks, spreading them. Cool air wafted along her cleft. Something thin and rounded pushed into her rectum. Gasping, she bucked, struggled for several moments to try to evade the intrusion before her mind finally accepted that she could not. Panting, she tried to force herself to relax as it was pushed slowly, but inexorably into her until it was deeply inside of her.

Something tweaked her nipples. She jerked, realizing it was the edge of sharp teeth. The teeth clamped down when she tried to jerk away, just hard enough to promise real pain if she continued to struggle.

Gritting her teeth, she forced herself to stillness.

Almost at once the pain and discomfort eased. A shiver went through her as the teeth nipped at her nipples, scraping over them until the blood engorged them almost painfully.

The rod in her rectum was slowly withdrawn and then pushed deeply again. Strangely, pleasure stirred to life as the motion was repeated and the teeth continued to pluck at her nipples, sometimes hard enough to send a flicker of pain through her, but then replacing it almost instantly with a jolt of pleasure.

Moisture began to gather in her sex. The expectation of pleasure replaced the fear of pain as her body burgeoned. She ceased to pant with fear and began to gasp with pleasure each time the hard shaft was pushed deeply inside of her, each time the teeth bore down on her tender nipples to the very brink of pain.

Fingers dug into her sensitive nether lips, pulling them wide. Something huge and hard pressed against the mouth of her sex, breached the opening. She gasped as she felt it stretching her, pressing deeper and deeper.

Fingers tangled in her hair, pulling her head up and a cock was pushed into her mouth. She might have bit down on it except that it filled her mouth so completely she couldn't close her jaws.

The cock behind her pressed inexorably deeper and deeper, thrusting past her resisting flesh until it could go no deeper. It was withdrawn, slowly, as the rod was withdrawn from her rectum, and then pressed deeply inside of her again, more rapidly than before.

In sync, the thrusting began in earnest, plowing into her from behind, forcing her mouth over the cock until it butted the back of her throat and then retreated. She groaned, partly in distress, but mostly in mindless ecstasy as she felt her body assaulted on every front, stimulated almost beyond bearing by the mouths that ceased to tease her with the edge of teeth and began to suckle her nipples hard, by the piston like thrusting of cocks into every exquisitely sensitive orifice.

An orgasm rolled over her and through her without warning, and then her body began to build again toward another one as the hard thrusting continued, pounding into her, and the suckling on her breasts became almost a torment, refusing to allow her heated body to cool. The cock in her mouth jerked, began to spew seed down her throat even as a second, far harder, climax hit her. She choked, swallowing in self defense although she might have been revolted if not for the fact that she was so caught in the grips of rapture she could not even think. The thrusting behind her continued, harder and faster until abruptly, she felt the cock jerk and hot seed bathe her channel.

She gasped weakly when the mouths ceased to tease her and the cocks were withdrawn, hanging limply against her bindings, struggling to catch her breath.

Her heart and lungs had barely regained their normal rhythm when the pleasurable assault began again. She groaned, not in fear this time, but because she wasn't certain she could endure any more pleasure.

She discovered she had no choice in the matter. Her body responded to the stimulation regardless of her wishes. Tension coiled inside of her as she felt the hard shafts penetrating her sex and her rectum, pounding into her aggressively. Pleasure escalated as her breasts were gnawed, suckled, licked. When the cock was shoved into her mouth, she was already so excited, she began sucking at it almost feverishly.

She was barely conscious by the time her body had peaked twice more and she was allowed to catch her breath.

She moaned in dismay when she realized, however, that that was all that it was, a moment to catch her breath. They began again almost as soon as she had, pumping into her and teasing her breasts until her weary body responded and she came again.

The more weary she became, the slower her body was to respond and the more determinedly they teased her until she did respond.

Finally, when she had lost count of the number of times she had been penetrated, taken to the heights of pleasure and found release, the manacles were unfastened. She sprawled weakly on the stone floor, her legs refusing to hold her up.

Hands lifted her and carried her. She roused slightly when she was lowered into a pool of steaming water and bathed, enough to open her eyes a fraction and glance around, but the heated water seemed to leach the last of her strength. She lost consciousness long before she was laid upon a cot.

Jala roused her some time later, picking at her until she got up to attend her needs. It was all she could do to walk from the cot to the chamber pot and make it back to collapse on the hard cot again. Listlessly, she lifted her head and looked around, discovering in the flickering light of the single torch that lit the room that she was in the cell she'd first been taken to.

Jala shoved food into her hands. "Eat."

She stared at the bread and cheese without interest.

"Eat, or you will be too weak to survive this," Jala growled.

She ate a little, more because Jala wouldn't leave her in peace than because she had any interest in the food or any concern about her weakness. When she had appeased Jala, she collapsed on the bunk again and felt almost instantly asleep.

It seemed to her that she'd barely closed her eyes when she felt the insistent tug of hands again. She made an attempt to struggle, but it was even more short lived than her first attempt had been the day before--she thought it had been the day before.

She was not blindfolded. Instead, they led her down the corridor and she was able to see what she had not seen the day before. The chamber they took her to was vast, as she'd thought. Once inside, the sight that caught her gaze at once was Nuri, chained hand and foot to a wall.

This then, was his punishment, to watch while others enjoyed the pleasures of the flesh he had claimed for his own.

Dragging her gaze from him with an effort, unwilling to examine the emotions that warred inside her at that knowledge, she looked around.

The demon that had seized her and tortured her with pleasure the day before sat upon a great throne. Surrounding him were lesser demons.

She was forced onto her knees at the foot of his throne.

His eyes glowed as he studied her. "Did you accept his seed with pleasure mortal?"

Colette swallowed. She had, but she had a feeling that wasn't the answer he wanted to hear. "We made a bargain. I kept my bargain," she said finally.

He growled, low in his chest and leaned forward. "And once again, he deprived me of my due. He toyed with you, mortal. His blood is tainted with that of a mortal woman and it has made him weak. He could not sacrifice the virgin meant for me before. This is why he was banished, why I demanded two in her place to earn my favor once more.

"Instead, he fell under your spell--though I can not see why--and planted his seed inside of your frail human flesh."

Colette stared at him blankly, trying to assimilate what he'd said. He was saying that Nuri would not have sacrificed her and her sister anyway? That he had not the coldness, or the cruelty in his heart to do so?

"He did not tell you he placed a Halfling in your belly?"

He had misinterpreted her look of stunned surprise for Colette had barely registered the comment about Nuri's seed. A shock wave traveled through her at that, however. The room seemed to recede around her. She had a demon growing inside of her, she thought in horror.

"Do not worry yourself, little morsel. I will not leave it there," he growled, leaning back once more and lifting his hand in a signal.

A blindfold was secured around her head again. Still too stunned to react, Colette was hauled to her feet, walked across the room and pushed back against cold stone. Her wrists were grasped, her arms pulled straight out at her sides and clamped against the wall. She felt hands on her thighs then, something wrapped around her legs that felt like a wide band of leather and then her legs were lifted.

Briefly, she hung from her arms. She was so focused on that pain, she was scarcely aware of what they were doing with her legs until she felt her thighs forced wide apart, so wide the muscles of her inner thighs strained and she felt her nether lips part. Her legs were pinned so that she couldn't move them. In the next moment, she felt fingers grasping her nether lips. Something was clamped on the flesh. She felt a tugging and cool air along her tender exposed inner lips.

Her heart began to pound in her chest with a mixture of fright and excitement she shouldn't have felt. Moisture gathered in her sex.

Something hot and wet slid over her exposed flesh. She jerked instinctively, but she was pinned effectively. She couldn't move at all, couldn't avoid the touch. She could do nothing more than try to close her mind to it.

She found that impossible as the tongue continued to lap her hungrily on and on until she was dizzy with the rioting sensations inside of her. A mouth closed over one of her breasts, suckling it hard and a shaft of pleasure cut through her painfully, joining the tension already growing in her belly. She bit her lip, trying to contain the pleasure she knew she shouldn't be feeling, but found when her other breast was siezed that she could no longer hold it in. A moan escaped her.

As if that was all the encouragement they had been waiting for, they began to torment her with more fervor. The tongue ceased to lap her cleft and delved into her opening, driving deeply inside of her and curling against one spot that sent a jolt of excitement through her. She swallowed with an effort, struggling as she felt her body rising rapidly toward release.

She had reached the peak, was hovering on the brink, struggling against the war inside of her to yield to its siren call, when they moved away from her almost as abruptly as they had started.

A sense of disappointment filled her. She lay panting, trying to catch her breath for many moments. Before she could do so, the hot mouths and rough tongues began to tease her again. Once more she was brought to the brink and abandoned. Shuddering, she struggled to regain her composure when they left her body cooling, throbbing with unrequited desire.

She realized after a time that this was not something that would cease, that they meant to tease her as mercilessly as the day before, except that this time she was not allowed to find culmination. She spent part of the time fighting to reach it, and part of the time struggling against it. It seemed not to matter. Either way, she was not allowed to reach her peak. They suckled the tiny bud at the apex of her thighs. They suckled her nipples. Time and again, the tongue was pushed deeply inside of her, lapping her, stroking that place that drove her into mindlessness but always ceasing before she could reach release.

After a time, she was feverish with the need. Desperation drove everything else from her mind as the itch became maddening.

She almost felt like weeping when she felt the manacles removed. Her body ached and throbbed all over. Tension was coiled so tightly inside of her that she could barely stand the touch of the hands that pulled her away from wall.

Her knees buckled. She was lifted and carried.

Certain that they were returning her to the cell, surprise flickered through her when they halted after only a few steps. She was lifted again, her thighs seized and pulled wide. Fingers dug into her fleshy nether lips, pulling them apart. Something huge and hard pressed against her opening.

She gasped, panting for breath as they bore down on her, impaling her on the hard shaft that stretched her almost painfully. Dizziness washed over her as her legs were released at last and the weight of her own body slowly impaled the hard shaft deeper and deeper as her arms were dragged behind her back and her wrists bound together.

Her toes touched the cold stone. With an effort she balanced on them.

Mouths plucked at her nipples, teasing them to attention and then suckling them hungrily. Groaning, she felt her knees buckle, felt her weight drive the huge shaft to the hilt inside of her. Slowly, as the mouths teased her, moisture gathered in her channel, heat, tension. Her flesh began to relax and flex around the hard shaft. Scarcely aware of what she was doing, she pushed herself up and allowed her body to slide slowly over the shaft again, sheathing it to the hilt.

The need rose inside of her again, more painful that before.

Hands caught her ankles, forcing her to bend her knees until she was resting fully on top of the hard shaft. She was held tightly, unable to move. Distress filled her as the relief she needed was once again denied.

Abruptly, the shaft began to withdraw from her clinging flesh. She whimpered.

It returned, slamming deeply, impaling her to the hilt and her heart leapt. She began to moan in desperate need as she felt her body impaled on the hard shaft over and over. Her culmination caught her unaware, tearing through her so hard she screamed at the agony/ecstasy of it.

And still it continued to pound into her, on and on until her body began to crave the hard, deep thrusts, responded, the tension coiling more and more tightly until she came again.

She was shaking from weakness by the time she was lifted away at last, barely conscious as she was carried back to her cell.

As before, Jala appeared after a time, pestering her until she got up and attended her needs, ate, bathed. Finally, she left in peace to collapse naked on the cot and sleep the sleep of the dead.

She didn't even try to struggle when she was dragged up again and carried to the chamber where she had spent two days in pleasurable torment. Her body quickened with need even as they dragged her down the corridor.

She wasn't blindfolded as before, but it was hardly necessary. She was too exhausted to feel any fear at all and her body was already screaming to be fed, to be tortured endlessly, craving the pleasure it had come to expect.

She was pushed onto a tilted slab of stone with her head at the lower end. Her wrists were manacled out to either side of her. Drawing her legs up, the imps pulled her thighs apart and secured them so that she couldn't close her legs or lower them. The demons fell upon her then, as hungry for her flesh as she was for the pleasure they'd taught her. They nipped at her with the edge of their teeth, licked her, suckled her flesh all over. She gasped and moaned beneath the assault, falling at once into a drugged stupor of pleasure that made awareness of anything beyond that recede.

A cock was pushed into her mouth. She suckled it feverishly as she felt a tongue thrust inside her, lapping hungrily at her passage and sending jolts of exquisite sensation through her each time it stroked the most receptive spot along her channel. Her body convulsed within moments. Unable to cry out for the cock in her mouth, she sucked it greedily, milking it until it was withdrawn.

The feeding upon her did not cease and her body hardly touched down before it began to climb toward release again. Another cock was thrust into her mouth. Her jaws ached, but she accepted it with no more than a soft moan. Enthusiasm replaced her weary acceptance as her body coiled toward another explosive release and she began sucking with desperation. She had almost reached her second peek when the tongue was withdrawn from her pussy and a hard shaft speared her, plowing past her resisting flesh and burrowing deeply. Even as he began pounding into her, her body siezed and began to convulse with release. When she had milked them both of their seed, they withdrew from her.

She lay gasping for breath, aware of nothing but the dull pounding of her heart and her struggle to fill her lungs with air.

The manacles were removed and she was rolled onto her stomach and dragged halfway off the stone slab before she was manacled again. Her legs were pulled apart and her ankles manacled as her wrists had been. The stone bit into her lower belly as her hips were seized and a cock thrust inside of her, its possession eased by the juices already coating her channel.

The beast hammered into her mercilessly, slamming into her so hard each thrust sent a jolt through her. Despite everything, even without the pleasurable assault on her breasts, her body responded, climbing again toward a release that hit her so forcefully she cried out.

When he had reached his own release, he moved away and another took his place.

She groaned, but it seemed that no matter how weary she became, her body had become addicted to the drug of fulfillment and it struggled on and on, culminating over and over again until she reached oblivion.

Chapter Eight

Every muscle in Colette's body seemed to have turned to jelly. They quaked weakly when she was taken at last to her cell. She was hardly even aware of reaching it and collapsing on her cot, hardly aware of Jala's efforts to rouse her. After a while, Jala ceased trying to rouse her and left. Dreams invaded her sleep, tormenting her even there with the carnal pleasures she was trying hard to block from her mind.

Nuri's face invaded her dreams, as well, drawn, haunted, glittering with impotent fury, but she shied away from it.

She didn't want to think about him or what he'd done to her.

His seed was growing in her belly. Why had he planted it there? Why?

She pushed that question from her mind, too, unwilling to consider it, reluctant at the same time to consider that his overlord had promised to see to it that the demon's seed did not prosper in her womb.

Endure, Jala had said. She wasn't certain she could endure much more, and yet the word had barely formed in her mind when her body warmed with remembered pleasure, grew damp with need.

She was sore all over when she woke at last to Jala's determined efforts to rouse her. Somehow, she knew that she had slept for a very long time, perhaps because despite the soreness, she felt almost as weak and disoriented with too much rest as she'd felt before from the lack.

When Jala had bullied her into seeing to her needs and bathed her, the imps Enis and Pell strode into the room and siezed her.

Dismay filled her. For all the difference it made, she resisted as they dragged her down the corridor and into the great chamber again.

Her heart skipped a several beats as they brought her to a halt and a cloth came down over her eyes. When it had been tied securely, she was led from the doorway and deeper into the chamber.

She was pushed back against something solid. Cold stone bit into her back as her arms were jerked out to either side and secured there with manacles clamped around her wrists. When she felt the hands on her thighs, her stomach tightened, but she thought that she knew what to expect and in any case, resistance was useless.

Her legs were drawn up and outward until her inner thighs protested and then wider still until she could feel the fleshy lips of her sex part and a breath of cool air caressed the inner lips or her sex.

Her first inkling that it would not be the same as before came when she felt something pinch down almost painfully on her nipples. She heard the cling of chain and felt a tug. She strained then against her bindings but the more she strained the harder the tug on her nipples and she went still, panting, feeling a strange combination of fear and desire colliding inside of her.

Something similar to the thing that had been clamped to her nipples was clamped on the flesh of her nether lips and she felt them drawn wide, exposing her most intimate flesh completely, leaving her totally vulnerable.

She gasped as she felt a finger delving her cleft and parting her buttocks, felt something harder and uncomfortable pushing slowly into her rectum. Panting, she squeezed her eyes shut against the discomfort, willing her muscles to relax as it was pushed deeper.

At last, the thrusting stopped and she relaxed fractionally, but held herself perfectly still, fearful any movement would cause her pain. The shaft was slowly withdrawn and then pushed inside of her again. Pleasure blossomed tentatively, built as the thrust and withdrawal continued.

Something tugged at one of her nipples, making her jerk reflexively as pleasure akin to pain shot through her. She realized after a moment as she felt the heat of a mouth and the rough texture of a tongue that some sort of ring had been clamped around her nipples so that they'd engorged to near painfully intense fullness and sensitivity. After a few minutes, the nearly unbearable tugging ceased.

The thrust of the shaft did not. It continued to move slowly inside of her and out again, stirring harder and harder currents of pleasure.

A hot tongue was dragged along her cleft. It sent a jolt through her as it brushed the tiny nub at the top. She jerked instinctively sending triple bolts of pleasure and pain through her body as the movement pulled at her nipples and her body tightened around the shaft.

Groaning, she tried to hold herself perfectly still as the tongue dragged slowly along her cleft again. A mouth closed over her other nipple, sending another hard shaft of keen sensation through her. This time, she gritted her teeth and held still.

The tongue ceased to lap her and a mouth closed over the nub, sucking. She bucked, groaned as equal parts pleasure and pain went through her. The stimuli intensified, as if they had achieved the goal they'd been aiming for. A mouth fastened over the first nipple, sucking it vigorously. The thrusting began to move faster. The mouth on her clit sucked harder.

She began to pant as her body tensed all over. She was nearing her crest when the mouth released her clit and a tongue was thrust deep into her passage. Rapture rocked her as her body exploded in release.

Her head fell forward weakly as the shaft was at last withdrawn. Before she had even caught her breath, she felt something huge pressing against the mouth of her passage. Her head swam dizzily as she was tilted, felt herself being pulled downward. Her body, still convulsing in the aftermath of release, resisted the press of hard flesh against the walls of her sex. She groaned as she was drawn downward until she was impaled to the hilt on the huge shaft, groaned as she felt her body quicken again, felt moisture saturate her passage as she was lifted up until only the head remained inside of her and then pressed downward again until she'd fully enveloped the shaft.

Hot mouths covered her nipples, tugging insistently, driving her into mindless pleasure as her body was brought down upon the shaft faster and faster until bliss erupted again and her body convulsed almost painfully around the hard shaft. Almost the moment the convulsions began, two great hands caught her thighs, lifting her and driving her down again harder and faster. The pleasure intensified instead of dissipating until it tore a weak scream from her throat as the cock inside her jerked and coated her passage with hot seed.

She went limp when her body at last stopped shuddering, her head swimming dizzily as she felt herself lifted up and righted again. Under other circumstances, she might have been repulsed when she felt a mouth cover her cleft, sucking hungrily at her, licking her, delving deeply inside her to lap her. As it was, the jolt of heat it shot through her only sent her reeling closer to oblivion.

Before she could grasp the darkness of nothingness, pleasure began to escalate inside her again. She groaned, knowing there would be no end to it until the demon had thoroughly sated himself.

She didn't know if he deliberately tormented her by not allowing her to rest, or if he was enjoying himself too much. In any case, she was not allowed even a few moments to catch her breath.

She knew it was the demon. The cock she was impaled on was huge and she had seen how enormous his erection was.

He toyed with her when her body had been rocked over and over until it was too weary to respond, tormenting her until it began yet another sluggish climb to completion and then another after that until oblivion finally reached up and grabbed her, hauling her into the depths of blackness.

Colette lost all count of time. Days blurred one into another. Weeks might have passed. She had no clue. She only knew that no matter how weary she was, she would be teased endlessly until her body responded.

And it was never same. Each time she thought she knew what to expect, something different was done to her. One day, she would be brought to service the demon. Another, she was dragged to the great chamber and his minions toyed with her, giving her both pleasure and pain as they gnawed and sucked her flesh, pounding into her frantically until they spilled their seed and then passing her to the next. And when she would think she was to be with the demon again, she was bound hand and foot and tormented ceaselessly and given no relief at all until she was close to begging them for it.

After a time, she stopped looking for Nuri, forgot what Jala had said completely, but each time she grew so weary she thought she would die the very next time her body exploded with pleasure, she was left to her exhaustion until they decided she was up to playing again.

The day came when she was carried to the chamber and found it empty of all save the demon. Numb, she didn't even protest when she was pushed down to lie on her back on the floor and her wrists and ankles manacled. She tensed when her nipples were pinched and rings pushed through them, but she felt little more than a twinge of discomfort. Drawing her nether lips back, they pierced her clit, as well, then strung a thin chain through the loops.

Her nipples and clit were still throbbing when they removed the manacles and hauled her to her feet. Handing the ends of the chain to the demon, the imps departed.

The demon studied her broodingly for several moments and finally tugged on the chain. Pain and pleasure shot through her. "I've grown--partial to my little pet," the demon growled. "Come."

Wincing as he tugged at the chain again, Colette followed him. Leading her from the chamber, he climbed the stairs from the dungeon and then up another flight, dragging her finally into a small chamber off of the upper corridor.

The room was empty save for a mattress on the floor against one wall that had been piled with pillows. Pushing her down upon the mattress, he knelt, grasped her thighs and pushed them wide. She gasped as he opened his mouth over her, trying to fight a moan of pleasure as he began to lap her greedily with his tongue. It could not be contained for long. As his mouth closed upon her clit, sucking, she caught his shoulders, stifling a moan. Grasping her wrists, he pinned them to the mattress and continued, sucking and licking her clit and her cleft and finally thrusting his tongue deeply inside of her and lapping her until her muscles began to convulse around his tongue and she groaned as her release caught her.

He ignored that, as well, suckling and lapping at her until her body reached its peak twice more and she was screaming with the intensity of it. He rolled off of her and onto his back, giving the chain a tug. "Mount me," he growled.

Shakily, Colette responded more to the tug on the chain that she couldn't ignore than the command. Straddling him, she caught his cock in her hand and lifted away from him, straining to push him inside of her. Impatient, he caught her hips, pressing her relentlessly down until she was gasping with a mixture of pleasure and pain as he stretched her almost beyond bearing, impaling her to the hilt on his shaft.

Slowly, lubrication flowed into her passage, easing his possession as he lifted her and pushed her down again. Uttering a growl after a few moments, he tipped her onto her back and thrust into her again, buried himself deeply and then began pumping into her furiously. When he had spent himself, he pushed away from her and sprawled on the mattress beside her.

Too weak to move, Colette didn't even react when he began to toy with her body, squeezing her breasts in his great paws, flicking at the rings in her nipples until warmth began to gather in her.

She didn't know whether it was better or worse that the demon had decided to keep her only to himself, but she discovered after a while that it was neither. She could not tell any difference. He held her down and tormented her endlessly, allowing her to rest only briefly before he used the chain to tug her to him and began again.

She was relieved beyond measure when at last he lay back upon the mattress and began to snore loudly. Crawling as far away from him as the chains would allow, Colette collapsed weakly on the floor and allowed her mind to drift toward slumber.

She was teetering on the brink of exhausted sleep when Nuri abruptly appeared. He stared down at her for a long moment, and she thought at first that she must be dreaming. He lifted his head after moment, his eyes narrowing as they focused on his overlord.

He began to chant in a voice that was barely above a whisper. The fine hairs on Colette's body lifted. Something stirred in the room. The overlord twitched.

Slowly, the chanting gained in volume, becoming louder and louder. As it did, the 'something' Colette had sensed grew stronger until she could see swirling particles of light. The swirling pinpricks of light formed above the sleeping demon, became brighter, more visible, and then intense, changing colors.

Alarm chased her exhaustion away as the demon opened his eyes. Nuri's voice grew louder still, echoing off the walls. The demon uttered a growl, tensing, his muscles straining as he tried to rise. "Release me," he said, his voice coming out slow, distorted.

Instead of responding, Nuri lifted his arms, extending them, his fingers splayed wide. Blue forks of power shot from his fingertips, encircling the demon, binding him as tightly as if they were ropes. He struggled against them. "I am your overlord," he growled, his voice so distorted Colette could barely make sense of them at first.

Ignoring the demand by his overlord to recognize him as his superior, Nuri continued the strange chant that increased in volume until Colette covered her ears with her hands. "Your si--re," the demon growled as his image began dim, began to grow transparent. "Re--lease me!"

"In hades," Nuri growled, gritting his teeth as the blue light snaking from his finger tips became blue fire, and then white. A black cloud began to rise around the demon. The demon faded until Colette could see the pillows and mattress clearly through him and finally disappeared altogether.

The moment he vanished, Nuri began to chant a different spell. Around him, the room crackled with energy. The radiance of the lights seemed to spread, intensifying until the room glowed and Colette squeezed her eyes closed against the blinding light that seemed to pierce straight through her eyes and into her brain.

At last, the light began to dim and Colette opened her eyes cautiously and looked around. Nuri swayed slightly where he stood. His knees buckled abruptly and he hit the floor, falling forward on his face. Anxiety filled Colette, but she felt herself slipping away even as she struggled to find the strength to rise.

* * * *

Colette surfaced from oblivion a number of times and immediately sought it again before the sounds around her began to intrude so persistently that she finally opened her eyes. Moments passed before familiarity set in and she realized she was lying alone in Nuri's bed, in his chamber.

Jala was cleaning, which mostly amounted to slamming things around, muttering under her breath.

"Showed him, we did. Sent us away and then come sticking his nose in *our* business."

Colette put her hand to her aching head and closed her eyes again. The movement caught Jala's attention.

"Lazy mortal! Lying abed days on end."

Days? Colette thought it over and realized she had not, as she'd thought, roused over and over again during the night, but had slept for many hours between the times. Disoriented by the thought, she searched her memory.

Nuri's overlord! That thought brought her eyes open again and she sat up. "The demon's gone?"

Jala sent her a look. "If'n you mean my master, no. The other one, yes."

It hurt to move. The soreness reminded her of all that had transpired in the days when the overlord had held her captive, but she had no clear idea of how long that had been. A combination of heat and fear washed through her, though, as the memories surfaced--and embarrassment. She had not thought that she was capable of experiencing pleasure under such circumstances, and yet she could hardly deny that she had--to herself or anyone else. She reddened when she remembered how vocal she had been.

"Nuri sent him back?"

Jala beamed. "My master is a powerful demon, and wise! Yes! He outsmarted the master and sent him packing--back to hades, he went, and can not open the portal now, for my lord placed a powerful spell upon it. Ha!"

Colette studied Jala doubtfully. Wise and powerful? If he was so wise and powerful why had she had to 'endure'? She asked Jala as much.

Jala growled at her. "Mortal, fool! Know nothing, you do. Halfing is not so powerful as demon whole! Had to bide his time and wait, gather power to himself and jump when the overlord was weak."

Colette thought that over. "You mean I weakened him," she muttered, feeling a mixture of anger and embarrassment when she realized how she'd weakened the demon.

"Take a lot upon yerself, mortal! Overlord not come atall if not for you! Came because you enticed the master to lust when he owed his overlord a sacrifice. It was only right and fair. Anyways, no other way to weaken the overlord. Master was not happy to share, fool!"

Despite the insult, Colette was slightly mollified that Nuri had not used her so much as he had taken advantage of something he could not prevent. The comment about him not being happy to share intrigued her beyond the explanation, however.

She dismissed it, unwilling to examine those feelings at the moment, particularly when her rambling, disjointed thoughts settled on other comments she'd heard before when she was too weak with exhaustion to consider them.

"He said sire! The demon. He demanded that Nuri release him."

Jala sent her a speculative glance. "Aye. Sire he is, overlord, too."

"His father!" Colette exclaimed, horrified. "That--that horrible creature *sired* him?"

She could tell from the look Jala sent her that Jala suspected her master was being insulted and she didn't like it at all.

"Malik always had a taste for mortals. Bred a Halfling on a mortal fool. She dropped it in the woods. Lord Nuri was strong then, too, though, didn't die. Malik decided he was pleased and took the Halfling. Banished him here when he saw the human side was stronger--called him weak. Showed the old bastard, he did!" She said and cackled. "When you drop that one, we'll take it and send you on your way, fool."

It was too much information too fast, and stunning information at that. Colette merely stared at the malformed imp, her mind too disordered to sort through the myriad of thoughts and emotions roiling through her.

"Brought food to keep the master's son strong," Jala continued after watching Colette for several moments, obviously disappointed that no argument was forthcoming.

Colette glanced in the direction Jala had indicated, but a wave of nausea washed over her. "I'm not hungry," she said with difficulty, laying down once more and closing her eyes to fight the queasiness.

Jala glared at her. "Master won't be happy you try to starve his son. Better eat, fool!"

Chapter Nine

Colette was angry when her condition became a certainty in her mind. Nuri had tricked her. She supposed she should have considered that becoming pregnant was a possibility if she were forced to uphold her end of the bargain she had made with the demon to save herself and her sister and mother. Maybe in the back of her mind, she *had* considered it and had simply dismissed it because she had known she might have no choice in the matter, and possibly because she had not really believed that a demon could get a child on her.

What made her angry, however, was that she had really *had* no choice even if she'd considered the possibility, that she was ruined, whether the demon freed her or not, and that she suspected he had somehow used his powers to *make* it happen when it might have been a remote possibility otherwise.

Jala had said as much. After thinking it over, she remembered the demon Malik had *known* it, which also seemed to her to indicate that Nuri could have *not* made her pregnant, but did so for some reason that escaped her.

She couldn't imagine why he would have except that he had been determined to win in their battle of wills.

She felt ill only thinking about it. It would have been bad enough to find herself in such a condition under any circumstances at all, but to be carrying a demon's seed?

She could not help but empathize with the woman who had borne Nuri. No doubt she, too, had been a helpless captive of Malik's, forced to endure all sorts of sexual acts she would never have willingly agreed to, her life utterly ruined, and she could not have carried a demon child home. She might manage to talk them into taking her back without such a thing, but with it?

She was almost as horrified, though. Regardless of the circumstances, how could any woman abandon a helpless creature to die, she wondered?

Despite her anger at Nuri, pity filled her when she thought about the way he had been abandoned to die by his own mother. Small wonder he hated mortals. And possibly he hated them because he was only a Halfling, despised by both humans and demons for something he could not help-- for the demon, Malik had banished him because of his human side and certainly he was not accepted in the world of humans for they would not go near him if they could avoid it.

One thing she could not understand was why he would do that to another after what he had suffered.

Jala had said she would be sent away once she had borne it. Had he done it only because he wanted a son of his own? Because he was weary of being alone?

She frowned at those thoughts, wondering if there was any possibility of truth to them. After all, he was a demon. Whatever Malik said, he seemed more demon than human to her and he did not seem to feel things as humans did. He had even scoffed at human emotions, behaved as if he could not understand why she was willing to risk all to save her mother and sister when she had told him it was because she loved them.

She had dreaded seeing Nuri again, dreaded the confrontation she expected, and yet when nearly a week passed without a sign of him, she began to feel very let down and anxious.

Was it only that he had no further use for her? Was it, as Jala had said, that he was angry that he had had to share her with Malik?

Had he felt possessive toward her? And, if so, did it mean anything beyond that?

Was he avoiding her because he was angry with her about it?

Or was he avoiding her because he was ashamed that he had not been able to overpower Malik until the demon had expended so much energy ravishing her that he'd weakened himself?

Maybe he wasn't avoiding her at all. Maybe he had just tired of her?

She woke one morning to find that her trunk had been brought to the room again.

She wasn't certain what to make of that, but she was glad to have it--right up until she discovered that her belly had already swollen until she could not even fasten her dresses up. She wept then, railing against Nuri, against fate, against the unwelcome thing growing inside of her.

All she wanted was to go home. It was all she'd ever wanted, and now, more than she ever had before, she wanted her mother. She might well have found the prospect of bearing a child frightening under any circumstances, but she certainly did now--unwed, knowing the creature inside of her was a demon.

The books, needlework, and tablets her trunk contained were some comfort to her. At least she had something to keep her hands and mind occupied.

Right up until the very moment Nuri appeared, Colette was certain that she hated him, was furious with him, couldn't wait until she could leave the abbey and never look back.

Such gladness filled her when she looked up from her needlework one evening and found him standing before the fireplace that she had to remind herself to breathe.

She'd forgotten how handsome he was, she realized, feeling warm all over as images filled her mind of his caresses.

She couldn't think of anything to say. An awkward, uncomfortable silence settled between them as they gazed at each other.

"You look--well," Nuri growled finally, his face darkening as he looked away from her and stared down at the flames on the hearth.

Colette's disappointment was crushing, all the more so because she had felt so thrilled to see him. She wondered what he had meant to say. Pregnant? Ugly and bloated? Recovered?

She returned her attention to her needlework, finding her long lost anger at last.

"Yes. I have recovered from being fucked senseless," she snapped, and then was horrified by the words that had slipped out. What made it worse was that she desperately wanted to be fucked senseless again. She hadn't realized that part of her restlessness was because she had grown all too accustomed to being thoroughly rutted with extreme regularity and her body now knew the lack.

"I would have--stopped it if it had been within my power," he snarled.

That hesitation gave her pause. She didn't know why, but she had the feeling he had meant to say protected. It was absurd, of course, mere wishful thinking on her part, because to want to protect her he would have had to have actually cared, which was not the same thing at all as merely feeling possessive. "Would you?" she asked, trying not to sound hopeful.

He glanced at her sharply. Instead of answering her, however, he moved to the high backed chair across from her and sprawled in it.

Colette tried not to notice the way his breeches clung to his manhood, faithfully outlining it--if her memory served her, and she was no longer certain it did--damn it! The only thing she was certain of was that her femininity instantly clamored to be filled.

"Malik is a powerful demon, one of the most powerful. He was not easy to dispatch," he said finally, anger still threading his voice but no so much as before.

The comment resurrected memories she was trying very hard to forget, mostly because of the discomfort she felt about her behavior and lack of control, not because she felt any particular horror over it. She knew she should have. The fact that she didn't was a dark secret she would take to her grave. She was uncomfortable enough with the self knowledge. It was not something she wanted to share.

He studied her for several moments and seemed to take her silence as condemnation. "Believe it or not, as you will," he growled, his face hardening with anger again.

"I didn't say I didn't believe it," Colette retorted. The fact was that she did, but that didn't make it any more palatable to her. It was easier to have a target for one's anger than none at all--or worse, only oneself.

She was very sorry, now, that she had flown in the face of providence and suggested the short cut through the woods, but it could not be undone. And Nuri was hardly innocent, for if he had not taken her none of it would have happened.

And if she had not been taken, then she could have looked forward to a long, dull and boring life as a spinster. Her honor would be intact and her virginity and they would have brought her cold comfort in her twilight years.

Or, perhaps, she would have wed some respectable gentleman who looked like the south end of a north bound mule and bred a new image of himself on her every year.

"But you hate me anyway."

Surprise flickered through Colette. "Why would you care if I did?"

He muttered something under his breath that she did not catch. It irritated her. She had asked on impulse, but she wanted to know. "Do you care?" she prodded.

"No!" he snarled, getting to his feet again and pacing before the hearth for several moments before he disappeared as he had come.

Colette gaped at the swirl of dark mist for several moments before anger filled her. "I *do* hate you!" she yelled at the ceiling, stamping her foot.

She flounced in her chair when there was no response, uncertain of whether she most wanted to scream and throw something or weep. In the end, she did neither, contenting herself with wrecking the needlework she'd been working on so painstakingly and then spending several more hours carefully removing the ruined stitches.

After nearly a week of alternating between blaming herself and blaming Nuri for her woes, Colette decided she had sulked long enough. If she had to remain pinned up in one room with no company other than Jala's, she was going to choke the life out of Jala.

She was trying her best not to think about her condition. She didn't want to think about it at all, let alone consider what she would soon be facing or what her life would be afterwards. Jala was either delighted at the prospect of welcoming a new Halfling into the world, however, or if she simply gloried in tormenting Colette.

Leaving was no longer an option even if Nuri had allowed it. She was not noticeably pregnant--yet--but she knew she would be before long for her waist had already disappeared and her belly had begun to round.

Regardless, there would certainly not be anyone around to see who did not already know and she saw no reason to stay cooped up in one room day in and day out. The air had a bite to it that she had not noticed the last time she had ventured out. Winter was upon them and soon the ground would be covered with snow.

Clutching her wrap more tightly about herself, she walked anyway, feeling vaguely disoriented as she stared at the near naked trees of the forest when the leaves had only just begun to turn the last time she'd noticed.

How long had she been at the abbey, she wondered?

What was her family doing? Were they mourning her death? She doubted that they still searched for her. They would almost certainly have given her up for dead by now.

Would they be joyful when she returned? Or would they be mortified at the scandal her return would no doubt generate?

Finding a bench at last, she settled on it, staring absently at the dead leaves stirred by the wind. Jala had made it clear that she would not be expected to stay after-- afterwards. She had not received the news with the thrill she would have expected, in fact, just the opposite. She had felt--unwanted and unneeded, though even she thought that was a completely unreasonable attitude for someone who had struggled so hard to escape her captivity--done things she would never have thought herself capable of only to achieve that end.

She might have questioned whether the imp knew her master's plans, except that Nuri had not led her to believe any differently.

Why, she wondered, did that bother her so much? Was it no more than a natural reaction to being rejected? Or was it a deeper cut than that?

Realizing that her fingers and toes were growing numb with the chill, she got up from the bench and finished her circuit of the abbey, returning to the main entrance once more. She was not ready to return to the bed chamber, however, nor did she particularly want to linger in the main hall. She saw no sign of him, but she knew that Nuri was generally there when he wasn't in his room and she had no desire to give him the impression that she had deliberately sought him out.

Remembering that she had found a library on that long ago day when she had searched the abbey for her mother and sister, she considered it for several moments and finally turned down the corridor of the east wing and followed it until she came to the double doors she remembered. She hesitated as she reached for the knob, wondering if this, too, was a place Nuri spent a good deal of time in. After a moment, she dismissed it.

He did not strike her as the type of person who found joy in books. The library had undoubtedly been designed and stocked by whoever had owned the abbey before.

She knew the moment she entered the room that she had misjudged him. A fire crackled on the hearth. Everything about the room told her that it was a room well used for there was not a trace of dust.

She was tempted to leave again at once, but she had read all of her own books and had come in search of something new to read. When she'd assured herself that Nuri was not in the library, she crossed the room and began to search the spines for a tempting title. Most of the books were works of non-fiction, volumes on every subject imaginable from animal husbandry to metallurgy and scientific theory. There were several books of poetry but she was not fond of love sonnets and certainly in no mood for such things now. Finally, she selected a book on gardening and horticulture. Discovering a novel about a seafaring adventure among the tomes, she took that, too.

As she was turning to go, she saw that there were a number of books stacked upon a table near a high backed overstuffed chair that sat in front of the hearth. Several more books lay on the floor nearby.

He had been reading. He would not be pleased if she took any of the books he had selected for himself, she knew. Curiosity drew her to examine the volumes anyway, partly because she wondered if she might find anything more to her taste, and partly because she wondered what his interests were.

She was more puzzled than enlightened once she had examined the books. Only two of the many stacked around his chair were of an 'enlightening' nature, both of them collections of magical spells. The rest were novels and purely for the sake of entertainment. That in itself wasn't nearly as perplexing as the type of stories, for each of those were romantic in nature, tales of great adventures and daring do of brave knights and their ladies.

Replacing the books carefully in hopes he wouldn't notice that they had been disturbed, Colette gathered her own books up again and left the library. Was he merely assuaging his own boredom with the adventures? Or was he trying to understand something he did not?

Jala had said that Nuri was a Halfling, but whatever his overlord seemed to believe, she had seen no sign at all that he felt the gentler emotions of his human side. He had made it fairly clear that love was certainly not something he grasped. Was that it? Was he trying to understand? And did that mean he felt them but simply didn't understand them? Or that he did not feel them and was curious?

It saddened her in an indescribable way to think she might be right, for whatever he thought, he could never grasp those things he was not capable of feeling. It almost seemed worse to think that he was aware that something was missing and desperately seeking it, than for him to have no awareness of it at all.

Finding once she'd settled with her books that they could not hold her interest for the thoughts rambling through her mind, Colette left the chamber again after a while and wandered about the great echoing halls of the abbey. She hadn't realized that she had any particular goal in mind until she found herself in the dungeon.

Flaming torches flickered and sputtered in sconces along the damp corridor. Knowing now why she'd come, Colette followed the corridor and found herself at last in the chamber she had spent so much time in. A shiver skated down her spine as she wandered about the cavernous room, examining the pillars and tables where she had been bound and tortured with exquisite pleasure.

It almost seemed now as if it had happened to someone else and not her, and yet if she closed her eyes, the images and sensations she had felt were almost as vivid as if she were feeling them all over again.

The girlish fantasies of passion that she'd entertained for so many years paled beside the actuality of it, but it made her realize that that capacity and yearning for passion had always been inside of her. She had learned things about herself that she hadn't particularly wanted to know, but it had been there all along, waiting to be tapped in to or she would not have experienced such raptures, she realized.

She wouldn't miss it so desperately now.

She sighed, frowning. She didn't just miss passion in general. She missed Nuri. The things that had been done to her in this place had forced her body to respond and she had experienced pleasure that was as much torture as enjoyment, as repellent as it was attractive.

She had not felt that way when Nuri had taken her. It bothered her that he had felt nothing but passion, that there had been no softer emotion attached to it. She could not lie to herself that it didn't, but she still wanted what she'd had.

After a few minutes, she shook the thoughts off and left the chamber, continuing her search. Finally, she pushed open a door and found what she had been looking for--the heated pool.

She'd begun to wonder if she had imagined its existence, for she had not been in any condition to remember anything about that time very clearly. Pleasure filled her as she moved toward it.

Kneeling on the edge of the pool, she tested the water. It was hot, almost uncomfortably so, but she knew this was the source of the unending supply of heated water that was brought to her with regularity for her baths. It was undoubtedly fed by a hot spring.

She had not thought to bring a towel, but the water was too inviting to ignore and she didn't feel like going all the way back upstairs in search of a linen to dry herself. The water heated the room itself. She could simply sit by the pool when she'd bathed as long as she wanted and wait until her skin was dry.

Peeling her clothes off, she left them far enough from the pool to keep them from getting wet and moved to the steps leading down into the water. A cake of soap lay on the lip of the pool and once she'd submerged herself, she picked it up and sniffed it.

A tangy, woodsy scent filled her nostrils. Currents of pleasure wafted through her.

Nuri bathed here. If she closed her eyes, she could vividly recall the light scent on his skin.

Emerging from the water, she stood on one of the steps and rubbed the soap slowly over her arms, her belly, her breasts, and finally her thighs and between them. Scooping water into her hands, she rubbed the soap into her skin then, creating a sudsy foam.

She wasn't even startled when she looked up and discovered Nuri standing beside the pool, watching her, his legs braced in a wide stance, his arms folded over his chest, his expression hard and uncompromising. She realized instantly that that had been in the back of her mind all the time she had wandered about the abbey, that she had not been wandering idly or without purpose. She had been searching for Nuri, invading his private spaces in the hope that he would not be able to ignore her intrusion.

Chapter Ten

Hiding a smile of satisfaction, she returned her attention to her bath, setting the soap down and working her hands slowly over her soap slick body. When she glanced at him again beneath her lashes, she saw that his gaze was on the movement of her hands, his eyes glittering with need. Satisfaction filled her. The fear she had refused to face, that he had grown tired of her and that her burgeoning body would have no appeal to him, vanished as she saw the tension in him.

Doubts returned to plague her when he made no attempt to move closer. Finally, realizing that she could not continue to soap herself without becoming painfully obvious, she moved deeper into the pool to rinse herself.

A shiver of anticipation moved through her when she heard his boots drop to the stone floor and the soft rustle of cloth as his clothing followed suit.

She turned to face him when she heard the splash of water behind her. He caught her upper arms, dragging her against his body. For several moments, he merely stared into her eyes. Abruptly, he tightened his arms around her. Her head swam dizzily. Darkness engulfed her.

She opened her eyes again when she felt herself falling, catching a glimpse of Nuri's bed chamber as she impacted with the mattress and then his face and broad shoulders filled her view as he moved over her. Pushing her thighs wide, he settled his hips between them, his engorged cock digging into her cleft as he caught her wrists, pinning them to the bed on either side of her head and arching against her. Lowering his upper body until her breasts were crushed against his hard chest, he covered her mouth almost brusingly with his own, forcing her lips to part. And when he had breached the fragile barrier of her lips, he thrust his tongue into her mouth with a ravenous ferocity that sent a thrill of excitement through her.

Uttering a sound of need, she struggled to free her wrists from his grip to hold him tightly against her, to caress him.

His hands tightened. A low, rumbling growl of fierce need vibrated from his chest as he lay claim to every tender surface of her mouth with the rough stroke of his tongue.

When he broke the kiss at last and moved along her throat, Colette was gasping for breath, writhing feverishly beneath him in mindless need. She felt the edge of his teeth as he opened his mouth along the side of her neck, sucking it until he brought stinging sensation to the surface before he released the patch of flesh and explored her ear with his lips and tongue.

She dragged in a panting, shaky breath as he abandoned that assault and nipped a trail along her throat to her breasts. Blood flowed into her nipples, engorging them to almost painful fullness as he ran his tongue over her breasts. She gasped as he caught one turgid peak between his teeth, raking them along the tender flesh in a way that made her fingers curl into claws as nearly unbearable pleasure shot through her and finally sucking it into his mouth.

She arched her back as he ceased to tease that nipple and moved to its twin to torment her, gasping, bucking against him.

"Please," she moaned shakily. "Nuri, please!"

Releasing his grip on her wrists, he burrowed an arm beneath her back and wrapped his fingers tightly around her opposite arm, pinning her arms to her sides and arching her back upward for his hungry caresses. Lifting his hips, he slipped an arm between them and guided his cock head along her cleft until he had wedged it firmly into the mouth of her channel. Shifting his arm beneath her hips then, he curled his, thrusting deeper, plowing into her in hard, aggressive thrusts that forced his erection past the clinging resistant flesh of her body until she began to feel as if he would split her in two.

Thoroughly pinned by his weight and his arms, she could do nothing more than shake and pant with need as he drove into her, withdrew slightly and pounded into her again, glorying in his forceful possession, feeling her body rush blindly toward release. She welcomed it, moaning with the force of her burgeoning, squeezing her eyes tightly to hold the sensations to her.

All too soon, it seemed to her, her body reached its peak and burst in a fiery culmination that drew hoarse, keening cries of rapture from her. The sounds and the convulsing of her body seemed to drive him over the edge, as well. A tremor traveled through his length and he uttered a harsh growl as his own body began to jerk and quake in ecstasy as his hot seed flowed into her.

Thoroughly sated, Colette went limp beneath him, struggling to catch her breath.

His grip on her eased. Breathing raggedly, he lifted away from her and looked down at her for a long moment.

She felt him stiffen. Slowly, he withdrew his flaccid member and rolled off of her.

Colette made a half hearted sound of complaint in the back of her throat when she felt his fingers trail lightly over her, unwilling to let go of the haze of repletion at the moment. Confusion filled her, though, when he snatched his hand back as if he'd been burned and she heard his feet hit the floor beside the bed.

With a great effort, she lifted her eyelids to look at him curiously.

His face was ashen as he stared at her, his gaze fastened on her thighs, and her heart skipped a beat at his expression. The alarm was sufficient to galvanize her. Still weak in the aftermath of her exquisite climax, she struggled upright and looked down at herself. Blood was streaked along her thighs. Horrified, she merely stared at it for several moments before her head jerked upward and she met Nuri's equally appalled gaze.

She placed a shaking hand on her abdomen when she realized what the blood might mean, but she felt no pain at all. Surely, it could not be anything serious if she felt no pain?

With an effort, she pushed herself to the edge of the bed and stood up. The muscles in her thighs gave her a twinge of discomfort, but despite the fear she'd been trying hard to ignore, she still felt nothing to cause her any great alarm. When she glanced up again, she discovered that Nuri had vanished.

Frowning, she looked around for several moments and finally moved away from the bed and went to stand before the mirror above the dressing table.

She saw then why Nuri had looked so appalled. As thoroughly as she had enjoyed his rough caresses, she saw now that they had left their marks. Bruises were already beginning to form on her wrists and arms, her hips, her throat, her breasts and thighs.

He thought he'd hurt her. Maybe he even thought he'd unseated his child with his roughness.

He hadn't hurt her, though. She'd thoroughly enjoyed it, and, despite the small amount of blood on her thighs, she could not believe the child had been harmed.

Dismay filled her, though. It didn't matter what she thought at this point. Nuri was convinced that he'd brutalized her. She knew that from the look on his face when he'd left.

She would not be getting another serving of pleasure-- maybe ever--unless she could convince him she looked far worse than she felt.

She suddenly felt like weeping. Sniffing the tears back, she looked around the room dully for several moments and finally moved to the washstand to clean herself up. She felt no better once she had clothed herself, though, and settled in the chair she had claimed for herself before the hearth.

What if she was wrong? What if she had enticed Nuri and ended up loosing the child he wanted?

When a day passed without incident and then another, Colette finally relaxed. They had only played a bit too rough. There was no reason why they could not share their bodies with each other so long as they curbed their enthusiasm only a little.

Nuri did not give her the chance to reason with him. After waiting almost a week for him to show himself, she finally decided to take the matter into her own hands and began to search the abbey.

She finally ran him to ground in the library. He was seated in the overstuffed chair in front of the fire, staring at the flames instead of the book that lay open on his lap.

"The babe has come to no harm," she said tentatively when he refused to acknowledge her presence.

When he looked at her at last, she smoothed her hands over her belly, showing him the rounded mound.

Nuri swallowed a little sickly and returned his attention to the flames. He could not bear to look at her, for each time he did the image rose in his mind again of the bruises he had left upon her when he had taken her with so little care for her frail human form. It mattered little that he had not intended to harm her. He had done so, and it tormented his days and his nights, made worse by his nearly overwhelming urge to take her again, and his fear that he would yield to the demon inside of him and hurt her again if he allowed himself to go near her.

He had not expected her to yield to him gladly. He had thought that she would struggle and, in his mindless quest to fill his senses with her, he had thought that he was preventing her from hurting herself fighting him when in truth it was the strength of his body and the force of his lust that had hurt her.

"I can not change what I am," he said harshly. "There is more beast in me than humanity. Still, I regret ...."

"I don't regret it," Colette said earnestly.

His gaze flickered over her. "Only that I did not succeed in removing the demon's seed from your belly?"

Colette felt her jaw go slack in stunned surprise. Hurt quickly followed. She was not happy about her condition, but regardless of what he'd come to believe about mortal women, she would not deliberately harm it. "No! It's true that I was angry about it--at first--but I would not harm it or want it harmed. How could you think that?"

"Easily. I may not be familiar with the full spectrum of human emotion, but I have no trouble understanding hate. I felt that when I was forced to watch ...."

He didn't finish the sentence, but he didn't have to. Colette felt a little sick herself. "You hate *me* for that?" she demanded, torn between disbelief and anger.

His lips tightened. "Nay," he growled. "Myself, because I could not stop it. Malik because of what he did--fate. I do not know. I only know that I am sick with the anger inside me and it will not go away."

Whatever he said, he was angry with her, too. She knew that. She had to wonder if he had believed she was taunting him. She hadn't been, but she had--mostly--enjoyed it and that was enough of an affront, she supposed.

Well, she could not help what she was either, she thought angrily. She had not asked for it. She had not been able to prevent it any more than he had. "What Jala told me was true then? You mean to …," she stopped abruptly when she realized she had been about to say 'send me away', for that was all too revealing a comment, "…release me once it is born?"

His face hardened. He swallowed audibly and looked away. "If it is--healthy," he growled finally.

Meaning he still believed she wanted to harm it? Hurt and angry over the not so subtle accusation, she had to swallow against a hard knot of misery before she could speak. "It was not I who threatened it!" she said angrily. "You did that!"

He slammed his hands against the arms of his chair and stood abruptly, kicking the book that had been in his lap into the flames angrily. "I know this! How does your revenge taste, mortal? Is it sweet? Does it warm your nights to know …." He broke off. Pushing past her, he stalked from the room, slamming the door so hard behind him Colette wondered that the hinges held.

She'd been staring blankly at the door for several moments before it occurred to her that it was the first time he had been so furious with her that he had not seemed even to think of using his magic to remove himself from her presence.

She avoided him after that, not because she was afraid of him, although she had no idea when she had ceased to feel any fear of his volatile temper, but because she was too furious with him to want to see him.

After a time her own anger cooled, but she had had two very unpleasant confrontations already and decided that was enough. She tried not to dwell on her misery, but it was difficult when she had so much time on her hands and no real outlet for her restlessness. She spent a good deal of time altering her clothing as her belly grew, letting out the waist as far as it would go and then raising it when even that was no longer enough to allow her breathing room.

The first time she felt the child inside her stir, she laughed for a little while and then cried when it dawned on her that she was not going to be around to cuddle it. Nuri would not allow her to take it with her even if she could, and he did not want her to stay.

The sorrow she felt at that made it impossible for her to ignore what she had been trying to hide from herself--that she had ceased to think of it as something unwelcome and unwanted.

She knew why, though she'd tried to deny that, as well.

She loved the demon. She didn't know how or why, and it didn't matter. Knowing wouldn't change anything. She felt it in the ache in her heart every time she caught a glimpse of Nuri.

Unfortunately, there did not seem to be anything that she could do about it, either to stop it, or to try to seek Nuri's affection in return. Regardless of what he'd said, and she had once believed, she did not think that he was incapable of feeling love. He might not fully understand his human emotions, he might have a very hard time controlling them, but he *felt* them. He had been jealous when Malik had claimed her, maybe mostly from pure possessiveness, but she thought if it had not been for that he might have come to care for her.

Had he wanted to hurt her because of that, she wondered? Was that why he had been so filled with guilt? Or was it only that he had given his desire full reign and it had not occurred to him until afterwards that she was mortal and far more frail than he'd realized?

She thought it mattered, that it was important to make him understand that he had not hurt her as he'd thought, but she had already tried to make him see that and he had only growled at her like a wounded beast. As tempted as she was to try to lure him into her bed again, she thought that was probably no better an idea than trying to talk to him, probably worse, particularly when she knew she was indeed more fragile now that she was so far along in her pregnancy.

As she drew nearer and nearer to her time, she did her best to put it from her mind as a tangle that was impossibly snarled and could never be made right again. It was not easy, but she realized that some things simply could not be changed and had to be accepted.

She did not want to think of the babe at all, fearful of feeling the pain of separation when she had to leave and yet that was as impossible as accepting that she had lost all chance of finding a way into Nuri's heart.

Her time came upon her early and without warning. She knew that she still had weeks to go, nearly a full month, and her first reaction was fear. She tried laying down, but the pains did not subside even a little. They steadily became worse until she was hardly even aware of Jala when she came in to bring her noon meal and tidy the room until she heard the crash of the tray as it hit the floor.

"Babe comes?" Jala demanded, her voice squeaky with fright.

Colette groaned. "Yes!" she said with an effort.

Jala screamed, ear splittingly and dashed into the hallway. "Master! Master! Come quick!"

"No!" Colette gasped, but she saw almost at once that it was too late, for Nuri appeared beside the bed while Jala was still jumping up and down in the hall screaming his name.

He studied her for several moments and finally settled on the edge of the bed beside her, placing his hands on her swollen belly. "I can take the pain away," he said finally in his deep, rumbling voice.

Colette grasped his wrist. "No! It'll hurt the baby!"

He shook his head. "It will come to no harm," he told her, pulling his hand from her frantic grasp and leaning over her to stroke her hair from her face.

Dizziness washed over her and then a swirling gray mist that seemed to envelope her mind. The pain receded, but with it went much of her awareness. Dimly, as if she was standing outside her body and only watching what transpired, she saw her belly contracting, her body struggling to expel the infant.

She didn't want to be distanced from it. She did not want to feel the pain either, but she knew if she allowed herself to be pulled away that she would not know when the infant was no longer cradled in her womb, that she would not know when it was taken from her.

She fought the spell Nuri had woven around her until at last she no longer had the strength to fight it anymore. Then, darkness claimed her and, as she had feared, she knew nothing at all.

Chapter Eleven

Colette knew even before she opened her eyes that something was very wrong. She did not feel as she should. She didn't know why she felt unlike herself. She just knew that something had changed drastically.

She opened her eyes and pushed herself up on her elbows when she heard Jala burst into the room with her usual clumsiness.

"Wake, good! Now you go!"

Colette stared at the ugly imp blankly. "What?"

"You go now! Follow the drive, you will find the road."

Colette's hand moved to her stomach. It was flat as if nothing had ever been there. "The babe?"

"Nuri's son!" Jala growled. "Not matter, you. Go! Before Master changes his mind and gives you to Malik."

Colette's eyes narrowed. She didn't believe for one moment that Nuri would consider handing her over to the demon Malik. Jala was lying. She was in a desperate hurry to rush Colette from the abbey.

"He wouldn't do that!"

Jala's eyes narrowed. "Know him, do you?"

Colette's lips tightened. "Well enough to know that's a lie."

"Suit yourself," Jala snarled, slamming the tray she was carrying down on a table. "Night soon, though, if you not go."

When she'd left, Colette got out of the bed. Dizziness assailed her once she was on her feet, but it passed fairly quickly. It still took an effort to walk the distance between the bed and the washstand to clean up.

She was in no shape to leave now, she thought angrily. She had only just given birth! A day might have passed since, perhaps even two, but Nuri surely could not expect her to be able to *walk* out?

Maybe he just didn't care so long as he was rid of her?

She thrust that thought aside. Maybe he didn't, or maybe he was just too damned single minded to remember that she was mortal?

Her clothes, altered to suit her burgeoning body, hung on her. She was so near to fainting by the time she'd managed to dress herself that she was tempted to simply climb back into the bed. Her anger had not abated, however. Resting briefly, she moved to the door and went into the corridor.

In the distance, she heard the wail of a baby. Her breasts tightened instantly and began to throb painfully as milk surged into them.

Her original purpose forgotten in that moment, Colette lifted her head, listening. Finally, she began to move slowly down the corridor, pausing now and then to make certain she was going the right way.

The wails grew steadily louder. The would pause for a moment and then began again, louder and angrier than before.

Puzzled as much as she was unsettled, Colette paused at last before the door at the turn of the corridor, listening for several moments before she twisted the knob and pushed the door open.

The sight that greeted her rooted her to the spot for many moments.

Nuri was sitting on the floor with his legs crossed. In one hand, he held a screaming, red faced infant. The entire front of his shirt was stained. Next to him on the floor was a bowl. As she watched, he dipped his small finger in it and lifted it to the infant's mouth. The squalling instantly stopped and the baby sucked his finger. The minute he pulled his finger away, the infant screamed furiously.

Something seemed to fist around her heart as she watched Nuri and the baby.

Without even realizing it, she crossed the room and knelt down in front of Nuri.

He looked up at her then, apparently so deafened by the infant's squalling he hadn't realized she was there until he caught the movement as she knelt, or perhaps he had thought that it was Jala returning?

Colette was fairly certain she had never seen a more miserable being in her life, for there was fear, desperation and wavering patience collided in his expression and in his eyes as he looked at her.

On impulse, she placed her palms on his cheeks and leaned toward him, kissing him lightly on the lips. "I love you," she said, misty eyed as she pulled away from him and took the squalling infant from his arms, ignoring the stunned expression that washed over his face.

"Shhh!" she said soothingly as she moved to the bed nearby and laid the infant down. He had thoroughly drenched his nappy, which accounted for much of the stains on Nuri's shirt. Poor darling!

Removing it, she looked around and finally simply dropped it on the floor, grabbing the cloth Nuri placed beside her and covering the baby's bottom again. When she had unfastened the dress she wore and bared her breast, she lifted the screaming infant to her.

He quieted instantly, snuffling as he searched briefly for her nipple and then clamped down on it once he'd found it hard enough she winced. Humming to him to sooth him, she glanced around and finally moved to a chair and settled in it, chuckling at the infant as he opened his eyes to glare up at her as if he was wondering what the hell she was doing perched over his dinner.

He had a shaggy thatch of hair on his head, she saw, and eyes just like his father's. On either side of his head, beneath the hair, she felt a tiny nub--horns, no doubt--she decided, running a hand along his back where she discovered another two nubs--wings?

"He is the image of you," she murmured, looking around finally for Nuri and discovering that he was still standing near the bed where she had left him, his expression unreadable.

As if her gaze brought him from his preoccupation, he shrugged out of his wet shirt and dropped it next to the nappy on the floor, kicking the bowl of milk over as he strode toward her and knelt in front of her.

She studied his face, but she could tell nothing about his expression. "I won't go," she said evenly. "He needs me and I love him and I'm not going to leave him here."

An almost comical mixture of emotions chased each other across his face. "You said you loved your family."

Colette gave him a look. "I do, but now I have a new family to love."

"You said you hated me," he reminded her tentatively.

Surprise flickered through Colette. "When? You mean when I was so angry with you? But--you weren't even there! And I didn't mean it. I was just furious that you wouldn't tell me what I needed to hear."

He tilted his head curiously. "What?"

Colette reddened uncomfortably. "It doesn't matter now. I want to stay. Don't send me away."

He swallowed hard. "I never meant to send you away. I only wanted to give you the choice of whether to go or to stay."

Relief flickered through her. She lifted her free hand and stroked his hard cheek, smiling faintly. "Jala was right. You are a wise man."

He looked disconcerted. "Am I? Do you think of me as a man and not a beast?"

"I think that I love you and it doesn't matter to me what you are, man, or demon, or Halfling."

He rose after a moment and began to pace the room restlessly while she moved the baby to her other breast and fed it. When the infant had drunk its fill and drifted to sleep, she rose and tucked it carefully in the cradle that sat near the hearth, humming and rocking the cradle gently until the baby quieted.

Nuri ceased his pacing and moved to stand behind her, peering down at the infant.

"He is not fond of me," he growled when she turned to look at him questioningly.

Colette smiled. Impulsively, she turned to face him and tweaked his nipples. "Because you have no dinner for him," she said, chuckling at the look on his face.

He looked disconcerted, but after a moment, he slipped his arms around her and pulled her tightly against his chest. "I think I love you, too," he muttered against her hair.

"You think? You don't know?" Colette asked teasingly.

"I am fairly certain," he said a little doubtfully. "I have felt as miserable and hellish as they describe it in the books."

Colette couldn't help but chuckle. She tightened her arms around him. "Then it must be love."

Epilogue

Colette smiled faintly at his bemused expression as she knelt on the floor in front of the chair where Nuri sat. "That went well," she said wryly, reaching for his shirt and slowly dragging the tails from the waistband of his trousers.

His stomach tightened as she slipped her hands beneath the fabric and caressed the hard muscles of his belly and chest. "You are pleased?" he asked doubtfully.

Subtlety wasn't one of Nuri's strong suits. She chuckled. "I was very pleased to see my family. I have missed them. I don't think they were terribly happy that you brought them here to see me. They looked very confused and just a tiny bit nervous and frightened."

He frowned. "They made you unhappy?" he asked, anger dawning.

"No," Colette said soothingly, pushing his knees out of her way and leaning close so that she could explore his flesh with her lips and tongue as she explored him with her palms and fingers. "I enjoyed the visit, even though they were jumpy and fearful about being brought here. I'm just not sure they enjoyed it as much--though, they did seem almost as taken with little Kimi as they were horrified to discover they had a grandson that was a Halfling--until he bit Brigit.

"He *did* let her go almost at once when I popped him on the head, but he is a very naughty boy. Very much like father," she murmured as she worked the opening of his trousers and delved inside, pulling his engorged cock out.

He grunted, sliding his hips forward on the seat, his eyes closing tightly as she began to stroke his member, moving her hands over him with a practiced touch that had him struggling to control himself within moments, breathing harshly. His fingers tightened on the arms of the chair as she began to alternate between massaging his scrotum and his shaft.

Her eyes narrowed with satisfaction and her own rising desire as she watched his face. When she felt tremors begin to radiate through him, she opened her mouth over the head of his cock and began to suck him. He speared his fingers through her hair, clenching them almost painfully against her scalp, obviously torn between the need rising inside of him and the unwillingness to culminate so quickly.

She allowed him no respite, moving her mouth and hands over him with increasing vigor until she felt his cock jerk and his hot seed flooded her mouth, sucking him until his body ceased to convulse in release and he uttered a groan of near agony at her continued caresses.

Releasing his flaccid member at last, she burrowed beneath his shirt once more, kissing and licking her way upward until she could reach no higher. She got up then, straddling his lap and nuzzling her face against his neck before she tilted her head back and nipped at his earlobe. "I adore you, demon lord," she murmured.

Catching her buttocks in his palms, he stood with her and strode to the bed. Tossing her upon the mattress, he followed her down, settling beside her and studying her face as he stroked his hands down her body. He swallowed thickly after a moment. "My need for you--scares me," he said finally.

Colette lifted a hand and caressed his cheek. "It thrills me."

He swallowed again, frowning. "I am a beast. I can not seem to control myself. When I touch you I can not think. All that I know is that I want to burrow deeply inside of you and stay there, but I would rather cease to exist than hurt you."

"I am not nearly as fragile as you seem to think, and I will be very disappointed if you do not love me thoroughly."

He studied her doubtfully. "You are well enough?" he asked tentatively.

Her gaze flickered over his face. "Did you plant your seed in me purposefully? I mean--could you have prevented impregnating me?"

His skin darkened. An expression of guilt crossed his features. "I wanted you to bear my son. I thought--I thought it might make you want to stay and I knew you would not give me what I needed from you until you wanted to stay."

"What did you need?" Colette whispered, tracing his lips with one fingertip.

"Your love."

"Because?"

"I love you," he said gruffly, sucking the tip of her finger into his mouth and curling his tongue around it.

Heat blossomed low in her belly. "Let's wait a little while before you give me a Halfling daughter. I'd like to enjoy it being just the three of us for a while," she murmured, lifting her head to nuzzle her face against his neck.

The End

BELLY OF THE BEAST

I really pushed the envelope here, for me, at least. I feel this should come with a warning--don't try this at home--any of it! My world is a fantasy world, my characters pure imagination and, as god of the world I created, no one gets hurt unless I will it--which, of course, I don't, because this is all in fun. Beware, there are many elements in this work that could offend and/or possibly repulse those not 'in' to seriously kinky sex!

Chapter One

The summons at the door of their cottage was so abrupt, so fierce a demand, that it startled Lady Mariel Champlain. She jerked reflexively, burning her hand on the pot she'd been on the point of pulling from the cook fire. Whirling, she glanced fearfully at her father, wondering if he knew who it might be, or if he would deal with whomever it was. He had been drinking steadily for days now, though, and scarcely seemed to register the pounding, even when it came again.

Realizing that she would have to deal with whatever the situation was, she turned to look at the pot of thin stew and quickly moved it away from the fire, setting it on the hearth. It was all they had to eat and, regardless of what calamity might wait on the other side of the door, she couldn't bear to allow the little food it held to go to ruin while she was distracted.

Sucking the burn on the side of her palm, she set her spoon and the folded cloths aside and hurried to the door before whoever stood on the other side broke it down, fearful that it might be more creditors that she would have to try to fend off.

The setting sun dazzled her for several moments, making it difficult to make out the dark figure who stood upon the threshold. Slowly, her eyes focused upon him, however. A debilitating wave of shock went through her as her mind registered who, or rather what, he was.

A Trull--a demon soldier of the dark Lord Valdamer, the warlock who ruled Daeksould. Once they had been human, but the demons who inhabited their bodies had erased all traces of humanity from them beyond the human shell they inhabited. They were not evil so much as they were soulless creatures, without pity, without remorse, without emotion of any kind, but they were the minions of Lord Valdamer and they did as they were commanded without question.

As numb as if she had suddenly been frozen and separated from thought, emotion, and even physical feeling, she fell back instinctively as he stepped into the tiny cottage she had shared with her father since they had fallen upon hard times and lost all that they had once had.

Closing the door behind him, the Trull folded his arms over his broad, muscular chest, his stance wide, his back guarding the door as he glanced around at the stark furnishings. "I am here to see Lord Champlain."

Swallowing with an effort, unable to speak, Mariel glanced at her father again. He'd roused from his drunken stupor enough, she saw, to look around. The look of terror on his face mirrored what should have been her own, except that she could feel nothing at all. He seemed paralyzed by his fear, for he made no effort to rise. "I am Lord Champlain," he responded hoarsely.

The Trull nodded. Stepping forward, he grasped Mariel's arm. "I am Behsart, sent by Lord Valdamer to accept your offering. Is this the female?"

Weakness washed through Mariel as she stared at her father uncomprehendingly.

For perhaps a second, their eyes locked and then he looked away from her. "Aye."

Without a word, the Trull pulled a set of manacles from his belt. Fastening one to the wrist of the arm he held, he grasped her other arm and manacled it, as well. Pulling a bag from his belt, he tossed it to Lord Champlain. "Your pay for your offering."

The bag landed in her father's lap, jingling. He grabbed it up with shaking hands and pulled the tie from it, pouring the contents into his lap--a pile of golden coins.

Mariel was still staring at him blankly, in complete disbelief, when the Trull pulled on the chain attached to her manacles and turned toward the door once more. She stumbled as she was dragged across the threshold. Instinctively, she righted herself once more, struggling to keep pace with the man who led her away. As he tugged her through the gate that fronted the tiny yard, she glanced back at the cottage, still unable to accept that her father had sold her for coin, hoping that she would at least see denial in his face, concern, shame--but there was no sign of her father.

Catching her around her waist, the Trull lifted her up onto the black fire steed he had tied at the gate and climbed up behind her. Holding the prancing beast to a walk, he urged it along the road and through the streets of the village. Some of Mariel's numbness began to wear off as they rode. A flicker of thought here and there entered her mind.

She had been sold by her father as sacrifice to the demons the warlock Valdamer owed his powers to.

She was going to die. She had not even lived yet. She was only twenty. She had never been courted, never gone beyond the village, never wed--though she should have long since and would have if her father had not squandered their fortune. Now she would not get the chance of any kind of future at all.

She shied away from that thought.

Why had her father done it? Only for the coin?

Sickness welled inside of her. He had gambled away his fortune and now used her to rebuild it?

She had never felt her father loved her, but she would not have believed he felt so little that a bag of gold coins was worth more to him than her life. Surely, she had least had some value to him above that? If nothing else, she had cooked and cleaned for him.

She thrust the thought aside, unwilling to accept it, certain there must have been more to it than that. Perhaps they had demanded that he make sacrifice and the coin was something offered as recompense?

In any case, did it truly matter? For whatever reason he'd done it. He had not even warned her. He had allowed her to go about her chores with no notion that any moment a knock would fall upon the door and she would be told her life was over.

She found it nigh impossible to grasp that she was to be led away to her death without warning of any kind, without ever having done anything to deserve such a fate.

After a time, it occurred to her that they were many days ride from Valdamer Castle. She would not be sacrificed until they reached it. The Trull had said that. She might have a chance to live if she could only gather her wits about her.

She was still too stunned to do so. With the best will in the world, she could not seem to think beyond her father's betrayal. As she looked up and saw that the Trull was leading her to the Demon Temple, what little wit she'd gathered deserted her.

The priestesses of the temple were assembled on the piazza that fronted the temple, awaiting her. Mariel's heart began to hammer in her chest with fear as the Trull pulled the horse to a halt and dismounted by the steps. Four priestesses with mallets began to hammer at the two drums suspended on either side of the temple door as the Trull reined his horse to a halt at the foot of the temple. Pulling her from the saddle, the Trull wrapped the end of the chain connected to her manacles around one fist and began to ascend the stairs, towing her behind him.

She could walk, or she would be dragged.

She concentrated on keeping step with him, mindlessly counting the stone treads as they climbed--twenty, and they reached the piazza. The High Priestess stepped forward. Taking the chain from the Trull, she turned Mariel so that she was facing the village. Mariel saw that a crowd had gathered below, drawn by the summons of the drums.

"Behold--the bride of the Demon Sheenigan, the demon of many mouths!"

She nodded then to someone beyond Mariel's view. The priestesses surrounded Mariel, tearing at her clothes and ripping them from her body piece by piece. Within moments, she had been stripped completely bare for all to see. Catching her by her arms, the priestesses paraded her back and forth along the edge of the piazza so that all might see that the bride offered to the Demon Sheenigan was without flaw.

Numbly, she walked and turned at the priestesses command, still too numb to feel anything at all, even embarrassment at being displayed in such a way, wondering a little hysterically what they meant by "flawless." She was certainly no great beauty, but perhaps they only meant that she was not lame, not hunchbacked, not twisted or deformed in any way?

When the High Priestess had offered a prayer to the Demon Sheenigan, she was surrounded by the priestesses and led into the temple. Torches lit the stone corridor that she was led down into the heart of the temple itself. The procession halted when they reached a large room at the end. In the center of the room was a pool. Steps led down into the crystal clear water. Around the pool were several stone benches. At the end, taking up most of one entire wall, water spilled into it from a statue of the Demon Sheenigan himself. She swallowed uneasily as she stared at the nightmarish creature, wondering if it was only her imagination that he seemed to be staring down at her lasciviously.

Leading her to the 'purification' pool, the priestesses bathed her. When they were satisfied, she was taken from the pool again and made to lie down on a stone bench. Anointing her body with oils, they rubbed it into her skin from her neck down--her arms, her body, her legs--between her legs. Next, they took scrapers and worked them over her body, removing the hair from her entire body, until her flesh throbbed and burned with the abrasive scraping.

She lay still until her legs were grasped and parted. Unfortunately, they had apparently anticipated that she would be reluctant for them to touch her private parts. They held her, pried her legs apart and scraped the hair from her mound and between her legs.

When they had finished, they took her into the pool and bathed her again.

This time, when she emerged, she was dried. Still naked, she was escorted from the chamber. Instead of returning the way that they'd come, the procession turned as they left the bath and Mariel saw that there were stairs leading downward into the bowels of the temple.

The air grew cooler as they descended, whispering over her throbbing, heated skin and pebbling it until shivers began to quake through her. When they reached the foot of the stairs, Mariel saw that they had emerged at one end of a large room. Torches flickered in sconces around the stone walls, showing a vast, empty chamber--bare save for a perpendicular slab of stone that protruded from the floor. She was led to it and all save two of the women departed. The two who remained turned her, pushing her back against the slab. The cold stone against her back sent a hard shiver through her, piercing the numbness that she'd begun to cling to, to welcome since it prevented her from feeling the terror that hovered at the back of her mind.

The two women lifted her arms up until they were above her head, attaching the end of the chain to something Mariel could not see. When they had secured it, they bent down and lifted leather cuffs from the floor. Wrapping the cuffs around her thighs just above her knees, they tightened them and then knelt and picked up another, smaller set of cuffs. These were secured around her ankles.

Mariel stared down at them in consternation, feeling the first twinges of fear working their way through the numbness, wondering what it was that they meant to do her.

It was not something she truly wanted to know, but she was not left to wonder long.

When the two priestess had finished securing her, they stepped back. The slab Mariel had been attached to was tilted and she discovered that it was a table--an altar. For several moments as it began to tilt backwards, she hung by her arms and then the tilting table caught her and she was slowly lowered until she was lying completely flat.

She closed her eyes, willing herself to remain calm, desperately seeking the numbness of before, telling herself that she was not to die today. The warlock Valdamer would sacrifice her. His priestesses would not dare to kill her. Whatever it was that they meant to do she could endure it knowing that she would not die.

She felt a tug on her legs and opened her eyes. The chains attached to the cuffs around her thighs and ankles were being tightened, bending her knees upward even as her feet were lifted.

The cranking stopped. The two priestesses who'd bound her, grabbed her and dragged her down the altar until Mariel could feel the edge of the stone biting into her buttocks. When they were satisfied with their positioning of her body, the cranking began again. Slowly her knees were drawn upward until they were perpendicular with her body.

The lifting stopped. Then, just as slowly, her thighs were spread. Mariel jerked at the chains, trying to pull her arms down, trying mindlessly to hold her legs together and succeeding only in causing herself a great deal of pain. The pulling continued until she felt the petals of flesh that protected her sex yield to the tug and part, felt cool air caress the sensitive flesh of her cleft--and still the chains were tightened until it reached the point where she began to feel a burning as the tendons were stretched and her mind instantly shifted from the discomfort of being so shamelessly exposed to the fear of pain.

To her relief, the pulling stopped. The chains that held her ankles were tightened, holding her feet in place. Then the women moved up her body and tightened the chains that held her wrists until her arms were resting on the table above her head and she could not move them at all.

When the tightening of the chains stopped, she relaxed fractionally, thinking, perhaps, that they would stop. Instead, they pulled leather straps from beneath the altar stone and bound her hips to the table and then bound her chest, just beneath her breasts, so tightly she could only breathe shallowly.

She lay panting with fear, unable to move any part of her body except her head and her arms prevented her from twisting her head more than a few inches. She saw, though, that the room was filling with the priestesses, all wearing the hood and half mask of the Demon Sheenigan. They had discarded their robes and now stood along the colored circle of stones that surrounded the altar as completely nude as she was.

The Trull stood near the entrance, the fire from the torches throwing off blue and silvery highlights in his pure, black hair, throwing harsh shadows across his rugged features. He, too, was completely naked now, his arms folded over his chest, his expression impassive.

A shiver went through her as her gaze was drawn inexorably toward the obscenely huge cock that jutted from his belly before she, resolutely, looked away again.

The Trulls were the most feared beings in all of Daeksould, the realm of the dark Lord Valdamer. She had never seen one of them except from a distance, but, even without Lord Valdamer's colors, she would have known the moment she saw the one who called himself Behsart that he was a Trull. There was no softness in him, she knew, despite his starkly handsome features, no pity, no mercy. He did not study her coldly. He studied her dispassionately, without emotion of any kind.

She would never escape him and she had no hope that she could convince him to free her. Why had she even considered that she had a possibility of finding a way to save herself? Was there any tiny speck of reasonable hope? Or was it merely that she could not accept that her fate was sealed and she could not change it?

The High Priestess appeared in the doorway beside him carrying the headdress of the Demon Sheenigan. He knelt and she placed the hooded mask upon his head. When he rose once more, Mariel saw that the mask covered all but the lower portion of his face, making him seem, if possible, even more forbidding than before.

Stepping away from him, the High Priestess turned to face the chamber and lifted her arms.

The priestesses of Sheenigan began to chant, offering their bodies to serve him, calling him to receive the offering. Slowly, they shuffled in a circle around the altar where Mariel lay, following the circumference of black stones. She closed her eyes, trying to close her mind to the world around her, trying to shield mind and body from the unknown terror that awaited her.

She jerked when the first hand touched her, her eyes opening wide with fear. The priestesses had closed in upon the table, she saw. As they moved around her, they skated their hands over her body, touching her everywhere. Mariel's skin prickled. A shiver raced through her.

After a few moments, they moved back once more, chanting, still performing the slow, shuffling dance, calling Sheenigan to enter their bodies and use them for his purpose. Calling upon Sheenigan to come and taste his bride.

The cool touch of a hand on her thigh made Mariel jerk all over. She lifted her head and saw that the High Priestess was standing between her spread thighs. Without a word, she placed a hand on Mariel's mound, spreading the flesh that surrounded her sex with her fingers. Mariel gasped as she felt the intrusion of a finger. For several moments, the priestess felt around inside of her. Finally satisfied, she stepped back. "She is a virgin, emissary of Sheenigan."

Mariel saw then that the Trull stood just behind the priestess. As the High Priestess moved away, he stepped forward. Laying his hand on her mound as the priestess had, he parted the flesh with his fingers and thrust the middle finger of his other hand inside of her. Mariel winced, her body flinching even though she was unable to jerk away. Gasping, panting, she stared up at the ceiling, trying not to think about the finger she could feel moving around inside of her.

After a moment, the finger was withdrawn and Mariel let out a sigh of relief.

They'd checked to make sure she was a virgin. She told herself they would release her now. She knew that must be what this had all been about, to make certain that they had a virgin to sacrifice.

They didn't.

Instead, as the Trull stepped back once more, the High Priestess moved between her thighs once more and the others began to circle closer to the altar, still chanting. Abruptly, the chanting ceased.

"Demon Sheenigan, we welcome you! Come! Sample your bride!!" the High Priestess cried out.

At once, the women crowded close. Bending toward her, they began to lick and suck her flesh. Mariel was too stunned at first to feel anything at all, but the shock did not protect her long. Two of the priestesses had covered her breasts with their mouths, sucking at her nipples hungrily. As revolted as she was, nothing she could do could stop the heated sensations that began to filter through her body to her brain.

She jerked, trying to struggle away from them at first, but she was pinned so tightly to the altar that she couldn't move more than a hair's breadth in any direction and soon lost the strength to struggle at all.

She squeezed her eyes closed, trying to block the sensations from her mind, but they invaded insidiously as the priestesses continued to lick and suckle her all over. Heat pelted her from every direction, from her nipples, from her arms, her belly--even her fingers and toes.

Despite the assault of sensations, she flinched all over as she felt the heat of an open mouth on her inner thigh. Her heart, already pounding, began to beat in her chest so hard she thought it might burst. Slowly, the hot, moist, sucking torment moved downward toward her sex. She strained uselessly against the leather than bound her hips, trying to evade the touch she knew instinctively--feared was coming. It changed nothing, availed her nothing. The hot mouth settled over her sex, sucking, licking the tender flesh. The breath left Mariel's lungs as if she had been punched in the stomach as pleasure so intense it was almost painful shot through her.

Sheenigan, the demon of many mouths, she thought dizzily as she stared at the priestesses and realized their eyes had gone blank, that they no longer controlled their bodies, their hands, their mouths or their minds. Sheenigan had entered them and taken possession.

As repugnant as the thought was, it was almost easier to believe that it was women who touched her so intimately than to consider that it was a demon who moved over her flesh. She tried to focus her mind on the fact that it was women who caressed her and that she should feel nothing at all beyond disgust, but her body did not know the difference. Her body only felt the pleasure and that pleasure built and built until she was mindless with it. Her mind clouded with ecstasy. Her body felt fevered. The pleasure reached the edge of pain. She found that she couldn't breathe enough air into her lungs. She lay gasping hoarsely, still fighting the pleasure that surged through her until she felt as if she was reaching a point of crisis.

As abruptly as they had begun to torment her, they pulled away. Bending, they picked up small vessels and began to chant once more.

When they poured the contents over her, Mariel lost her breath, felt blackness swarm around her, for the liquid was so cold against her heated flesh it felt like fire. The tension and pleasure vanished abruptly, her body seizing, clenching. She lay shivering as they began to circle her once more.

Slowly, the painful chill eased. Her heart ceased to hammer painfully against her chest and she began to breathe more easily. As if they had only been waiting for her body to return to normal, they moved close once more. This time, she knew as they leaned toward her what they intended. She cried out, lurched against her bindings. The two who had captured her breasts in their mouths bit down on her sensitive nipples just hard enough to warn her that resistance meant pain. She subsided abruptly, trying to close her mind to the stabs of pleasure that went through her as they sucked her nipples, licked them, sucked again, teasing the sensitive buds with their tongues until the drug of bliss filled her again.

The demon had many mouths, and each was a torment to her, sucking, licking, teasing her to the edge of madness. She gasped hoarsely when she felt the heat of a mouth covering her clit, sucking it hard as her nipples were sucked, licking it. Within moments, she reached the state of mindlessness that they'd brought her to before.

Try as she might, she couldn't close her mind to the sensations. No sensitive area of her body was ignored. Pleasure assaulted her from every direction. Within moments, she was gasping so hard her head swam with dizziness. Blackness skirted her consciousness, but remained beyond her reach. They sucked her flesh until it became pure torture before they withdrew once more.

Again they tipped the freezing liquid over her body, jerking her from the sharp edge of pleasure so abruptly that she lost her breath for several moments.

Desiree Acuna

She lost track of the number of times they moved forward to violate her senses. Hours seemed to pass in a haze of heat and desperation. Finally, she reached a point where her body failed to cool even when they poured the chilling liquid over her. It continued to hum, to throb all over until she felt as if she was in the grips of a high fever, lost awareness of anything beyond her torment and an absolute desperation to find surcease.

Abruptly, the chanting stopped and the priestesses moved back. Dizzy, completely disoriented, Mariel lifted her head with an effort, wondering if her torture had at last come to an end.

She saw that the Trull had come to stand between her spread thighs. As she watched, his ankles were seized and his legs parted and manacled. Next, his wrists were manacled. He leaned forward over her body as the chains that bound his wrists were tightened, hovering inches above her, suspended by the chains so that the muscles of his chest and arms were taut and bulging with the strain. The High Priestess began to dance around the altar where she and the Trull were chained. Mariel stared at her blurrily, trying to figure out what seemed strange about the woman.

She realized when the Priestess had made her second circuit that the woman had strapped a garish red penis to her lower belly that bobbed obscenely as she danced around the altar.

When the High Priestess had circled the altar thrice, she stopped behind the Trull. Mariel met the Trull's gaze in confusion. Something flickered across his face and he let out a harsh breath, gripping the chains as he moved forward.

He'd jerked forward twice before Mariel realized that he wasn't moving forward. He was being thrust forward as the Priestess forced the cock she was wearing inside of him. Before that had even fully sunk in, she felt something nudging against her cleft. Looking between her body and the Trull's, she saw that the Priestess had grasped his cock. In a moment, Mariel felt something huge and rounded being forced inside the mouth of her sex.

She panted as she felt her muscles resisting the intrusion, bucked, trying to evade the determined pressure. For a second the pressure stopped. Mariel had just drawn a breath of relief when the Priestess slammed against the Trull once more. The force of her thrust impaled Mariel on the Trull's cock, ramming his turgid cock deeply inside of her. She cried out with a mixture of pain and pleasure as she felt his engorged flesh rammed so deeply inside of her she felt as if he would split her in two.

The painful throbbing in her body that had only just begun to subside, tore through her as he drove into her over and over, slamming so hard against her she felt his groin grinding against her clit.

Abruptly, something inside of her seemed to shatter. Ecstasy such as she'd never known exploded within her, tearing a scream from her throat, dragging her down into blackness.

As she fell into the black void, she heard the Trull's harsh cry of ecstatic pain as he, too, was forced over the edge, felt his cock jerk inside of her and a warmth bathing the channel of her sex.

Chapter Two

Her first awareness afterward was of a sense almost of weightlessness. Swimming upwards slowly to consciousness, Mariel realized finally that she was being carried. She felt the solidity of an arm behind her back and another beneath her knees, felt the heat and strength of a hard chest against her cheek, heard the pounding of a heart not her own against her ear.

The sense of moving ceased after a few minutes and she felt herself being lowered onto something soft. The softness beneath her shifted and a body pressed against hers.

Dimly, she realized that it was the Trull, Behsart who lay beside her, his arm and leg holding her prisoner, but she could not find the will to care. Within moments, she drifted downward into nothingness once more.

When she woke, she found that she was alone on the bed. Still groggy and disoriented, she sat up as she saw that the priestesses of Demon Sheenigan had filed into the room.

Fear surged through her. She would have leapt from the bed and fled, but pain shot through her the moment she tried to stand and a wave of blackness threatened to engulf her.

She was seized by the priestesses and led from the room. A sense of panic invaded her as she saw they were leading her to the bath once more. She struggled, but she was greatly outnumbered. They merely surrounded her and dragged her into the pool. Two grabbed her arms. Two grabbed her legs and the others proceeded to bathe her despite her efforts to elude them.

When they were done, they dragged her from the pool and dried her.

The Trull entered the room with the High Priestess.

The High Priestess moved toward her, carrying a length of sheer, red fabric. The other women took it from her and slipped it over Mariel's head.

She saw then that it was a robe of sorts, loose and flowing, the sleeves loose also.

Her body was perfectly visible through the fabric, however.

When they had settled the robe around her, Behsart stepped forward, grasped her wrists and fitted the manacles over them once more. A sense almost of relief flooded her as he led her down the corridor they had traversed the day before and out onto the piazza that fronted the temple.

She glanced over her shoulder as they began to descend the stairs, but there was no sign of the priestesses. Settling her before him on the saddle, Behsart turned his horse and headed west through the streets of the village. Everyone stopped as they passed. Most averted their gazes, too terrified of the Trull to look at her. She saw pity on some of the faces, however, lascivious interest on others. Finally, she simply lifted her head and ignored them.

There was no hope for her among them. Even those who felt pity for her plight would not intervene.

When they had cleared the village and entered the forest beyond, Behsart urged the horse toward a small clearing beside the narrow road and dismounted. When he'd tied the beast, he grasped her around the waist and lifted her down.

She stared at the chain he'd hooked to his belt as he dug through the saddle pack. He'd lain with her the night before, as naked as she was. If she had not been so exhausted from her ordeal, she might have slipped away.

She had not thought that she was such a weakling. It angered her that her body had failed her so completely that she'd missed what might well have been her only chance to free herself.

When he'd found what he sought, Behsart pulled a wine skin from his saddle horn and turned, striding to the shade of a tree and settling beneath it. She had, perforce, to follow, settling beside him.

Withdrawing bread and cheese from the bundle he held, he broke off a portion of each and held them out to her.

Mariel's stomach growled the moment she saw the food, her mouth watering instantly and she realized that she hadn't eaten since early the day before. No wonder she'd had no strength to fight them, none to take advantage of a possibility for flight! She'd been so terrified the day before, she hadn't even thought of food after she was taken.

In truth, she was hardly less frightened now than she had been then, but her body clamored for sustenance just the same. She took the food he offered, nibbling at it, glancing at him from time to time from beneath her lashes.

The threat his mere presence represented could not be ignored, but she saw as glanced at him that the man he had once been was far more handsome than she had realized before. His features were all hard angles and planes, but pleasingly masculine, his nose a straight blade, his lips thin, but well formed.

His eyes, when he wasn't looking directly at her, were beautiful, a deep, gemstone blue, surrounded by thick, black lashes.

She shivered as he looked directly at her, for she could see the demon in his eyes.

"Why was I taken to the temple?" she asked hesitantly. "I thought I was to be a virgin sacrifice."

"You are. No man has touched you. Only the demon Sheenigan."

It was the man's flesh that had claimed her maidenhood, but she didn't think the demon would react well to that. She supposed the High Priestess had received the demon Sheenigan into her body and Sheenigan considered that he had claimed both her and the man, but she knew little about demons, in truth, and wished she knew far less.

"I am not to die?"

His head tilted curiously. "We are on pilgrimage to the temples of the seven demons who rule Daeksould through Lord Valdamer. Each will sample your flesh before you are taken to Valdamer, who will separate your spirit from your flesh so that you may join with the seven demons."

Mariel felt her throat close with terror. She coughed, choked and finally managed to swallow the mouthful of food she'd taken. "I must... I'm to be used in six more rituals? And then to die?"

"Sheenigan found the taste of your passion appealing. He was gratified that you received him with such pleasure. If you please the others, perhaps they will allow you to keep your body."

Mariel fought down a wave of nausea. It sounded no better that way. She didn't think she could bear more of the same as she had already endured. It was true they had wrung pleasure from her body in spite of all that she could do, but it shamed her that they had. She certainly felt no glory in it, no desire to go through anything like that again.

Her body called her a liar, burgeoning with heat at the thought of the forbidden pleasures, her mind filling with images of all that had happened to her in the temple of Sheenigan. Resolutely, she thrust it from her.

She was uncomfortable that Sheenigan had chosen to use women's bodies to wring pleasure from her body. She wasn't certain, though, that she would have felt much, if any, better about it if it had been men--except that it would have seemed more natural to her. It would not have seemed quite so wrong to enjoy it.

She didn't want to be the bride of the seven demons of Daeksould! "Did he take pleasure in that body you wear, demon?" she asked sharply. "That was Sheenigan, guiding them all, wasn't it?"

Something flickered in the eyes. For a moment, she thought she glimpsed something that was not demon, but it was gone so quickly she wondered if it was no more than wishful thinking.

"It was Sheenigan. He used this body to plant his seed inside of you."

Mariel's mind went perfectly blank for several moments, but the thought that finally erupted was denial. The demons were spirits. They could subjugate the spirits of others, chain them and use their bodies, but the man's seed was his. She could not, would not, believe that there was any possibility that a demon's seed might be growing in her belly.

"Who is the man?"

This time, she was certain she saw something flicker in the demon's eyes. "He was known once as Cavan, Lord of Reugal, but he is no more. I have sent his soul away and taken the shell for my own."

He was lying. Demons always lied. But perhaps a part of it was true? She didn't believe the man's spirit was gone. She thought it was there with Behsart, enchained by the demon's power, but too strong to be ousted. Perhaps the demon actually had given her the name of the man? But would it be of use to her?

He handed her the wine skin and she drank. When she'd finished, he pulled her to her feet, put the remains of the food away and lifted her to the saddle once more. He set the horse to a canter then, following the road westward.

It could not be said that Mariel's fear vanished, or even diminished a great deal, but she could not maintain it for any great length of time. Instead, it rose and fell inside of her, rearing up to strangle her and speed her heart whenever thoughts crept into her mind of what lay ahead, slipping to the back of her mind when she became focused on her discomfort.

They stopped again when the sun reached its zenith. Despite her hunger, Mariel managed to eat very little more than she had earlier. She tried, knowing that if she continued as she was she would grow weaker and weaker.

Not that her strength was of much use to her against the demon Behsart, but she knew she needed to keep her strength up in case an opportunity arose for freedom.

As the sun sank toward the horizon, they left the forest behind and began to pass farms, and then houses clustered more closely together. Ahead of them, silhouetted by the setting sun, the temple of the three horned demon shed a black shadow across the village it commanded.

Mariel's stomach clenched at the sight. Her heart began to beat more rapidly, in time to the rhythm of the horse's galloping hooves as they moved nearer and nearer the temple.

When they reached the outskirts of town, Behsart slowed the horse, forcing him to a walk and she realized that she was to be displayed yet again, this time as the bride of the Demon Trihern, the three horned god.

The priests of the Demon Trihern began to beat the temple gongs as Behsart pulled his horse to a halt at the base of the temple. Dismounting, Behsart dragged her from the saddle and led her up the stairs. Her knees trembled, threatening to give way beneath her and send her tumbling down the stone steps once more. By the time they reached the piazza, she was shaking all over.

The robe, thin as it was, was stripped from her as a crowd gathered below.

"Behold," the High Priest called out, "the bride of the Demon Trihern!"

As before, she was tugged along the edge of the piazza, turned, walked all the way to the opposite end, so that everyone could see her. As much as she hated being gawked at by all those below, she was reluctant for it to end. When they had finished displaying her and the priests surrounded her, she resisted, pulling back against the chain. The priests on either side of her grasped her arms, dragging her toward the entrance of the temple, lifting her when she stumbled.

The temple to the Demon Trihern looked much the same as the temple to Sheenigan. Torches lined the stone walls of a long corridor. She was marched down it and at the end she saw that there was a room with a pool as there had been in the other temple. This time, the statue hovering above the pool was a likeness of Trihern.

They bathed her as the priestesses had. When she was led from the pool, she was forced down on a bench. Because she had struggled, one priest knelt at the head of the bench and held the chain to her manacles tightly. Two others grasped her ankles and held them while another priest spread oils over her body and scraped her flesh, though she thought it impossible that she could have so much as a follicle of hair left.

It was worse, she supposed, because it was men this time, realizing wryly even as the thought occurred to her that she had thought it worse before because it was women. Perhaps, though, it was only because her shock had abandoned her allowing her absolute clarity of perception. Inwardly, she cringed when her legs were spread wide and her genitals scraped as the rest of her body had been.

It would've been a relief when they finally finished and led her into the pool again, except that she knew she was to be led to the altar. Despite her fear of Behsart, who, as ever, guarded the door and watched, she fought them, trying to break free in a mindless panic that took no consideration of the fact that she had no where to run to and no real chance of escaping all of them even if she managed to break free for a few moments. They caught her, lifting her up into the air and carrying her down the stairs on their shoulders.

She did not see an altar such as the one in Sheenigan's Temple. She looked around in confusion when they'd set her on her feet. The chain attached to her manacles was seized and her arms lifted above her head. Seeing their intent, she began to struggle again, tugging at the chain. She was caught and held while the chain was attached to the hook hanging from the ceiling. When the two men released her, they caught her legs. She kicked out at them, but the struggle was all too brief. Within moments, they had captured her legs and fitted a manacle around each ankle. Chains pulled her legs apart until she was forced to stand on her tiptoes or hang from her arms.

She couldn't see the High Priest as he entered the room, but she heard him as he called the priests forward to pay homage to the bride of the Demon Trihorn with the use of their bodies to his service. The priests, wearing hooded masks with that bore the face of Trihorn, dropped the robes they were wearing to the floor and moved toward her, chanting. Each wore an obscene red penis strapped to their bellies above their own cocks.

Mariel stared at them, horrified, as they began to shuffle around her, striking her with some sort of whip-like instruments, except that the fibers hanging limply from the tips didn't hurt--not precisely. As they slapped them against her breasts, her belly, thighs and buttocks, her skin began to tingle, to grow more sensitive the longer the 'thrashing' went on. They'd moved around her three times when one of the priests stepped from the line and knelt before her. Grasping the lips of her sex, he parted them and began to suck at her tender flesh.

A jolt went through her. She jerked, lost her precarious poise, and the weight of her body tugged painfully at her arms. With an effort, she caught her balance and rose up on her tiptoes once more. She'd barely regained her stance when another man detached himself from the group and caught one of her nipples between his teeth, tugging at it almost painfully, forcing fiery sensation through receptive tip and into her body.

She closed her eyes, fighting her body's response, but knowing even as she tried that she could not really fight it. Pleasure surged through her despite her best efforts.

She groaned in despair as another man detached himself from the group and began to tug at her other nipple. Behind her, yet another grasped her buttocks and parted them, licking the cheeks and the cleft between them.

The man sucking at her clit moved away. Before she could draw a breath of relief, another took his place. As the priestesses had, the priests moved over her body as if they meant to devour her, gnawing almost painfully at her flesh at times, licking, sucking any part of her body that was sensitive to stimulation and she began to think every part of her body was sensitive, some more than others. They came and left again, moving steadily around her, taking turns driving her almost to the breaking point. Her nipples quickly began to throb incessantly. Her belly clenched and unclenched, saturated with warm moisture. Her clit pulsed with need when no one touched it and pounded harder when they did.

By the time the third had knelt between her legs, pushed the fleshy petals apart and began to suck her clit, she was so drunk with the haze of lust filling her that if they had not surrounded her, holding her in place she would have fallen and hung from her arms until they separated from their sockets. The third rammed a large finger into passage, thrusting it inside her over and over as he caught her clit in his mouth and sucked it. He'd barely begun to sucking the achingly sensitive bud of flesh when her body began to convulse in waves of keen rapture.

Unable to stop herself, she groaned as it seized her in an uncompromising grip.

Either he was unaware of the fact that she'd reached culmination, or it was immaterial to him whether she did or not and the demon that controlled him was only interested in his own pleasure. He continued to lick and suck her clit, driving his finger into her over and over until she was screaming with the jolts of pleasure that continued to wrack her body as long as he stimulated it. She collapsed weakly when he moved away, struggling to catch her breath. Her body was still pounding with the hard echoes of her release when another stepped from the circle.

Her nipples ached from the almost constant fondling. The muscles along her passage continued to spasm many minutes after her climax began to fade. Blood beat in clit to the pounding rhythm of her heart, making it almost painfully sensitive.

It almost seemed more devastating to her senses than having release denied her for so long and she tried to move away from the man who opened his mouth over her breast and began pulling at the nipple.

A man knelt between her thighs, pushed the flesh apart, and fastened his mouth over her clit, thrusting a finger inside of her. One knelt behind her, parted her buttocks and pushed his finger into her rectum.

That intrusion was such a surprise that it shifted her focus abruptly. She flinched, struggled to evade the invasive touch, pressing more tightly against the man in front of her who was tugging at her clit with mouth. Despite the discomfort, pleasure began to radiate through her body from the fingers thrusting into both orifices. Within moments, her body surged swiftly toward release. She was still hovering on the edge when both withdrew. She slumped, gasping, feeling almost as stunned as if she'd stepped inadvertently onto nothing but air when she'd expected something solid.

She was still struggling to come to terms with the abrupt withdrawal when another took his place. Almost the moment his mouth closed over her clit, her body began to tremble with impending release. She cried out as he rammed his finger inside of her passage, coming. Blind and deaf to her jerking, convulsing body, her desperate, gasping cries as she passed beyond her endurance, the ritual proceeded without pause. The man continued to thrust in finger in and out of her, tugging and sucking on her clit as if he'd found a particularly succulent berry and meant to suck it dry. His stimulation, and that of the others who fondled and sucked her breasts and belly, forced her body to continue to spasm with release until she was screaming.

She fainted, she thought, for several moments, completely loosing awareness of her surroundings. The ritual continued unabated. Mariel surfaced to consciousness once more as the pleasure coursing through her body began to wind the tension inside of her toward release again.

Over and again, they brought her to culmination that was so intense, devastating to her senses that she would reach a point where she couldn't bear it any longer and swoon. She had climaxed until there wasn't an ounce of strength left in her body by the time they finally ceased to torment her. Only half conscious, she was barely aware of being released until she collapsed into someone's arms. Lifting her head with an effort, she saw that it was Behsart who held her and relief went through her.

She'd begun to think she would die from the pleasure, but it was over. They would allow her to rest.

To her stunned surprise, she was set on her feet and pushed down on a cold stone slab that bit into her belly and ribs. Weakly, she tried to rise as she felt her ankles caught in two hard hands.

Her legs were pulled apart and her ankles manacled once more. When she felt a tug on her wrist manacles, she looked up and saw that Behsart was in front of her, removing them.

As her arms dropped limply on either side of the bench, they were caught and her arms manacled once more, this time to either side of her.

She felt a hand skate of her buttocks. Despite her exhaustion, she twisted, trying to look behind her. She could only move far enough to get a glimpse of the man, however. Her heart began to pound as she felt the man behind her pushing her buttocks wide, felt, a finger she thought at first, probing her rectum and one probing her vagina. Both were a good deal larger than a finger she discovered. The moment he had aligned both penises, he thrust inside of her.

Mariel gasped at the double penetration, feeling more surprise than either pain or pleasure at first. Behsart seized her hair, turning her head so that she faced him and shoved his cock into her gasping mouth. Belatedly, she tried to struggle but found with little surprise that she had been bound so tightly she could not move in any direction, could not escape the penetration of the three horned demon as he rammed into her body.

If she'd had the energy, or even the ability to think, she might have tried to bite the cock Behsart had shoved into her mouth, but she had neither.

As both men began to pump into her body hard and fast, however, she remembered what Behsart had said about pleasing the demon and it flickered in her mind that Behsart was only the demon that inhabited the body of Cavan. If she pleasured the man's body, would he know it? Would it reach his humanity?

Instead of remaining docile and allowing him to move his cock in and out of her mouth, she cupped her tongue and cheeks around his engorged member, sucking him. She felt a shudder go through him. It sent an answering wave of pleasure through her, joining with the rising tide of pleasure she could not stem from the man pounding frenziedly into her vagina and rectum.

Within moments, her body exploded with ecstasy. Almost mindless with the pleasure, she sucked Cavan's cock ravenously as the convulsions swept through her. Abruptly, he caught the sides of her face in his hands, jerking as he reached his crisis. She sucked harder, felt his hot seed hit the back of her throat and kept sucking until she'd milked him dry.

When she released him at last, he was trembling with the effort to remain standing.

Gasping for breath, he finally knelt and released her hands. To her relief, her ankles were released, as well, and Behsart hauled her limp form from the stone and cradled her against him as he left the chamber and ascended the stairs.

She struggled to retain her consciousness, but she was only vaguely aware of being lain on the bed and the heat of Behsart's body as he settled beside her and threw an arm and leg over her.

When the sound of movement woke her, Mariel realized that it was morning. Blearily, she lifted her head and stared at the priests who'd filed into the room. She didn't protest or struggle when they caught her up and walked her down to the pool. The bath was soothing, almost enjoyable after her ordeal of the night before. It would've been more soothing if her body had not hummed to life almost the moment they began stroking her.

She began to have her first inkling that her ordeal wasn't over when she was dried, but led from the room naked. She didn't fully grasp the implications, however, until the procession turned toward the stairs once more. By then, it was too late to offer any resistance.

She was almost relieved when they didn't chain her as they first had the day before. Instead, she was placed on her back on the altar. Her wrists were manacled to her sides. A strap was placed over her ribs just below her breasts and tightened. Another was strapped across her hips. They caught her ankles then, secured a manacle to each and her legs until they were almost perpendicular to her body before they spread them wide. The chanting and dancing began almost at once.

The stone altar they'd placed her upon was too short to support her entire body. Her hips dangled over the edge of one end, her head and neck the other. She strained to hold her head up for a time and finally allowed it to fall backwards, resting, her eyes closed.

Except for the difference in her positioning, the ritual began much as it had before, with the dancing and chanting and the chafing of the hoarse hair flails. When they had completed three circuits of the altar, one by one they detached themselves from the group. Mariel lay limply as she felt a mouth cover one breast, and then the other, felt fingers part the flesh of her sex and a mouth settle there and begin to suck at her as if they would draw her essence through her flesh. For a time, the discomfort of her position kept her focused away from what they were doing to her.

Slowly, the stimulation penetrated her mind, bringing it to focus on the pleasure rather than her discomfort. With dread, she felt her body skating upward toward culmination as they continued to tease her flesh. She'd begun to groan and struggle feverishly against her bindings when she felt a probing of her lower orifices. She was penetrated simultaneously. It wrung a gasp from her and as it did, someone caught her head, shoving a cock into her mouth. They pumped into her with almost mindless frenzy, driving her body rapidly toward the pinnacle. Both priests came almost simultaneously as her body crested and the first tremors began to quake within her passage. Withdrawing, they left her hovering on the edge.

She gasped, shuddering, stunned by the sudden cessation.

She'd long since lost any concept of pleasing the demon. She could think of nothing but the teasing that left her on the edge, unfulfilled, desperate to have her ache appeased. She knew the demon that controlled them was teasing her so much as he was deriving his own pleasure. He'd found release. He wanted more.

It was still nearly unbearable as the priests teased her with their mouths, bringing her to the edge again and again, but leaving before they'd given her surcease from the throbbing ache that only grew worse the longer they tormented her.

She almost felt like weeping with relief when she felt one moved between her legs, felt the prod of cocks in her body's openings, penetrating. When a third cock was thrust into her mouth, she began sucking it at once, felt her body struggling to reach the peak. They pounded into her like pistons, jarringly, forcing their bodies to rapid culmination--forcing hers over the edge at last into the bliss she'd been frantically seeking.

She gasped in relief when they left her, sated, basking in the aftershocks that rippled through her and, for many moments, only dimly aware of the ritual continued around her even more frenziedly than before.

She groaned in protest when they began to prod her passion from her body once more. They alternated, sometimes penetrating her body, at others merely licking and sucking her until she was ready to scream. Dimly, she began to realize that the ritual would not cease until all had used her body to find release.

In time, she was only conscious of her body. The sound of the drums became the sound of her heart. The chanting was the rasping of her breath, in need, in torment, in blessed release. She drifted in and out of even that much awareness, prodded to focus by the demands of her body in response to the stimulation that was ceaseless, remorseless, almost unbearable.

When she was finally released, she was lifted from the altar and carried to the bath once more. The bath was almost as much torment. As many times as her body had found release, it still hovered on the brink, still trembled with the aftershocks. She didn't even know when she was deposited on the bed once more.

She was too sore and exhausted to feel fear when she woke once more to discover the priests had come for her again. A good deal of dread suffused her, however.

To her surprise, they merely dressed her, this time in a sheer, flowing blue robe, and left. Before she could consider whether or not she was up to attempting flight, Behsart stepped through the doorway, the manacles in his hands.

Numbly, she watched as he secured them around her wrists. Her legs folded under her when he pulled her to her feet. Without a word, he bent down, scooped her into his arms and strode from the temple. When he'd climbed up behind her on the horse, he slipped an arm around her waist and pulled her back against him. She twisted, looking up at him in surprise and caught a flicker of something very human in his eyes before the demon surfaced once more.

A tiny ray of hope filtered through her despite her weariness. She had thought even when the notion occurred to her that she might be able to reach the man held captive by the demon Behsart that it was no more than wishful thinking. She began to think, though, that Behsart was not nearly as strong as he believed himself to be--either that, or the man was far stronger that Behsart believed.

They were still many days from Valdamer castle. Perhaps there was a chance of saving her life after all.

Instead of stopping as he had before, Behsart merely pulled food from his pack and handed it to her. As she nibbled it, she considered the situation carefully, realizing that she had never before heard of a sacrifice being taken on pilgrimage to the different temples before she was taken to the castle and offered as sacrifice to the demons.

Of course that didn't necessarily mean a great deal. As far as she knew, there had been no sacrifices for many years, not since Lord Valdamer had first come to power.

She frowned, realizing after several moments that there had actually been none since Valdamer had come to power. The other sacrifices had occurred when Lord Belean had been in power, the warlock Lord Valdamer had defeated to gain control of Daeksould.

What, if anything, she wondered, might it mean beyond the fact that Valdamer had his own way of performing sacrifices to the demons?

Perhaps it was the demons who had demanded it?

Realizing finally that that line of thought was leading her nowhere, she went back to puzzling over the emergence of the man whose body Behsart controlled, wondering if it was possible the pleasure itself was what seemed to be weakening Behsart. Demons were evil creatures who took pleasure from pain, inflicting or receiving it. As difficult as the rituals had been for her, though, she had not suffered

pain--some discomfort, more pleasure than she felt like she
could bear at times--but still pleasure.

Even though the rituals had summoned the Demons
Trihorn and Sheenigan, their hosts had experienced
pleasure, which meant that Behsart had. And if it had, as
she thought, weakened him, what effect had it had on the
great demons? Had they been less affected because they
were so powerful? Or had they, because they had entered
the bodies of each of their worshippers, weakened
themselves?

The thoughts occupied her until they stopped to rest midday. When they'd refreshed themselves, Behsart sprawled
beneath the shade of a tree, watching her through drowsy,
heavily lidded eyes as she removed the food from the pack
and tore off a portion for each of them. She pretended to
concentrate on her own meal, but she couldn't help but
notice that his gaze moved over her body hungrily and she
made no attempt to block his view. When she'd finished,
she stretched, and finally lay down on the grass on her
back, dropping her arms onto the grass on either side of her
head.

She'd begun to drowse when she felt his presence beside
her. Lazily, she opened her eyes and looked at him. His
gaze locked with hers, his face taut as he grasped the robe
and began to push it up her body. She lifted her hips,
allowing him to push it all they way up. Catching her
thighs, he parted them, kneeling between her legs and
leaning forward to suckle her breasts.

Her breath caught in her throat as she felt the heat of his
mouth enfold the tight bud that tipped her breast, felt sharp
desire flood through her, but she remained perfectly still,
allowing him to do as he pleased.

He was breathing heavily when he abandoned her breasts
and moved down. Cupping her buttocks, he lifted her hips
to his mouth and dipped his tongue into her cleft, parting
the flesh with his tongue, licking her, delving deeply and
running his tongue along that most sensitive flesh. Her
scent seemed to drive him into a sort of madness. He
moved his mouth over her hungrily, sucking and licking her
until she felt the first tremors of her climax gripping her.
Her gasps and moans spurred him on and he continued to
suckle the bud of her clit until she was screaming his name,

begging him to stop. He moved over her then, shoving his cock inside of her to the hilt, pumping his hips frantically, driving his cock into her so hard he lifted her from the ground with each thrust.

Abruptly, another climax caught her. As her passage began to spasm around his turgid flesh, he growled, jerked and slammed into her hard, grinding into her as his seed flooded her passage.

He collapsed on top of her, gasping for breath. Even as she felt her body float downward toward the mellow warmth of her afterglow, however, he pulled away from her. Grasping her, he rolled her onto her belly, lifted her hips until she was on her knees and then thrust into her again. She groaned, feeling her body surge upward instantly as he rammed into her with almost painful thrusts, burying himself so deeply inside her she felt as if she would split, then pulling slightly away and hammering into her again. Her body quaked, spasmed, exploded with ecstasy. The convulsing muscles dragged him over the edge with her and he cried out hoarsely, surging into her as his seed bathed her passage once more.

When he pulled away at last, he lay back on the grass, gasping for breath. Mariel wanted nothing so much as to drift into oblivion, but she thought the demon might be at his weakest and if he was she needed to try to reach the man she believed still dwelt within that body with the demon. With an effort, she rolled onto her side and studied him with an expression of interest. "You must be a very powerful demon to have destroyed the spirit of such a powerful man," she murmured, reaching out to stroke the hard, bulging muscles of his chest and arms.

He opened his eyes and looked at her and she saw the demon vanish from his eyes for several moments. Swallowing, she shifted closer to him. "Cavan?"

The moment she called to the man, the demon rose once more. "This man was weak. His body is weak. It demands rest when I want to find more pleasure," Behsart muttered, almost angrily.

Smiling with an effort, Mariel placed her palm on his chest, over his pounding heart. "The body will rest and we can find more pleasure in a little while."

The comment didn't seem to appease him much, but he turned thoughtful. "We lingered too long in the Temple of Trihorn. We can not reach the next temple tonight. I will take my fill of you when we make camp tonight," he said, rising abruptly and adjusting his clothes.

Still weak in the aftermath of her explosive release, Mariel rose without objection and allowed him to place her on the horse once more. He pulled her against his chest possessively, wrapping one arm snugly about her waist when he'd mounted behind her. Mariel wasn't certain whether the possessiveness was the demon or the man, Cavan, but she allowed herself a faint smile as she leaned trustingly against his hard chest and closed her eyes.

Chapter Three

Contrary to what Behsart had believed, they reached the edge of the forest before nightfall. Mariel saw a wide plane. Rising up from it in the gathering mists of evening, was the dark shape of the Temple of Hezifath, of the snake tongue.

Instantly, her belly clenched in dread anticipation. She didn't know if it would have been worse if she'd known what she would face here, or not, but not knowing made her heart pound painfully in her chest. Despite that, her body burgeoned with anticipation. Until only a few days ago, she hadn't known carnal pleasure at all, but the rituals of the demons had enslaved her body to the pleasures of the flesh and no matter how much her mind shied from it, her body welcomed the possession of her body in carnal torment.

She glanced up at Behsart uneasily. "They will be expecting us?"

"Yes."

His voice was grim. She could sense the reluctance in him to give up what he'd promised himself, and yet she didn't think he dared disobey the demons more powerful that he. After a moment he seemed to come to some decision. Looping the reins of the horse around the saddle horn, he grasped her, turning her to face him and drawing her legs over his so that she sat astride his lap. Dragging her robe up, he bent her backwards over one arm and fastened his mouth over the peak of one breast, raking is teeth over the distended tip almost painfully. When it began to throb with the rush of blood into the swollen flesh, he sucked it into his mouth, tugging on it with his mouth and tongue until Mariel was gasping dizzily. Releasing it, he moved to its twin, raking that nipple with his teeth before he pulled it into his mouth. As he sucked her, he reached between her legs, parting the flesh of her sex and thrusting a finger deeply inside of her, spreading the creamy moisture that had gathered there.

She saw when he released her nipple that he'd pulled his cock from his loincloth. It stood stiffly erect, pulsing. Grasping her around the waist, he lifted her up and speared her flesh with his hardened member, bearing down on her until he'd forced his cock past the resistant flesh of her passage and buried himself to the root inside of her.

Grasping her manacled wrists, he looped her arms around his neck and wrapped one arm around her hips, pulling her tightly against his belly, shifting slightly and grinding into her and drawing a low moan from her throat. Taking the reins once more, he kicked the horse into a gallop.

The bounding motion of the horse beneath them bounced Mariel upward so that his turgid cock slipped almost completely from her body, then slammed her down against him, impaling her on his cock, before bouncing her upward again. Despite the painful depth of his possession and the brutal pace with which his hard flesh was rammed repeatedly into her body, heat flashed through her with his first ramming thrust, soaking her passage so that her body slipped more easily over his erection. It spiraled upward rapidly, until she was gasping and shaking with impending orgasm.

Her belly clenched around him as the muscles began to convulse with release. The continuous, rapid pounding of his cock drove her to the edge of darkness, forcing her body to convulse on and on in release without cease or even a lessening. She was near to weeping when she felt his cock jerk inside of her and begin to spasm as he found his own release.

When his own body had ceased to convulse with his climax, he slowed the horse and finally brought it to a stop. Quivering, only dimly aware of her surroundings, Mariel gasped as his spent flesh finally slipped from hers and she slumped against him, resting her forehead on his chest as she fought to catch her breath.

Her breathing had barely returned to normal when he grasped her hips and lifted her and she felt his hardened cock probing her once more, thrusting deeply inside of her as he pulled her tightly against him again. Wearily, she lifted her head to look at him, feeling her passage clench around him as he urged the horse forward once more into a fast walk that moved her gently along his turgid length, then a jog, that began to jounce her a little harder, and finally a gallop.

By the time he'd urged the horse into a gallop, her body was already high on the scale to completion. Within moments, the ramming motions of his cock inside her set off another wave of bliss.

His body climbed slower toward completion the second time. Hers convulsed in blinding rapture until she blacked out for many moments. Slowly awareness began to drift back into her mind. Still, she lay limply against him, completely spent, unable to lift her head for some time. When she finally managed to pull away and look around, she discovered that they'd reached the outskirts of the tiny village that dwelt in the shadow of the Temple. She stiffened, trying to move away.

His arm tightened, holding her against him. "You are mine," he growled into her ear.

As she looked up at him in surprise, she felt his cock harden inside of her again. He set the horse to a trot. The animal's gait jogged her up and down on his cock in a quick, hard rhythm that stirred the ashes of her passion. Aware that the curious were glancing at them as they passed, she tried to hold the sensations at bay, but they quickly overwhelmed her, driving her upward toward her peak. She bit down on his shoulder to keep from crying out as her body began to convulse once more in spasms of pleasure.

She was hardly aware of the cessation of movement until Behsart lifted her arms from around his neck and loosened his grip on her, allowing her to slide from him. She looked around then and discovered he'd reined the horse to a halt at the foot of the temple steps.

Without a word, he adjusted his clothing and climbed down, dragging her off with him and settling her on her feet. When he'd tossed the reins to a waiting priest, he led her up to the piazza. They were halfway up the stairs before the priests began to pound the gong to call the worshippers of the Demon Hezifath.

She saw when she reached the piazza that the priests who waited looked both worried and confused. Behsart ignored them, passing the chain he used to lead her to the High Priest and stepping to one side.

Collecting himself after a moment, the High Priest began the ritual of display.

Mariel was still so dazed from their coupling she merely stumbled after them as they led her across the piazza. Finally, almost with a sense of relief, she saw that they had turned to enter the temple.

Mariel had thought she knew what to expect here, at least, if she still had no idea of what the Demon Hezifath would demand of her. She found that she was wrong. Instead of taking her to the bathing chamber, they took her to a small chamber, empty save for a narrow cot, a pitcher of water, and a chamber pot for her needs, and locked her inside.

At first, Mariel was too exhausted from her coupling with Behsart and the hard, multiple orgasms he'd driven her to to be greatly disturbed by the difference in her reception at this temple to what she'd come to expect. Bathing herself, she drank a little of the water and collapsed on the narrow bunk, falling asleep almost instantly.

She was awakened sometime later by a scraping noise. When she sat up, she saw that a tray of food had been set inside the door. Hungry from days of travel, little food, and the expenditure of energy in fear and the pleasure that had been wrung from her body again and again, she retrieved the tray, sat on the bed and ate.

She began to wonder why she'd been placed in the chamber, whether it was because she had arrived before they were ready to perform the ritual, or if it was because they had been in no doubt that Behsart had sampled the bride of the seven demons of Daeksould.

Slowly, fear began to creep inside of her as the thought took hold that that was exactly the case and that her 'pilgrimage' would be cut short and she would be sent directly to Valdamer's castle and put to death. Rising, she set the tray with the half eaten food by the door and began to pace the small chamber, wondering if there was any hope of escape if that was to be the case.

Behsart had reached a point where he could not seem to resist his desire for her flesh, but what little power that might give her over him, if any, would be of no use to her if the demons were angered with him and someone else was sent to take her to Valdamer Castle. She stood no chance of escaping if that was the case.

It occurred to her after a while that she hadn't even tried the door to see if it was locked. She knew it must be, but she moved to it and tried it anyway. Without much surprise, but with a great deal of disappointment, she found that it was.

Moving away from the door, she began to pace once more, glancing now and then at the tray. Finally, she settled to watching the door, deciding when it opened, if only one priest stood there, she would see if she could catch him off guard and escape.

She would've felt better for her chances if she were closer to the outer door to the temple, but she realized fairly quickly that her chances were virtually nil any way she looked at it. As long as she had felt that she had some chance of coaxing Behsart into lowering his guard, she had thought patience the wisest course. Any attempt to escape would put him on guard and make another attempt useless. She had to wait until the most opportune moment.

Behsart had said that if she pleased the seven demons they might consider allowing her to keep her life. She didn't really believe that in her heart of hearts, but she had clung to the hope that it was possible, that if she failed to escape she might still have a chance for life.

If, as she suspected, she had displeased them, she thought her chances less than nothing.

Despite her fear, or perhaps because of it, exhaustion finally got the better of her once she'd stopped pacing the room and settled to watch the door, but it was the sound of the door opening that woke her. She surged to her feet at once, swaying slightly with the grogginess of sleep. Two priests entered. Ignoring the tray, they seized her and dragged her from the room, down the long corridor that led to the bathing chamber.

She had already learned that trying to fight them was useless and yet she could not command herself not to. She struggled as they forced her down on a stone bench beside the pool. They held her, anointing her body with oils and scraping her skin until she throbbed all over. When they had bathed her, they led her from the pool and dried her.

As they left the chamber, they turned and followed the steps downward to the offering room. Below, she could hear the priests chanting and an almost hissing noise as they shuffled their feet across the stone floor. Mariel's dread grew with each step. As relieved as she was that it seemed that they would perform the offering anyway, she feared what she would have to face in the chamber. It might have frightened her less if the ritual had been the same each time, but each time it differed in every respect except that the demon, she knew, would whip his followers into a frenzy of carnality and that they would wring pleasure from her body until they'd sapped her of all strength.

Hezifath was the demon of the snake tongue. Her mind refused to supply her with how he might manifest himself in his followers.

As in the other temples, she saw that a stone altar stood in the center of the chamber. Instead of leading her to it, however, she was seized by the two priests who had walked beside her as they descended the stairs. Dragging her beyond the altar, they forced her down on the stone floor in the center of a circle made up of different colored stones so that it looked like the eye of a serpent. The stone was cold beneath her and she began to shiver as they knelt and removed the manacles that bound her wrists together.

Each man took one of her arms and pulled it straight out from her body, manacling her directly to the stone floor. They moved down her then. A third man approached, carrying a wedge shaped stone, and knelt beside her hips. The two who were binding her for the offering to Hezifath lifted her hips. The wedge was pushed beneath her buttocks. When she was lowered once more, she realized that it had curled her hips upward. Catching her legs then, they bent them at the knees and spread her legs wide, chaining her ankles to the floor.

She lay staring up at the ceiling, shivering from dread and the cold, listening to her heart hammering in her ears and the breath rasping from her chest in frightened gasps.

The High Priest came to stand between her legs. He lifted his arms. "Come, followers of the Demon Hezifath, of the snake tongue--pay homage to his bride."

As the priests advanced toward the circle where she had been chained, she saw they wore the hooded headdress of the demon Hezifath. There bodies were painted in a pattern that made their skin appear as serpent's skin. They wore no more than a cup over their genitals.

When they reached the outer ring of the circle, they began to chant and dance in a circle around her, writhing, moving their arms sinuously. After a time, the chanting began to sound more like the hissing of serpents than sounds from human throats. As she watched, they knelt to the floor and then lay upon their bellies, moving around her with the sinuous, undulating movements of serpents, resembling huge snakes.

One moved toward her, undulating around her, flicking his tongue over her breast until her nipple grew turgid, standing erect. He bit down on it, drawing a gasp from her. She relaxed fractionally when she felt no more than a twinge of pain, but even as he moved away again she wondered if the next bite would, or the one after that. She knew once it began that it would continue much the same and feared once the fever was fully upon them that they would begin to bear down on her harder each time, biting her in truth rather than merely simulating a bite.

As he left, another approached her from the other side, flicking his tongue over belly, nipping her flesh before he moved on. Both fear and heat surged inside her as another approached her, flicked his tongue over her other nipple and then, lightly, bit down on her, raking his teeth along the distended tip before he released it and moved away. Within moments, she felt them all over her, felt the flicking of their tongues over her skin, nipping her. Sometimes it bordered on pain, occasionally one bit her hard enough to draw a gasp from her, but she began to relax as pleasure began to far outweigh the discomfort and even the harder nips with sharp teeth sent heat spiraling into her belly.

She closed her eyes, but that only seemed to focus her mind more surely on the sensations flooding her. Her head began to swim as the drugging euphoria of bliss sucked her down. Despite the clouding of her mind, she tensed as she felt the heated flick of a tongue along one thigh. The licking moved lower, traced her nether lips and the seam where they met. After a moment, the tongue parted her nether lips, flicking along her cleft. Gasping, she pushed backward with her legs, moving away from the touch.

To her relief, instead of following her, he moved away.

Her relief was short lived. A moment later, Behsart knelt over her. Straddling her belly, he dragged her hips to the edge of the offering stone once more until it bit into her buttocks and her legs strained against the counter pull of the manacles around her ankles. Tightening his knees around her, he pinned her so that she could not move. As a tongue flicked along her thigh once more, he caught the fleshly lips of her sex and pulled them wide, stretching her so that the mouth of her sex opened.

She felt the flicking tongue move along the tender flesh of her cleft, sending sharp stabs of pleasure through her belly. Moving up her cleft, the hot tongue flicked the tiny, exquisitely sensitive bud of her clit, until heated desire had her belly clenching and unclenching. She gasped when he nipped her, sending a sizzling shaft of arousal through her. He did not linger. Once he had bitten her, he moved downward again and she felt the tongue thrust inside of her. It seemed to swell, to lengthen, undulating through her passage. As it began to slowly withdraw, Behsart's hold shifted, spreading her body's opening wider so that the tongue plunged more deeply inside her, curling against the walls of her passage, stroking her.

She shook, tried to twist away and discovered she couldn't. The thrusting continued until she was gasping hoarsely, her body trembling.

As he moved away, Behsart shifted once more. Bending his head, he opened his mouth over her exposed flesh and sucked and licked her clit almost savagely, punishing her for her attempts to escape the invasive tongue until she was gasping shrilly.

She was trembling on the brink of release when he lifted his head. She shuddered at the abrupt cessation of stimulation, feeling a shiver skate through her as her body began to cool. Moments passed. While she struggled to catch her breath, the priests began to nip and lick at her breasts and belly once more, her arms, her neck.

Her flesh quivered as she felt the skate of a hot tongue along her thigh. As the tortuous sensations neared her sex, Behsart caught her nether lips, pulling them wide and offering the exquisitely sensitive inner flesh for the delectation of the demon Hezifath.

The heated tongue moved back and forth along her cleft, nipping at her clit until she began to quake with imminent release. She fought it, dreading it, knowing that once it began they would not allow it to stop until they were ready to move on. As he moved down her cleft, Behsart shifted his hold on her, spreading the mouth of her passage wide to receive the tongue of the serpent. Two others approached her, flicked their tongues over her nipples and bit down on them as the tongue was thrust deeply inside of her. She gasped sharply, her body convulsing with pleasure. It continued to spasm as the tongue was thrust into her over and over.

The moment the priest withdrew and moved away, Behsart shifted again, burying his face against the tender flesh, sucking her clit into his mouth, teasing it with his tongue. The tremors of her climax, which had began to subside, mounted once more, tearing through her in almost painful waves until she was screaming with the nearly unbearable pleasure.

Darkness began to engulf her before he ceased to torment her.

She was still gasping, trying to catch her breath when they began moving over her again. Her body, heated now to the point of release, was not allowed to cool more than a handful of moments as they continued the ritual unceasingly, teasing her flesh to such sensitivity she felt faint, dizzy. Each time the serpent approached to spear her womb with his tongue, Behsart parted the lips of her sex, opening her wide for them and holding her. Again and again they brought her to culmination, until she was hoarse from crying out, until her flesh quivered and shook without cease.

She wasn't even aware that the torment had ended at last until she felt her ankles freed from the manacles and her legs dropped limply to the floor. When her wrists were freed, Behsart scooped her into his arms and lifted her.

She hung limply, too weak even to feel much dread as he strode from the circle and lay her face down on the altar. She was dragged back until her feet touched the floor. Her legs were spread wide, her ankles chained again. The manacles were placed around her wrists once more, drawn upward so that her arms were above her head, her cheek resting against the cold stone.

She'd thought that they had wrung every ounce of pleasure from her body that could be had, but as the first moved behind her, parted her buttocks and shoved his cock into her rectum, her body began scaling the heights once more. One after another, they drove into her frenziedly until she gasped hoarsely and came, and still the ritual continued until she lost count of the number of times her body was wracked by spasms of pleasure and fell finally into a deep black pit.

The shivering as her heated flesh began to cool roused her to dim awareness and she realized that she was cradled in Behsart's arms. Carrying her to a room with a wide bed, he laid her upon it and joined her. Instead of merely throwing one arm and leg over her, however, he gathered her close against his body, wrapping his arms around her.

"You will displease them if you fight it, my love and I can not allow it. Yield to them. Take the pleasure they offer you and soon we will both be free," he murmured, his voice sounding deeper, less harsh that Behsart's voice usually sounded.

"Cavan?" she whispered, but she didn't know if he responded or not. Within moments, strangely reassured by the steady pounding of his heart beneath her ear, she sank into oblivion again.

Chapter Four

When she had been bathed the following morning, the priests dressed her in a deep blue gown. She glanced at Behsart as he took the chain attached to her manacles, but there was no sign of the man. Behsart looked back at her, his eyes filled with nothing but heat and possessiveness.

She swallowed with an effort. The look should have heartened her, for it could only mean that she was right. Behsart, drawn by the pleasures of the flesh, was slowly but surely losing his control. However, she'd begun to realize that she was as much in control of Behsart as vice versa. He had only to look at her and her body responded with welcoming heat. His rough possession of her drove her into mindless bliss. Moreover, she had seen no more than a glimpse of what she believed to be the soul of the man inside. If she was, in truth, weakening the demon Behsart, why could she not see him more frequently? For longer periods of time?

When they had left the temple behind and set out across the plain once more, she remembered the words he had spoken to her the night before. She knew it must have been Cavan. The words, the way he had held her, spoke of human emotions.

She'd thought Behsart was punishing her for her resistance, but it seemed that Cavan had been saying that he was the one who had assaulted her senses so devastatingly. It confused her, but the promise of his words lifted her spirits, as well, added another ray of hope to the few that she had managed to gather to comfort herself.

She tried not to think about the fact that her time was growing short. They had made pilgrimage to three temples. The Demons of each had claimed her. Only four more lay before them and then she would have no more time. Then, if she had not managed to escape, she would be taken to Castle Valdamer and she would either die, or the seven demons would take her to them in her fleshly form and she would be theirs.

To her surprise, Behsart pulled the horse to a halt as soon as they had entered the forest at the edge of the plain. Her belly tightened with a mixture of dread and anticipation as he turned her to face him, spreading her thighs over his own. Without a word, he caught her arms, looping them around his neck and lifted her against his belly. She swallowed with an effort as she felt the probing of his cock. He bore down on her, sheathing his turgid flesh inside of her. She licked her lips. "Why? To punish me because I tried to resist?"

He studied her face for a moment. "Because I want my flesh buried inside of yours," he growled, kicking the horse into motion once more.

To her dismay, he rode with his flesh buried inside of her until the sun had reached its zenith. She could not stop her body from responding to the constant stimulation any more than he could. By the time he pulled the horse to a halt beneath a tree, she was hanging limply against him, too weak even to move. Holding her, he dismounted and finally allowed her to slide to ground. When he'd unhooked her arms from around his neck, her knees gave out and she wilted to the ground. Lifting her, he carried her to the shade of the tree and settled her beneath it.

She stared at him numbly as he turned and walked to the horse to pull their food from the packs, but she was in no condition to take advantage of his inattention--which he was probably well aware of.

They ate in silence. Mariel was almost too tied to eat at all, and certainly too tired to try to think of anything to say. He allowed her to doze for a little while after they'd eaten before he drew her to her feet and led her to the horse once more. To her dismay, the moment he mounted, he turned her and mounted her on his turgid shaft. Again, they set out and, despite her weariness her body responded to the ramming thrusts of his cock, building her to a fever, giving her release, and then building again until finally, late in the afternoon, she reached a point where her body was simply too exhausted to respond and she slept, slumped against him.

She woke when the horse stopped, lifting her head and looking around fearfully.

She saw that they were still in the forest, however, and relief flooded her. Behsart chained her to a small tree while he made camp. When they'd eaten, he led her into the woods and allowed her to relieve herself and then to a stream. When she'd bathed, he drew her robe over her again, manacled her wrists and took her back to camp.

He lay beside her on the pallet, pulling her closely against him, but, to her relief, he made no attempt to couple with her. The following morning, they rose and ate, then resumed their journey. To Mariel's surprise, he merely pulled her against his chest when they had mounted.

As relieved as she was, she puzzled over it, wondering if he had completely sated himself with her and what that might ultimately mean beyond the fact that her body was allowed to rest. At dusk, they stopped and made camp once more. When Behsart made no attempt to couple with her, Mariel's anxiety deepened, but when she noticed that he still watched her every move hungrily, she began to realize that it was not that he had lost interest in her but something else that restrained him. She finally decided that it must be his fear of the demon that he was taking her to, but that brought her no comfort at all.

Instead of stopping as dusk began to settle around them the following day, Behsart pressed on, slowing the horse for a time until the moon rose and then urging it into a brisk trot. They came at last upon a village and Mariel stared with dread at the tall, dark shape that loomed in the center of the village. When they reached the temple, she was taken to a cell much like the one she'd been locked in at the Temple of Hezifath and left.

The soreness and weariness from her coupling with Behsart, and the rituals, had worn away in the days she was allowed to rest, but she was weary from the travel and when they'd left her, she simply climbed gratefully onto the soft mattress and fell asleep.

She was awakened the following morning when the priests came for her. Grasping her arms, they led her to the main corridor and turned toward the main entrance of the temple.

She heard the banging of the gongs as they began down the corridor. They seemed almost to step in time to the pounding. When they reached the piazza, the robe was stripped from her. To her surprise and dismay, the priests lifted her up. Spreading her legs, they displayed her to the worshippers of the Demon Bileezal, of the horned cock.

Fear clenched inside of Mariel as the High Priest intoned the name of one the most feared demons of Daeksould, ousting her discomfort over the way that the priests had displayed her to the worshippers at the foot of the temple.

It came to her as they set her on her feet at last that the path of the pilgrimage that she'd been led on had begun with the weakest of the seven demons and that each successive temple they visited belonged to a demon more powerful and terrible than the last.

Her knees went weak as they led her inside so that the priests who held her arms had to support her with each step. She was too filled with dread even to consider struggling as they took her to the bath chamber and prepared her to receive the Demon Bileezal.

When they had finished, instead of leading her from the chamber, they lifted her onto their shoulders as they had when they'd displayed her and carried her down the stone steps to the offering chamber. Below, she heard the pounding of a drum. The priests moved in concert to the rhythm beat out, stepping, hesitating, stepping again. Mariel's heart seemed to beat at treble the pace. She was panting with fear by the time she was lowered to the stone floor and set on her feet.

She looked around fearfully as the procession of priests left the chamber. Her arms were pulled behind her back and her wrists bound together, then she was turned to face a doorway across the chamber. The altar lay between where she stood and the doorway and she stared at it in sick fascination.

A flickering light caught her attention, dragging her gaze to the door. A priest, wearing the hooded headdress of the Demon Bileezal appeared in the opening, holding a candle that cast the mask into frightening relief. He was bare, even of paint, except for the hood and the cod piece that cupped his genitals. His cock stood erect, protruding from his belly.

She saw as he stepped from the doorway that the priest behind him looked identical in every respect. In all, twelve filed from the doorway moving to stand on either side of the altar. When they'd lined up, they began to chant. The two who held her arms pushed her forward. Pushing her face down on the altar, they attached manacles to her ankles and then attached the chain to her wrists so that her legs were bent behind her.

When they had lifted her up once more, they turned her so that she was perched on her knees on the end of the altar. She wavered as the spread her knees, but they held her arms, preventing her from falling. She began to shiver with nerves as the priests began to move around the altar. Despite every effort, she could not prevent herself from staring at the erect cocks that stood out from their bellies. Each shaft was studded with small, rounded metal balls from the tip to the root and around the circumference of the cock. The cocks themselves seemed impossibly huge, nearly as big around as her wrist and almost as long as the distance between the lips of her sex and her belly button.

She swallowed against the knot in her throat, knowing the size alone was enough to cause her discomfort if not outright pain. She had no idea of what the hard, rounded 'horns' might do to her, but her belly clenched spasmodically as she stared at them.

She was jerked back to attention as the priests holding her arms, thrust her shoulders forward, bearing down on her arms at the same time until her back arched, and her breasts were thrust forward. One of the priests circling her stopped. Covering one breast with his mouth, he shoved the erect cock between her legs as he closed his teeth over the engorged bud at the tip of her breast. A mixture of pain and pleasure shot through her as he pulled away, holding her nipple tightly between his teeth. When he released her and stepped away, another took his place, tugging at her other nipple in much the same manner.

She flinched in anticipation when the third stopped. Instead of catching her nipple between his teeth, he suckled it, flicking it with his tongue until wetness coated her sex. When he had stepped away, a fourth took his place, suckling her other nipple until she felt weakness seep through her. The fifth caught her nipple as the first had, biting down just hard enough to send a shaft of pain through her pleasure.

At first, each time she felt teeth latch onto her, it jerked her completely from the pleasure the suckling mouths had instilled in her. After a time, her body began to react differently, flooding with sharper pleasure as she felt the pinch.

She was so dizzy and weak she would have collapsed long before they ceased to tease her if the two who held her had released her. Instead, when the procession around her finally stopped, they lifted her and turned her to face the altar. She saw that eleven of the priests had stepped back from the altar. The twelfth climbed onto it and lay down on his back. The High Priest approached carrying a vessel and poured the contents over the erect cock. The priest lying on the altar worked the liquid over his cock until it glistened from the rounded head to the root.

She was lifted and moved up the altar until she was straddling the man who lay there. Reaching between her legs, the priests who held her pulled the lips of her sex back and placed her over the cock, aligning her body so that when they settled her, the head of his cock was inside her. Mariel's heart slammed into her ribs as she realized what was coming.

The drum was struck. Catching her legs, the priests who held her impaled her on the cock the other priest held straight up. She gasped as it was rammed inside of her to the root, too stunned for several moments to realize that she'd felt very little pain as it was driven into her without allowing her muscles to adjust to the enormity of the size of the cock, that they'd anointed the shaft with oils that allowed it to be forced inside of her without ripping her apart.

The drum struck again. They lifted her, poising her on her knees so that little more than the head of the cock remained inside of her. Before she could catch her breath, the drum stuck again. Pulling her knees out from under her, they slammed her downward, impaling her once more. She gasped, feeling the rounded 'horns' rippling along her passage and sending out sharp jolts of pleasure that made her belly clench almost painfully around the hard cock that had stretched her to her limits.

Again they lifted and then forced her down, moving to the rhythm the drum set. By the time the huge, knobby cock had been slammed into her a half dozen times, her body was on fire, begging for release.

She was almost more dismayed than relieved when they lifted her from him and moved her to the end of the altar again. Turning her to face outward, they jerked her shoulders back, thrusting her breasts out in offering.

Again the priests began to move around her. She shook as the first stopped and caught one nipple, raking it with his teeth as he pulled on it and finally released it. When he had moved on, a second stopped. Bracing herself, Mariel was caught off guard when he caught the nipple of her other breast and suckled it. When he had moved away and a third took his place, she tensed, expecting the pleasure/pain of his teeth. Instead, he suckled the nipple that still throbbed from the first priest's teeth. The fourth caught her by surprise, biting down hard enough that it jolted her from the pleasure that had begun to make her thighs quiver with weakness. She cried out, panting for breath as he finally released her and moved away.

Expecting the next to suckle her, she was caught off guard once more as he, too, bit down on her nipple, tugging at it, raking his teeth over it. Her belly quivered.

She found very quickly that she could not brace herself. Each time one stopped, he threw her off guard once more, suckling and giving her pleasure when she expected pain, biting her painfully when she expected pleasure.

As before, her body ceased after a time to react any differently. Regardless of whether pain or pleasure was inflicted on her, her belly clenched with pleasure, her body shuddered.

When they ceased at last and lined up on either side of the altar once more, her nipples were pounding, her sex was throbbing, her back ached from being held so long with her back arched and her breasts thrust forward.

She gasped as they jerked her upright and turned her.

In a heated fog, she watched as a priest climbed upon the table and lay flat. Again the High Priest stepped forward, pouring oil over the cock that stood stiffly erect. She was moved. When they had set her on her knees above him, they reached between her legs and spread her wide, shoving the cock head inside of her.

She gasped dizzily as she felt the cock head stretching the mouth of her sex, caught her breath when she heard the drum, flinching instinctively. Grasping her knees, they impaled her on the shaft, slamming her down so hard against him she felt her clit grinding into his belly. Before she could catch her breath, the drum pounded again.

This time the rhythm the drum set was much faster. She was lifted and rammed down on the shaft over and over so hard and fast that she felt her body skating the fine edge of pain, felt it hovering near release despite the pain.

She was moved again just as she felt her body gathering itself toward culmination.

Her heart began to pound in both anticipation and dread as she was settled at the end of the altar and her arms pulled back once more. She tensed as the first stopped before her, but there was no bracing herself when she never knew whether she would be given pleasure or pain. Each assault caught her completely off guard.

With dread, she felt them turn her to face the next. Again, she was held and her body aligned. This time, the rhythm was so fast she came as soon as the cock was rammed inside her the fourth time. Her belly clenched, convulsing with spasms of pleasure that became almost more torture than pleasure as she was driven down over the rigid shaft again and again, without respite.

Her entire body was tingling with release as they moved her to the foot of the altar once more. She faced it with dread, sated, unable to bear the thought of being pleasured again so quickly.

To her dismay, as they settled her on her knees, they pulled her thighs wide so that her knees were on the very edges of the altar. As they bore down on her arms until her back arched, lifting her breasts and thrusting them forward, the priest on either side of her reached between her thighs and caught her nether lips, peeling them back to expose her clit. She jerked, tried to twist away from their grip, but she was still so weak from her release it was no contest.

She flinched as the first priest stopped, kneeling and placing his mouth over her clit. Considering that her body had only just found release, the sucking and licking was almost as much torment, she thought, as it would have been if he had bitten her. Her passage tightened, heat and moisture flooding through her.

When he had moved away, a second man took his place. He bit down on her breast so hard she cried out, gnawing at her nipple, pulling it. She looked down at herself when he released her at last, surprised to see he hadn't broken the skin. Even as she glanced down at herself, she felt the priests peel her nether lips back, offering her pussy to the one who knelt in front of her. He bit her, sending a shaft of pain through her and ripping a cry from her throat. Scraping the sensitive bud with his teeth, he pulled on it as they had her nipples.

Blood pounded in the sensitive flesh as he withdrew and the lips of her sex were released. She jerked reflexively as another priest took his place and leaned toward her. To her relief, he covered the tip of breast so recently abused and suckled it, lathing it with his tongue. The throbbing ache subsided and heated pleasure replaced it.

The next man knelt and Mariel felt her belly jerk as the men who held her drew her nether lips back and offered her throbbing clit to him. Instead of soothing the tender flesh as she'd expected, he bit down on her, raked his teeth across it and tugged. Even as pain spread through her, however, he released it and began to suck her. The pain was transformed abruptly to pleasure. The moment she relaxed, he closed his teeth over her again, tugging, and sending another shaft of pain through her. Then, he suckled until she was dizzy with the alternating sensations cutting through her body. Her nipples and clit throbbed without cease as each took a turn, giving her pain, and then pleasure, over and over until her body began to respond with need even to the pain.

By the time they had ceased tormenting her, her body throbbed all over, begging for release. Dizzy and breathless, she was turned once more to face the impaling. This time they didn't even rest her knees on the altar. Lifting her, they thrust the cock head inside of her and bore down on her. Pain and pleasure jolted through her as the cock was forced inside of her, withdrawn, slammed into her again. Her body convulsed with pleasure as the cock was rammed into her for the third time, and kept convulsing as they impaled her over and over.

She lost awareness of her surroundings as they lifted her away once more and positioned her at the end of the altar. Her whole body was still thrumming with release, felt boneless. When they arched her back, they had to hold her upright.

Briefly, the hope rose that she'd been assaulted so endlessly that her body had gone numb, moved beyond feeling anything. Instead, she discovered that it had progressed to a state where it rushed from satiation, to peak, and into culmination far more rapidly, where pleasure shot through her when she was given pleasure, and a sharper, harder pleasure shot through her when she was given pain.

She was barely even conscious as the dance of offering began to circle her. She didn't realize the first priest had stopped before her until those who held her curled their fingers into the lips of her sex and pulled the flesh back, exposing the sensitive inner flesh in offering. He closed his teeth on the throbbing bud, raking them along the flesh as he pulled and tugged at the clit and tender petals of flesh that surrounded it. The pain jolted her back to full awareness, sending stabs of pleasure through her and making her heart pound. He rose and stepped away and another took his place, kneeling as the first had. Again the priests who held her drew her nether lips back, offering her fully. He closed his teeth on her tender flesh, tugging, suckling for a moment and then biting into her sensitive flesh again.

As he moved away, another took his place. This one settled his mouth over her breast, gnawing on her nipple ravenously.

She'd come to expect that they would alternate, though there was no rhythm that she could find, no way to tell when she would be given pleasure, or when it would be pain. One by one, the twelve stopped. Each time, she thought that they would soothe the throbbing. Instead, each time her nether lips were drawn back in offering, stabs of pain and pleasure went through her as they moved over her tender flesh with their teeth. Each who took a nipple into his mouth, gnawed it hungrily. Each assault sent sharp stabs of pleasure/pain through her, until her body was humming for release.

When they positioned her once more for the impaling, she was looking forward to it almost with a sense of desperation. She'd begun to feel as if her body was on fire and she would die if she didn't find surcease. As soon as they had spread her flesh and wedged the cock head inside of her, she wanted to thrust herself down upon it. They held her. When the drum sounded, they bore down on her, grinding her against the belly at the root of the cock and her heart slammed against her ribs as pleasure shot through her in equal measure. A heart beat passed. The drum was struck again and she was lifted. Another heartbeat and they bore down on her, ramming the hard cock into her.

Despite the pleasure, the measure was too slow. Each time they moved her, her breath caught, her body quivered, but release remained beyond her reach. She was nearly sobbing when they moved her to the end of the altar and thrust her breasts and cunt out in offering.

They suckled her nipples and her clit, licked her. She bit her lips, trying to keep from moaning in frustration, needing more. When at last she felt the lips drawn away from her clit and the offering was taken with savage hunger, she groaned, feeling her body shoot toward climax. Before it had caught her, he moved away. She felt like weeping, was nearly mindless with need. The next three suckled her, teased her. The next caught her nipple and tugged at it, but it was not enough.

Almost as if they knew that she hung on the edge, desperate, needful, they merely tormented her.

When they positioned her above the cock once more, she was gasping so hard she felt faint. Spreading her flesh, the cock was inserted. She waited, poised, hoping, dreading. Catching her on the first drum beat, they bore down on her. Almost the moment she felt the root grinding against her, the drum sounded again and she was lifted. Again it struck, the rhythm so fast she'd hardly landed before she was pulled away. Her climax began to quake inside of her as they bore down on her again. It exploded shatteringly through her, almost painfully as they continued to pound the engorged cock into her over and over.

She was weak with relief when they moved her again, but it did not last long. She was positioned at the end of the altar once more. The torment began to seem endless. At last, however, when she had received each of his twelve minions, the Demon Bileezal allowed her to rest. She was unbound, lifted onto the shoulders of those who'd carried her to the chamber and borne away. She was settled on the softness of a mattress and she knew no more.

Chapter Five

Mariel was so disoriented when she woke, she had no idea of where she was beyond the fact that it was a cell. Rising, she attended her needs, glanced with little interest at the tray of food by the door, and fell into the bed and slept. She roused when the scrape of the tray against the stone floor penetrated her dreams.

Slowly memory returned as she drifted to full wakefulness. She sat up. To her surprise, she felt little tenderness. She frowned. Vaguely she remembered that someone had rubbed soothing oils into her skin, massaging the soreness from her. Her stomach growled and she got up. The food on the tray told her little, but she saw that it was not the same as before and wondered how long she'd slept.

Shrugging the thought off, she ate, set the tray by the door once more, and lay down on the bed again. She was awakened again when the door opened. Sitting up, still groggy, she watched as two of the priests entered. Without a word, they pulled her to her feet and escorted her from the cell to the bathing chamber.

When she'd been bathed and led from the pool, she looked toward the door expectantly, knowing that now the High Priest would bring a robe for her and she would leave the temple.

The High Priest did not appear. Instead, when she'd been dried, the priests lifted her onto their shoulders and carried her from the room. Her heart jerked painfully as they lifted her for she knew her ordeal was not over.

As she'd known they would, they carried her down the stone stairs to the offering room. When they set her on her feet, the two priests beside her caught her arms, turning her. With dread, she stared at the doorway on the opposite side of the room, hearing the beat of the drums, the scrape of feet as the favored priests of the Demon Bileezal appeared there, bearing candles. As they entered the chamber, they moved to stand on either side of the altar, extinguishing the candles and laying them on the floor at their feet.

The High Priest emerged last. Turning when he'd stepped from the door, he lifted a vessel and moved toward the altar. As he passed before each of the twelve priests, he tipped the vessel, pouring a glistening liquid over each cock. When he'd completed the circuit he held up his hands. The drumming stopped.

The two men who stood on either side of her caught her arms. Dragging her toward the altar, they lifted her and sat her on the end. Her arms were pulled behind her back and bound and they lowered her until she was lying on her arms, her back arched upward from her hands in the small of her back. Two other robed priests joined those who'd placed her on the altar. Catching her legs, they bent them at the knee, placed manacles around her ankles and attached them to either side of the altar so that she couldn't straighten her legs, resting her feet on the edges of the altar.

As the High Priest moved around the altar and came to a stop at her feet, the two who'd bound her ankles grasped her thighs and pulled them apart, then reached between her legs, parted the flesh. The High Priest tipped the vessel he carried, pouring the clear liquid over her genitals. Mariel flinched as the cool liquid poured over her warmth of her sex, sending a shiver through her.

When the High Priest stepped back, he lifted his head. "The Demon Bileezal has favored his bride, devoting the first half of the ritual to her pleasure. Take your devoted servants, Lord Bileezal and take your pleasure of your bride."

The drums began to beat again as the High Priest turned and moved away. Around her, the priests chanted, summoning the beast. Mariel's heart kept time to the drum beat, pounding in her ears as fear filled her at the priest's words. The four men who surrounded her lifted her, moving her toward the end of the altar until the edge cut into her buttocks. She was settled again, but instead of allowing her feet to rest on the altar, the two priests at her feet caught her legs, spreading them.

As the vessels of Bileezal began to move around the altar, Mariel's throat closed. They circled her three times before one stepped from the circle and stood between her legs. The men holding her legs pulled thighs wider and parted the lips of her sex with their fingers wide in offering.

Stepping forward, the man guided the head of his cock into her and leaned over her. Propping his hands on either side of the altar, he dropped his head and caught one distended nipple in his mouth, raking his teeth across it, pulling it, then moved to the twin, nipping her hard. Both pain and pleasure shot through her as he began sucking and biting her flesh almost frenziedly. Abruptly, he thrust inside of her.

Mariel cried out as he rammed into her, felt her flesh yielding reluctantly to the intrusion, spasming around the enormous cock. The force of his thrust would have pushed her up the table except for the fact that the four who surrounded her held her to receive as the man, keeping rhythm with the drum, pounded into her joltingly, grinding against her, biting and sucking her breasts. There was no measured number of strokes as there had been the day before. He rammed into her over and over until she thought he would split her in two--and in spite of the pain he inflicted, her body heated, drugged with the euphoria of pleasure, climbing toward release.

Abruptly, it ripped through her, dragging a hoarse cry from her throat and still he rammed his cock inside of her on and on, pushing her climax to the limits of her endurance. Suddenly, he jerked, shuddered, his seed pouring inside of her. Straightening, he stepped away and rejoined those who still circled her, chanting.

A second stepped from the group. Pushing his cock head into her, he thrust deeply inside of her and began to pump into her frantically, jarringly, wringing weak cries from her as her body began to climb toward release almost immediately. She came, her body wracked by excruciating spasms as he slammed his cock past the quaking walls of her sex. Mellowing heat washed through her and then her body began climbing again. The jerking of his cock as he climaxed sent her spiraling over the edge once more and into near oblivion.

Mariel lay panting for breath as he pulled his cock from her and stepped away. Something cold was poured over her heated, throbbing genitals, sucking the breath from her lungs. She was still trying to catch her breath as she was lifted until she was sitting nearly upright.

A man stepped from the moving circle, grasped both her breasts in his hands and began devouring them feverishly, biting, suckling, licking, and drawing her back from satiation to heated need once more. When he released her breasts at last, he knelt, feeding upon her clit as her nether lips were drawn back to offer it to him. Mariel was nearly mindless before he ceased and stood, shoving his cock into her and fucking her as feverishly as he had sucked and bit her. She climaxed twice before he pumped his seed into her and stepped away.

She was barely conscious by the time the fourth had pounded into her until he'd emptied his seed.

Removing her bindings, they lifted her and carried her from the offering chamber and up the stairs to the bathing chamber. The cool water revived her. The bathing was far from pleasant, however. Her body felt so sensitive she could hardly bear to be touched.

To her dismay, she was borne to the offering chamber once more where the drumming and pounding continued unceasingly. As before, she was bound and offered to Demon Bileezal. Four more times he took her, driving her into release over and over before he took his own.

She knew even as they took her to the bathing chamber that her ordeal was not yet over, but when they took her down the third time, she felt like weeping. By the time they bore her down the stairs the fourth and final time she was almost beyond knowing or caring--almost. They still managed to wring pleasure from her, and hoarse cries, over and over.

Her last thought before she was allowed to sink into the darkness was that she hoped she'd pleased the Demon Bileezal. He'd nearly fucked her to death and she hated to think she'd endured two days of offering her body in vain.

She was allowed to rest for two days before she was escorted to the bathing chamber, bathed, dressed in a golden robe and led away by Behsart. He said nothing. He rarely spoke, but despite his typical reticence, she immediately noticed the repressed rage in him as he settled her before him on the horse. Mounting behind her, he pulled her tightly against him, turned the horse and spurred it into a trot as they rode from the village.

They had not ridden far into the forest when he guided the horse off the road and into a clearing. Dismounting, he tired the horse and pulled her from the saddle. Leading her to the shade of a tree, he pushed her down and followed her, shoving her gown up and falling upon her as if he were starving and she a loaf of bread. The savagery of his possession heated her blood until she was moaning beneath him and when he parted her thighs and thrust into her, excitement surged through her. Within moments, her body began to convulse, closing around his thrusting cock and milking him so that his crisis jolted through him, as well.

Briefly, he rested and then he took her once more, as desperately as he had the first time, ravishing her hungrily, thrusting into her with frantic need until he brought her to culmination again and followed her, shuddering with his own release.

When he'd ceased to shudder, he rolled off of her, lying on his back in the grass and staring up at the tree above them. Mariel dozed. When she woke, she discovered that he was lying beside her, staring down at her, his expression almost puzzled. She gazed back at him, equally curious, wondering if she was seeing the demon, Behsart, or the man, Cavan.

He'd made love to her, she realized with a touch of surprise. Despite the desperation of his possession, he had held her, stroked her body almost worshipfully, pleasured her before he sought his own release.

Was it at all possible that the demon was capable of softer feelings?

She could not believe that he was. Cavan had begun to gain control of the demon as Behsart weakened.

But who was Cavan?

Behsart had said that he had once been known as Cavan, Lord of Reugal. The name meant nothing to her, but she had no way of knowing if it was because Behsart had lied to her and made the name up, or if it was purely ignorance on her part. Until the Trull had come for her, she had never traveled beyond her own village. For as far back as she could remember, they had been poor, for her father could never hold on to money long and the poorer they got, the more heavily he drank until that began to eat into the little that was left from his gambling.

As tempted as she was to try to reach the man she'd begun to feel emerging from the grasp of the demon, in the end, she held her silence, fearful that she would arouse the wrath of Behsart if she tried to summon Cavan and undo whatever good she'd gained. She thought that she would be far better off to pander to Behsart's lust for her and feed him upon it until he became so sated and weakened Cavan could supplant him and aid her in escaping her fate.

She had been surprised but tremendously relieved that she'd been allowed time to rest after the last ritual, but she knew that the worst trials were ahead of her. The ritual at the Temple of Bileezal had been by far worse than anything that had come before. It made her ill with fear only imagining what she might have to face at the temples she must face next.

The only thing that sustained her was the belief that, no matter what, they would see to it that she reached the Castle Valdamer. It was not much to find comfort in, but it was all she had.

Perhaps, since the Demon Bileezal had taught her that pleasure could be had, even from pain, she would be able to endure.

Abruptly, Behsart rose and moved to the horse, retrieving the food pack. When he returned, he handed her a portion and took some for himself. They ate in silence. Mariel glanced at Behsart several times from beneath her lashes and saw that his gaze had settled unblinkingly on her.

She was almost disappointed when he made no attempt to couple with her again. Instead, when they'd finished, they took their ease and returned to the horse.

When Behsart had settled behind her, Mariel turned and looked up at him. "Pleasure me as you did before," she whispered huskily.

His face went taut, his eyes blazing instantly with passion. His hands shook as he turned her to face him, settling her thighs over his as she looped her arms over his head. His cock was already hard and throbbing as he shifted his loincloth and released it. Tightening her arms around his neck, she lifted up so that he could push his cock head inside of her and, once he had, settled on his lap, feeling the dampness that remained from their coupling easing his passage. He caught her hips, thrusting upward as he bore down on her until her clit rubbed his belly.

His eyes glazed as he tightened his arm around her hips and set the horse into motion. Mariel clung tightly to him, welcoming the heat that began to build inside of her at once. The body, the scent, the touch belonged to the man-- not the demon Behsart and she knew the man was aware of her, desired her, drew pleasure from her body even as he wrung pleasure from her.

She relished the closeness, the sense of belonging, as much as she enjoyed the desire and clung to him as they brought each other to culmination over and over, until they were drunk with each other.

They stopped to refresh themselves, but each time they mounted the horse to go on their way, she mounted his cock and rode him. At dusk, they made camp. When they had eaten and bathed in the stream, they rolled together in Behsart's bedding, curling around each other and making love slowly. He pulled her across his chest when they had sated one another, stroking her back, holding her close. As Mariel drifted away toward slumber, he spoke.

"I grow stronger with each day that passes. Stay strong for me, my lovely Mariel. Together, we will banish the demons."

Behsart was sullen and withdrawn when they woke. Mariel was in no doubt that the demon was once more dominant, banishing Cavan once again, for she saw it with every glance. She wasn't certain whether he was angry with her because Cavan had escaped his control the night before, or if it was because he was looking forward to turning her over to the priests of the next temple with resentment. She thought it possible that it was a little of both and made no attempt to draw him into conversation or to tempt him to couple with her.

The following day, they reached a range of gentle, rolling mountains. They camped that night in the foothills and began the climb the following morning. By midday they had topped the crest and started down once more. Toward evening, she saw the towering Temple of the Demon Raezitath, the ringed demon.

She didn't know whether to be relieved or sorry when Behsart stopped to camp once more. She was certainly in no hurry to reach the temple, but the fear of waiting in dread was almost as bad as reaching their destination and knowing that she only had to endure the ritual and she would have it behind her.

At dawn, they rose and mounted the horse and set it toward the Temple of Demon Raezitath. The priests began pounding at the gongs even as they cantered the horse up the main road. By the time Behsart had tethered the horse and helped her down, worshippers had already begun to gather. When they reached the piazza, the High Priest took hold of the chain and Behsart departed once more.

Mariel watched fearfully as he strode down the stairs, mounted the horse and rode off, wondering why it seemed he would not even be allowed to enter the temple. Or had that been his decision? Did it mean she would be here many days, as she had at the Temple of Bileezal, she wondered fearfully? Or did it mean nothing at all beyond something so simple as a need to run some mundane errand, such as having the horse shod?

When they had finished displaying her, she was escorted inside. Despite the robed priests that surrounded her and the dimness inside the temple after the bright morning sunlight, she saw almost at once that the Temple of Raezitath was not laid out as the other temples had been. The corridor, instead of running straight and level through the temple, slanted downward, dipping more sharply as they reached the center of the temple and splitting off to the right and left.

The procession turned left as they reached the end of the corridor. Mariel saw as they reached the floor below that the bathing, or purifying chamber, was a part of the offering room. She tried not to think what significance that might have as they came to a stop and the manacles around her wrists were removed.

A priest seized her by each arm and walked her toward a mosaic on the floor near the pool, forcing her to lie down on her back. Kneeling on either side of her, they grasped her arms and positioned them straight out from her body, clamping a manacle that was set into the floor around each wrist. Uneasily, she watched as they moved back toward her, clamping a second manacle around each upper arm.

A leather strap was fed through a ring in the floor, across her body just below her breasts and into a second ring on the other side, then tightened to that she could barely breathe and could not move at all.

They moved down her body then. Grasping her ankles, they parted her legs so wide she'd begun to feel pain in her hip joints and groin and finally fastened her ankles with manacles connected by rings to the tiled floor. Moving up her legs, they secured two more bands around her upper legs, tightening them against the floor, as well. The two who had secured her stepped back.

Chapter Six

Minutes measured in pounding heartbeats passed. Finally, two other priests approached her. One knelt between her legs and the other straddled her, settling his buttocks on her lower stomach with his back to her. Mariel swallowed, panting in little gasps, unable to take a decent breath of air into her lungs as she waited fearfully to see what they would do.

In a moment, she felt fingers parting the seam of her nether lips, felt the flesh peeled back. Her clit was captured between two fingers and stretched. A moment later, fire shot through her. She screamed, jerking against her bindings, waiting in terror for the pain to be repeated. It wasn't. They continued for several moments to tug and pull at her clit, but the fiery pain began to dissipate to a dull throbbing.

Finally, the two stood. Moving to either side of her, one lay something cold and metallic on her stomach. The priest on her right grasped her left nipple and stretched it. The second thrust a thin, sharp needle through the flesh, running it all the way through and out the other side. Mariel screamed the moment the needle pierced her flesh, surging against her bindings. Ignoring her, the one with the needle set it aside, picked up a tiny ring and inserted it in the hole he'd made, fastening it. She stiffened as they moved to her right breast. Again, her nipple was pinched and the skin stretched. The one with the needle pierced it and a second ring was attached and fastened.

She watched in fear as they collected their tools and rose, wondering if they meant to pierce her anywhere else. To her relief, they turned and left.

The two who had bound her returned and began to release the manacles. When they had finished, they pulled her up and walked her to the pool. The pain of the piercings had subsided to a dull, pounding throb, but the bathing was an ordeal. The slightest touch sent new waves of pain through her sensitive areas and the scraping that followed was almost worse.

The drums began to pound even as she was led from the pool the second time. The priests began chanting. Mariel stared fearfully at the opposite end of the chamber as she was dried. There were perhaps a dozen robed priests besides those who attended her in the purification. As she watched, however, six others filed into the room. These wore the hood of the beast. They were naked beyond that except for some sort of harness-like contraption that cupped their genitals. Their cocks were erect, standing obscenely against their bellies and painted bright red. Mariel wasn't certain if it was fear that made it appear that their cocks were even bigger than those of the Temple of Bileezal, or the paint, or if they actually were bigger. The men themselves were massively muscled.

When her attendants had finished drying her, she was led to the offering area and toward three posts that stood up from the floor. She was pushed back against the center post. A strip of leather perhaps four inches wide was laid on the floor at her feet. At each end of the strip was a large ring. Chains were attached to the rings.

Her feet were threaded through the larger rings and they were drawn up to her thighs. She was told to sit then. When she'd settled, the two priests who'd escorted her pulled on the chains attached to the rings. Slowly, the chains grew taut and began to lift her thighs upward. The strap beneath her buttocks tightened. Her hands were placed on the chains and then she was slowly raised up from the floor until she was hanging several feet above it.

The lifting stopped. Taking another pair of chains from the floor, the two priests attached them to the rings around her thighs and moved to the posts on either side of her. Threading the chain through rings set in the posts, they began drawing them tighter and tighter until Mariel's thighs had been drawn so wide she felt the tendons pulling painfully. When they'd secured the chains and released them, it released some of the tension and her tendons, to her relief, ceased to burn.

Returning to her once more, one of the priests pulled her hand from the chain and pulled her arm behind her back, then reached for her other arm, twisting that around behind her as well and binding them behind the pole. The second took a pair of manacles from the floor, fastening one around each ankle. When he'd finished, he took a tiny chain and threaded it through a loop on the manacle of her right foot.

She stared at him in confusion, wondering what possible purpose so tiny a chain, which looked as if it could be snapped easily, could have. Reaching above her head, he threaded the tiny chain through a metal eye protruding from the side of the post. Pulling it taut, he threaded it through the ring piercing her right nipple, down through the ring in her clit, up again through the ring in her left nipple and to a second metal eye on the opposite side of the post before attaching it to the manacle on her left ankle.

Sensation that was part pain and part pleasure shot through her as he tugged on the chain, adjusting it and finally securing it. Mariel swallowed with an effort when he moved away. The slightest movement of her feet sent waves of sensation through her nipples and her clit. The greater the movement, the closer to pain it became.

She held still, hardly daring to breathe as they moved away from her at last, discovering that it was not only a matter of moving her feet that tugged against the delicate chain. Each rise and fall of her chest with breath, the slightest movement of her body, tugged at the rings and stimulated sensation. Heat burgeoned inside her body in response and she had not even been touched.

She looked at the two priests in dismay as they returned. One stepped between her legs. The other stood to one side, holding some strange looking devises. Taking one, the priest grasped the flesh of her nether lips. Clamping the metal end into her flesh, he wrapped the strap around her thigh, drew the flesh back, then clamped the other end of the strap a little lower on her fleshy lip. The second was attached as the first had been, holding the lips of her sex wide. When he'd finished, he ran his finger along her cleft, parting the thin inner lips. After studying her sex a moment, he and the other priest moved to the two poles on either side of her and tightened the chains spreading her thighs.

The tightening spread the lips of her sex wider and tugged on the chain running through her nipples and clit. Mariel gasped, panting as needles of pain went through her seemingly everywhere at once. The gasp sent a second wave through her and she squeezed her eyes closed, holding her breath, trying to slow her pounding heart. She opened her eyes as she heard the chanting grow louder and saw that the chanting priests were approaching her. The six who were bare lined up in front of her. The High Priest moved along the row, stopping at each and tipping oil onto the head of their cocks. When he'd reached the last, he turned, lifted his arms and offered her to the Demon Raezitath.

At once, three of the six moved toward. Instead of circling her, however, they began to stroke her body, to suck and nip at her with their teeth and lick her. Each time she jerked reflexively, sensation shot through her nipples and clit at the same time. The harder she jerked, the greater the pain and the less pleasure. By the time she realized she was inflicting most of the pain on herself, her whole body felt as if it was throbbing. She closed her eyes, willing herself to remain perfectly still.

She quickly discovered, however, that she simply could not control her reflexive actions. When they gnawed along the keenly sensitive soles of her feet, she jerked. When they sucked her toes, she jerked again. One knelt before her and ran his tongue along her cleft, teasing the ring in her clit with his tongue and both feet jerked at once. After a time, the pain and pleasure began to merge, turning her body into a throbbing mass of pulsing sensation.

One of the three stopped between her thighs, pushed the head of his cock into her and then thrust deeply. The abrupt invasion made her jerk all over, sending a hard wave of pleasure through her. Grasping the post behind her, he withdrew slightly and began to pump into her hard and fast, jolting her body and sending both pain and pleasure screaming through her. As her body began to convulse with the first tremors of release, tightening around his cock, he began to ram into her harder and faster until she was screaming with the sharp convulsions of pleasure. When he'd come, he moved around her and began to suckle one of her breasts. A second moved between her thighs, sheathed his cock inside of her and began thrusting into her as the other two moved to her feet and began to suck and nip at them, causing her to jerk reflexively. The cock thrusting in and out of her, the jolt of pain and pleasure that went through her when she jerked, set her body to spasming in another hard release. The moment the walls of her sex began to convulse, he grasped the pole and began to pound into her harder until his cock began to jerk inside of her.

She was gasping so hard when he finally stepped away from her that an almost constant stream of sensation ran through her as each breath pulled on the rings in her nipples and clit. When the third man positioned himself and pushed inside of her, she came almost instantly. The muscles of her passage convulsed around his hard cock and continued to spasm as he drove into her frenziedly, seeking his own release. By the time he reached his crisis, she was nearly hoarse and barely conscious.

Something cold and hard was pushed into the mouth of her sex, reviving her instantly. As cold liquid poured through her passage, bathing her hot sex, her belly clenched and she jerked hard against the chain. Pain erupted everywhere at once. When she was able to unclench her eyelids, she saw that the three who'd received her had returned to the line of priests. Several moments passed and then the other three moved forward.

Surrounding her, they suckled her breasts, nipped her inner thighs and sucked bites of flesh into their mouths, tormented the soles of her feet and toes, sucked and lathed her cleft and clit until once again she was a mass of pulsing flesh, dizzy with the heat that clouded her mind. One by one, they sheathed their hardened cocks in her flesh and thrust into her until they were spent.

Again, when they moved away, cold fluids were forced inside her sex, jerking her from the edge of unconsciousness. The first three approached her again, tormenting her with their mouths, and tongues and teeth, and then thrusting their cocks into her and fucking her until they came.

To her surprise and relief, when the second trio had received her again, she was lowered and her bindings removed. Leading her to the purification pool, the attendants bathed her, dried her and then lifted her to their shoulders and carried her up the incline to the main corridor. Instead of turning, however, they crossed the bisecting corridor and continued. At the end was a stout wooden door. When it was opened and she was carried inside, she saw it was a large chamber. Pillows were scattered about the floor and formed piles along the walls. Curtains lined the walls. A single narrow stone table stood near the door.

They lowered her onto pillows in the center of the room.

Instead of leaving, however, they extended her arms to either side of her and manacled them to the floor. Her knees were bent, her thighs spread wide and bindings were placed around her thighs and ankles, pinioning her legs to the floor. The clamps they'd used to hold her nether lips wide were attached to her once more.

They left her then. Mariel stared up at the ceiling, wondering what was to come next. As time passed, however, exhaustion got the better of her and, despite her discomfort, she slept.

The opening door woke her sometime later. As she glanced toward the door, three of the priests who'd received her entered the room and closed the door again.

Two moved to the mounded piles of pillows and sprawled out on them, lying on their sides, their heads propped on their hands. The third picked up a pillow and approached her. Kneeling between her thighs, he pushed her hips up, shoving the pillow under her so that her hips were tilted up. When he was satisfied, he settled on his stomach and opened his mouth over her cunt and proceeded to suck and fondle her genitals with his tongue until Mariel was squirming beneath the onslaught.

The other two merely watched for a time, but finally they rose and moved toward her and began to suckle her breasts until her body began to jerk and spasm in release. Before the last echoes had faded away, the one who'd been gnawing and sucking on her clit came to his knees, thrust his cock inside of her and began slamming into her. Within moments, her shocks of release began to pour through her again, spurred to greater and greater heights as he began to thrust more rapidly in search of his own release. Grinding deeply inside of her, he held himself still until his seed had ceased to spew inside of her and finally withdrew.

Rising, he moved to the curtains along one wall, disappeared for several moments and returned with a wet cloth. When he'd bathed her, he left again. A few moments later, he emerged from the curtained doorway, strode to a mound of pillows and sprawled atop them, composing himself for sleep. The other two fondled her for a while bringing her sated body to heat once more, and finally rose and returned to the pillows, dropping down on them.

Mariel swallowed convulsively. Before they'd begun to fondle her, her body had been sated. Now, she was a mass of unfulfilled desire once more. After a while, she drifted to sleep, however. She was awakened when the door opened again.

Blinking, she lifted her head and stared at the robed priest who entered, carrying a tray of food. Setting it on the table near the door, he turned and left.

His entrance had roused the three men. They rose and approached her. Releasing her from the bindings, she was told to attend her needs, bathe and return. Stiff and sore, she did as she was told. When she returned to the room, she was told to lie down again.

Her stomach felt as if it was caving in, but she saw no use in arguing. Once she'd lain down on the cushions, two of them set about binding her once more. When they'd finished, they settled cross legged on either side of her. The third lifted the tray and approached. Sitting down on the floor between her thighs, he took the bite sized chunks of food and laid them out on her body. When he'd placed all the food on her belly and breasts, he took a small pitcher from the tray and drizzled a thick liquid over the grapes and small chunks of apples scattered over her body. Almost as an after thought, he drizzled a small portion over her exposed genitals.

Once he had finished, he set the tray aside and got on his hands and knees. The others followed suit. Leaning over her, they plucked the food from her body with their mouths and teeth. Turning, the one to the right of her leaned down, his mouth hovering just above hers, offering her the grape between his teeth. Grateful that she wasn't to be left to watch them eat, she took it. The grape popped in her mouth and she swallowed the juices thirstily. As they fed her with their mouths and her thirst and hunger began to subside, she began to focus on the feel of their mouths moving over her. Heat blossomed, built. It built far more rapidly when they'd polished off the tidbits of food and began to lick the sticky liquid from her skin. A shock wave of sensation flooded through her as the one between her thighs lowered his head and began to suck and lick the syrup he'd drizzled over her genitals. When he'd licked and sucked every drop of it from her, he moved over her and thrust his cock into her, pumping into her feverishly until he came.

Mariel was still throbbing on the verge of release when he withdrew, bathed her sex and then lay down once more. She dozed, drifting upward sometime later as the heat in her belly reached flash fire from the mouth suckling her clit. She came almost as soon as he mounted her.

She dozed when he'd finished with her. She was released twice more to attend her needs but bound again for offering as soon as she returned. They pleasured themselves on her when the mood struck them, taking turns. Sometime later, another tray of food was brought and they ate the food from her body as before. She dozed off and on, was awakened sometimes by a mouth suckling one or the other of breasts, sometimes her clit and sometimes they merely mounted her and thrust into her until they came.

In the morning, the robed priests returned. Releasing her from the bindings, they carried her to the offering chamber once more. When they'd bathed her a thin chain was brought. Threading it through the ring on one nipple, they pulled it down, threaded it through her clit ring and then up again through the ring on her left nipple. The ends of the chain were then pulled over her shoulders and she was forced onto her hands and knees. Two of the six receivers approached her and got down on their knees, one at her head and the other behind her. The one behind her pushed her legs apart and thrust the head of his cock into her opening. Grasping the chains in his hands, he held the ends tightly as he pushed inside of her.

Pain and heat shot through her as the chain was pulled taut by his thrust. Even as she opened her mouth to cry out at the pain, her hair was caught and her head pulled up. The man kneeling before her shoved his cock into her mouth. The man thrusting into her pussy set the pace, slamming into her and forcing her forward so that the cock in her mouth slid deeper. Each thrust sent both pain and pleasure coursing through her as it tugged on her nipples and clit. As the heat rose inside of her, she began to suck more feverishly at the cock in her mouth. When she climaxed and her body began to quake, the man thrusting his cock into her pussy began to slam against her more desperately, sending more pain and pleasure ripping through her so that she sucked harder and harder on the cock in her mouth until it began to convulse, spewing his seed into her mouth and down her throat. She gagged, tried to pull away. The chain was jerked so hard she thought it would tear the rings from her. She swallowed convulsively at the command, feeling the man behind her come.

When they rose, they carried her to the pool, bathed her and returned her. Two more took their place, trusting into her until their crises erupted. Hours passed in a hot, throbbing morass of pain and pleasure until it was all she could do to remain on her hands and knees and receive them. One by one she received their cock into her mouth and then in her vagina.

She was almost too tired even to feel relief when she emerged from the pool and they lifted her, carrying her from the chamber. She was asleep almost before she fully settled against the pillows.

When she awoke, she discovered she'd been spread again and manacled. Three of the receivers were sprawled on the pillows around her, but she had no idea if it was the same three that had shared the room with her the night before, or the others. They still wore their hoods. She could see nothing of their faces beyond their eyes and mouths. She thought it was probably the other three, but it made little difference to her. They were mere shells. All them were the Demon Raezitath, who used their bodies to pleasure himself on her so that he was not subject to the limitations of one body. When one tired, he allowed it to rest and used another.

For a time, they seemed content to move to her and slake their lust as it suited them. When they'd released her the second time to see to her needs, however, she was not bound again. Instead, one caught the chains that were still threaded through the rings in her genitals and nipples and held it. When he wanted her, he pulled on the chains until the pain woke her and she crawled to him. Sometimes he would push his cock into her mouth and make her suck him and mouth fuck him until he came. At others, he would mount her from behind, or throw her to the pillows and thrust into her pussy until he found release. When he was sated, he would tug on the chains and pull her to the next.

She dozed for brief periods, but she was never allowed to sleep for long before she felt a painful tug on the chain that drew her to whoever held it to offer herself once more.

Chapter Seven

Mariel had never been more glad to see anyone than the two robed priests who came for her the following morning. If she had not been held by the chain, and too weak even to stand, she would have leapt to her feet to follow them. They came to her, lifted her and carried her down to the pool, bathing her.

Her body throbbed all over, ceaselessly.

Instead of dressing her when they'd dried her, they carried her to the offering room once more. She was bound against the post, her thighs and the lips of her sex spread wide to keep them from hindering access to her body in any way. As they had the first day, they took her by threes, expending themselves on her body repeatedly before allowing the other three to sate themselves on her.

When she was released, she was taken to the chamber of pillows once more. Again, she was pinioned to the floor. Three joined her, and again they exhausted themselves on her.

She was barely conscious when the priests bore her away to the pool the following day and the bath revived her very little. Apparently they saw that she would merely collapse if they forced her onto her hands and knees again, so she was taken to the post. She was barely conscious as they thrust into her over and over and yet her body convulsed regardless.

When she was finally released, she hung limply from the arms of those who carried her, barely aware of anything. She lapsed into complete unconsciousness as she was laid on the pillows. She was allowed, at last, to rest, barely aware of the passage of time. They roused her and forced her to eat periodically, but the moment they ceased to prod her, she fell over and slept once more.

When she finally awoke to full alertness, she had no idea of how much time had passed. The robed priests entered the room. She leapt to her feet and then went still with stunned surprise to discover that she was completely unfettered. Before she could recover, they moved toward her, lifted a black robe and drew it over her head, settling it around her.

Relief flooded through her, undiminished even as they placed the manacles on her wrists and led her from the chamber.

Behsart awaited her on the piazza. Without a word, he took the chain the priest held out and crossed the piazza, descending the stone stairs rapidly. Mariel hurried after him, fearing any moment she would be dragged off balance and roll to the bottom. When he reached his horse, he lifted her to the saddle, climbed up behind her and spurred the horse into motion.

Mariel settled against him uneasily. He was enraged. His eyes glittered with it. His entire body was taut with anger held barely in check. If she had doubted before what that anger signified, she no longer did.

He did not like yielding her to the temple demons. His sense of possessiveness was rapidly moving beyond his control.

They did not stop to break their fast when they had left the village behind as had become their custom. After a while, however, Behsart pulled bread and cheese from the food pack and handed them to her. She placed her hands over his as she took the offering. As innocent as the contact was, he hesitated for a long moment before he withdrew his hand.

When she had eaten, he took the wine skin and handed it to her, watching as she drank. The food and wine comforted her, easing some of her tension, but much of it still lingered. His anger was unnerving enough. The fact that he seemed to have withdrawn was even worse.

Only two temples lay before them now. That did not allow her much time to devise a way to save herself if Behsart did not succumb to her.

She had counted on it. There was nothing else. Since she had been taken, she had been bound, watched, or simply too exhausted from the offerings to have any hope of escaping.

At mid day, they stopped to refresh themselves. Behsart watched her hungrily, but he made no attempt to take her and she found she simply didn't have the nerve to try to approach him herself when she could see that rage was a good part of his hunger.

"Why are you angry with me?" she finally asked when they had set out once more.

He was silent for so long that she thought he wouldn't answer her at all.

"I am not angry with you," he said finally, his voice a low, husky growl.

He said nothing more and, jog her mind though she would, she could think of no way to keep the conversation going in the direction that she wished. After a time, he shifted, slipping an arm around her waist and pulling her back so that she lay against his chest. Breathlessly, she waited to see what he would do next.

He did nothing more, and her uneasiness began to grow once more.

She cleared her throat. "You do not want me anymore?"

"We want you."

Mariel shivered. Two voices had emerged from his throat simultaneously. "Then--I don't understand."

"It is forbidden," he growled, his voice as it had been before.

Startled, Mariel glanced up at him. "Why?"

He fell silent for a time. She had just decided that he had no intention of telling her when he spoke again.

"This man is an enemy to us. He is rebellious. Thrice, he has tried to banish us."

Mariel threw him another startled look, her heart skipping several beats as she realized he was talking about Cavan. She didn't know why, but it hadn't occurred to her before that Cavan had been captured by the demons while he had been fighting them.

Just how did one go about fighting demons, she wondered?

They were spirit creatures--powerful spirit creatures. Surely to battle them would require knowledge of magic? Had Cavan been powerful enough that he had had reason to believe he had a chance of defeating them? Or had he merely been too foolhardy to know better? Too arrogant to consider that he could fail?

"Us?" she finally prompted.

"We are one," Behsart growled. This time, his voice sounded like many voices entwined.

The sound sent another shiver skating along her spine, but the words were almost as frightening. "They know... all that you do?"

"No. I am not as powerful as they are, but I am still strong."

She digested that for several moments, wondering if she dared pursue it. Finally, she asked, "But they know about... They must know that we...."

He leaned down until his lips were near her ear. "They smell him on your body, taste him on your skin," he growled in a gravelly voice.

Mariel's nipples tightened almost painfully as his heated breath caressed her ear. She didn't have to glance down to know that it must be very obvious if Behsart cared to look down. Her body burgeoned, scattering her thoughts. She swallowed. "So... you cannot touch me again because he is an enemy of the demons?"

He slipped his hand upward from her waist, flicking at the ring on one distended nipple. "When I bury this flesh deeply inside your sweet body--when I taste this tender bud," he growled, pinching her nipple between two fingers, "he feels it as I do. He enjoys your taste and your scent, the smoothness of your skin, the softness of your body. He enjoys the heat at your core, the feel of your flesh wrapped tightly around his, feeling your body shiver and convulse in pleasure. He is not allowed surcease from his torment. He is not allowed to taste our bride."

Mariel swallowed with an effort, dizzy with the heat that enveloped her at his words, entranced with the sensations flowing through the nipple he toyed with and into her belly. She fell silent, too aroused to think, unwilling to distract him in any case. After a time, he ceased to toy with the nipple ring, ceased to pluck at her nipple. She didn't know whether to be relieved or sorry when his hand slipped down to her waist. It settled there for only a moment, however. He caught the robe, bunching it in his fist and slowly drawing it higher. When he had bared her lower body, he began to play with her clit ring and finally slipped his hand lower, pushing one finger inside of her.

A shudder went through her. She shifted, offering him better access.

He let out a harsh breath and began thrusting his finger as deeply inside of her as he could reach and then sliding it out once more. Removing the finger after a few moments, he teased her clit, then slipped his hand down and pushed his finger inside of her again.

She groaned, leaning against him and lifting her hips to meet the thrust of his finger, half fearing that he would stop before he brought her to crisis when he moved his hand upward once more. He pinched her nipples, tugging on the rings and flicking his fingers against them until he drew a moan from her throat. He slipped his hand down her belly to her clit then, teasing it for several moments before he pushed his finger inside of her again, thrusting into her quickly. A shudder went through her as she came. She groaned as his finger continued to thrust inside of her until her passage ceased to quake.

She slumped weakly against him as he withdrew his finger at last. Lifting his hand, he sucked her juices from his finger. After a moment, he slipped his hand between her legs once more, cupping her and pulling her back against the hard ridge of flesh she felt against her buttocks.

He made no attempt to touch her otherwise, but his palm remained cupped around her sex for some time before finally, almost reluctantly, he moved it up to her waist once more.

Near dusk, Mariel saw that they were approaching the mountains once more. They made camp near a pool fed by a waterfall. Mariel studied the falling water longing as she sat near the fire, eating.

"Would you like to bathe in the pool?"

She glanced at Behsart quickly. Doubt surfaced almost the moment he offered. "Is the pool deep?"

"It will not matter. I will go with you." He rose and began to discard his clothing.

After a moment, Mariel rose, as well, and pulled the robe off, following him a little nervously to the edge of the pool. Behsart waded in, halting when he discovered the chain had gone taut. He turned, studied her for a moment and finally waded back. Scooping her into his arms, he waded into the pool once.

She uttered a squeak of surprise when he set her on her feet and the cold water lapped her knees. "It's c-c-cold."

To her surprise, he chuckled. "It is mountain water."

Mariel stared at him for several moments and finally looked away, totally bemused by the fact that he'd laughed--the demon? She didn't think so. It was Cavan, and he was growing stronger. More and more, she heard him in the things that he said, and the way that he behaved.

Heartened, she ignored the chill of the water and waded toward the pool. The water was almost up to her breasts by the time they reached the water fall, and the chill made her breathless. She held out her hands beneath the falling water and finally moved closer, stepping beneath it and allowing it to pelt her for several moments before she stepped out again.

They had not brought either soap or cloths to wash with, but Mariel felt clean and fresh when at last they waded out once more. She shivered as the night air caressed her skin and Behsart drew her closer as he led her back to the fire. Taking one of the blankets, he wrapped it around her and urged her to sit on the bedding that he had lain out near the fire, then knelt behind her, raking his fingers through her long, dark hair until he'd removed most of the tangles and the fire had dried the dark mass.

Finally, his hands fell still. Mariel held her breath, waiting.

Clutching her hair in his fist, he tugged on it until she lifted her face to look up at him. "You are a fever in my mind. My body hungers for you until I can find no rest. Are you a sorceress?"

Mariel swallowed with an effort. "I am only a mortal woman."

Cupping the side of her face, he leaned down and opened his mouth over hers hungrily, thrusting his tongue into her mouth and exploring the exquisitely receptive flesh, sending flashes of heat through her. Mariel sighed into his mouth, stroking her tongue along his.

Breaking the kiss after only a few moments, he pushed her back against the bedding and followed her down, moving his mouth over her face, her neck, the upper slope of her breasts ravenously, as if he wanted to taste all of her at once. His breath rasped harshly from his chest.

Nuzzling her chest, he placed a kiss over her madly pounding heart and traced a path with his tongue to one nipple, teasing it with the tip of his tongue and the heat of his breath before he took the engorged tip into his mouth and sucked it. Keen pulses of heat rushed along her nerve endings to her sex, making it contract so tightly her belly ached with the tension.

Impatiently, he cupped her other breast in his hand and suckled the tip, moved down and sucked the flesh underneath it. Shifting, he nibbled a path over her ribs and down the center of her body to her belly, placing little sucking bites across the quivering flesh.

Abruptly, he shifted once more. Catching her legs, he parted them, sucking a trail of kisses along the flesh of her inner thigh. When he reached her pussy, he let out a harsh breath, parted her nether lips and opened his mouth over her hungrily.

Mariel cried out, arching up to meet him as she felt the heat of his mouth, the flick of his tongue. He finessed her tender flesh more lavishly, dragging his tongue up her cleft, flicking her clit with the tip, fastening his mouth over her and sucking until she was gasping hoarsely, her body trembling with imminent release, sucking until she began to thrash about mindlessly and finally began to jerk and shudder as her body convulsed in an explosive orgasm.

He moved over her then, propping his body on one arm as he reached between them and pushed his cock along her cleft until he reached the mouth of her sex. Thrusting the head of his cock inside of her, he hunched upward, claiming her wet channel by inches, withdrawing slightly and driving deeper each time until he had possessed her fully.

Lifting his upper body slightly away from her, he watched her face as he undulated his hips, pushing deeply inside of her, withdrawing, pressing forward again. Mariel parted her thighs wider, lifting up to meet him. A tremor skated up his arms and through his body. Groaning, he lowered himself fully against her, buried his face against her neck and set a more desperate rhythm. The stroke of his flesh along her sensitive passage, the urgency of his thrusts, sent heat spiraling through her once more, lifting her rapidly toward her pinnacle. As she felt his body jerk and shudder with release, her own soared over the edge once more.

Gathering himself after a moment, he slipped an arm around her and rolled onto his back, carrying her with him. When he had dragged one of her legs across his, he caught her hair and tipped her head back, kissing her without hunger, or heat, but instead with warmth and tenderness. He tucked her head against his shoulder then and sighed gustily, stroking her back. "Offer prayers to the ancient ones, my love. We need all the help we can get," he murmured.

* * * *

There was no warning, no sign that they had reached their destination until they broke from the forest. One moment Mariel lay against Behsart's chest, half drowsing, the next she saw the Temple of Annomiz looming ahead of them.

They had traveled for three days from the Temple of Raezitath, camping the first night beside the pool, the second on the eastern slope of the mountains they had scaled, and the night before, they had stopped beside a forest stream.

Cavan had not emerged since that first night beside the waterfall. She had drifted to sleep in Cavan's arms and woke with Behsart, who was almost as ill tempered over his lapse as he had been that he had been denied in the first place. He had taken her to the pool the following morning and told her to scrub herself, making her stand in the chilly water for nearly an hour before he was satisfied and allowed her to come out again.

His temper had mellowed very little since, but although Mariel took care not to stir it, she was inwardly pleased, for she had had Cavan with her much of a day before he vanished again--far longer than any time before.

That warmth had sustained her through the wearying travel.

It deserted her as she stared in dread at the temple they approached, the Temple of the Demon Annomiz, the stone demon, the demon of fire and ice.

Chapter Eight

The walls of the temple seemed to exude cold, but Mariel wasn't certain if that was actually the case, or if it was fear that made her bone deep cold as she was escorted down the main corridor into the temple and prepared to receive the stone demon of fire and ice.

The name alone struck terror into her heart. Try though she might not to think about the rites at the temples of Bileezal and Raezitath, she could not keep the fearful thought from her mind that each had been worse than the last, and at each she had had to endure longer.

Her mind skittered even from the thought of pain. Except for her deflowering, she had not really known pain until she had reached the Temple of Bileezal. There, she'd been forced to endure both pure pain and pleasure that had bordered on it until her body had quivered and exploded with devastating culmination regardless.

It had been much the same at the Temple of Raezitath.

She feared it would be as bad, and possibly far worse, at the Temple of Annomiz.

When the priests had dried her, a thin chain was threaded through the rings as they had been at the temple of Raezitath.

They placed a blindfold over her eyes next, tying it tightly around her head, and then bound her arms behind her back, no doubt to prevent her from tearing the blindfold away from her eyes--something she was instantly desperate to do.

Her heart fluttered, then beat a little faster. She was so dizzy and disoriented as she was lifted and carried from the room that she began to think that she might pass out.

She prayed for it as she heard the beating drums and the chants of the priests, summoning Annomiz. She was shivering with fear and cold when they stopped. She felt cold stone beneath her feet. She swayed, but she was not released.

She was neither commanded by voice or the pressure of the hands holding her. Instead, the chain connected to the rings in her nipples and clit was yanked down on hard enough to send pain shooting through her. Her knees went weak and the two priests who held her allowed her to drop to her knees.

Her fear increased. Blinded as she was, if they would not tell her what they required, she could not know what they wanted until they snatched on the chain.

She was bound. She had no idea of how except that her thighs were spread so wide she felt as if her legs would separate from her body and even that did not seem to be wide enough to suit them for they clamped her nether lips, peeling them back until she felt cold air caressing her sensitive inner flesh.

She was lifted and carried. Her knees settled on stone once more. Something cold, hard and stiff was inserted into the mouth of her vagina and she was forced down over it. Her belly clenched as it entered her. Her heart hammered so hard she might have fallen if they had not been holding her.

The pressure on her shoulders ceased when she felt something cold against her parted nether lips, when the thing they had pushed inside of her bumped against her womb, causing it to clench and sending spasms of pain through her. She panted fearfully.

The hands holding her released her and she heard the scrape of their feet on the stone as they moved away. She swayed. The chain was jerked upward and she righted herself with an effort.

Slowly, her body adjusted to the long, cold object.

She heard the scrape of feet nearby and jerked her head instinctively toward the sound. The movement caused her to sway again and again the chain was jerked. She went still, concentrating on trying to keep her balance.

Something touched her. She jerked reflexively and again pain was the response.

She was touched again and again as they circled her. Something covered her breast, seemed to suck, but it did not have the warmth of a mouth. Nothing that touched her had the warmth of living things. It was icy, so icy that it felt like fire if it lingered on her skin for more than a few moments.

Despite the pain and fear, the continuous caresses began to produce warmth inside of her, though why she couldn't imagine. Her body burgeoned, grew warmer. Moisture began to collect in her sex. Need grew inside of her.

The stimulus was not enough to bring her to culmination, only enough to make her begin to yearn for it as the minutes dragged into an hour.

When the touching ceased and the priests drew away, she was lifted and carried once more. Again, her knees settled on a cold stone surface. Fingers pulled at her sex and something cold and hard was pushed into her. It was bigger than the last. Despite the slippery substance that seemed to coat it, the object was hard and rigid as no human member and large enough it stretched her flesh as they forced her down onto it.

She was gasping for breath by the time they ceased to bear down on her, her belly clenching and unclenching around the unyielding thing wedged inside of her. The dance began again.

The burgeoning had vanished, however, as the cold object was forced into the throat of her sex. Again she jerked and quaked as fire and ice moved over her body, stroking her, sucking at her breasts until heat slowly invaded her again. She'd been impaled upon it so long, however, that she began to waver. The tugging of the chain became almost constant as she struggled to keep her balance, to keep from falling down upon it and forcing it any deeper inside of her. After a time, the pain became heat, sizzling along her nerves and she began to moan as pleasure numbed her mind to all else.

The fondling became more insistent, more persuasive as the minutes ticked past. She began to gasp as she felt her body tensing on the verge of release. Something covered each of her breasts, sucking determinedly until her body began to convulse and spasm around the hard shaft inside of her.

The contracting of her muscles in release had scarcely subsided when she was pulled from the shaft, carried a short distance and settled on her knees. Hands pulled at her sex. Again, something cold and hard was forced into the mouth of her sex. It was bigger around than the last and she whimpered in fear and pain as she was impaled on it. Her belly spasmed and clenched, resisting the intrusion. Ignoring her distress, they bore down on her inexorably until the huge thing spread her, filled her passage completely, bumping against her womb. Beneath her, she felt the lips of her sex touch the cold base of it.

She was hardly aware of the dancing and chants as she was released and left to hang upon the shaft. She panted as her body continued to fight the intrusion even after it was forced fully inside, refusing to adjust, quaking around the unyielding hardness and sending sharp pain through her belly.

They did not begin to caress her until she ceased to struggle and pant. Even when they did, her body was slow to respond. As before, the fondling became more demanding and determined, forcing her body to respond, until heat built, until she began to gasp and moan as her body struggled against the pain and iciness, and struggled toward culmination.

She screamed when she came, her body convulsing so hard and so endlessly around the rigid shaft that she felt blackness swarm around her.

She was barely conscious when they removed her from it. Dimly, she realized that hours had passed and the hope sprang that she would be allowed to rest. When they settled her on her knees once more, fear inspired her to struggle, despite the fact that her entire body felt like jelly. She cried out when she felt the enormity of the shaft they forced into the mouth of her sex, fighting them despite the sharp tugs on the chain.

It availed her nothing. She whimpered as she was forced down upon it, felt it stretching her to the point of pain and began to fear that it would rip her apart.

When she realized fighting was useless, she tried to concentrate on relaxing her muscles and accepting it. It helped, but not much. The impaling was still long, torturous, and painful. She began to feel as if her body simply could not hold it. She was weeping with pain and terror by the time they'd forced it fully inside of her. She gasped when she felt the lips of her sex meet the coldness, a tiny measure of relief washing through her when she realized she would not be forced to take more of it into her.

A sound, almost of rejoicing, or triumph went up from the priests.

A moment later, she felt hands touching her and her legs were unbound, her knees pushed from the stone so that the weight of her own body settled her more firmly over the hard shaft, sending a stab of pain through her that made her gasp. Her ankles were bound and chained to the floor--she thought. She only knew that her toes touched something that felt substantial. She could not reach it well enough to push herself up.

The manacles around her wrists tightened and she realized that the chain had been attached to something behind her. She stretched her fingers and touched something cold and hard. It helped her to balance, though.

The chain running through her clit and nipple rings tightened as it, too, was secured--in front of her.

Despite the throbbing pain of being impaled on something far too large for her body, she almost felt a sense of relief. She had taken it inside of her without being ripped in two. The fact that they were binding her seemed to indicate that she would not have yet another, larger shaft forced inside of her.

She knew that she could not have taken anything larger without being shredded. She was grateful that they had not tried.

Although she couldn't see them, she heard the priests moving around them as they began to dance almost frenziedly. Their chant became more like a song. The rhythm of the drum increased in pace.

In time, when the pain of being impaled on the huge shaft had begun to subside to a dull throbbing, the icy caresses began once more. With determination they stroked and caressed her until her body began to respond. Heat built inside of her, spreading moisture through her channel soothing the residual pain from the thing that had been forced inside of her. They teased and sucked and licked at her until tremors began to run through her and when she began to gasp hoarsely, they suckled her breasts more frantically still until they brought her to culmination.

The clenching of her body was excruciating. She screamed hoarsely as it rocked her almost endlessly. The moment she ceased to convulse, before her body could cool, they began prodding her body toward its peak once more. Within moments, her body began to spasm, clenching around the thing inside of her.

The moment she began to cry out and shudder, they began tormenting her again. Each time they did, because her body never fell far from the edge, her body responded faster, culminating in seemingly endless convulsions of rapture.

She had reached the point where she began to sway, felt blackness rushing up at her when the mask was abruptly torn from her eyes. She blinked, trying to adjust her vision. Slowly, her eyes focused and she stared down at the thing beneath her.

She saw that she had been impaled on the cock of the stone demon, Annomiz.

As she stared at the frightening image, she saw a ripple of movement. She blinked, certain her eyes were playing tricks on her that they had driven her mind past rational thought. When she opened her eyes again, she saw the thing moving. Slowly, as she watched in abject horror, she saw the Demon Annomiz sit up.

His hands reached for her, grasping her hips.

The priests scrambled forward, releasing her manacles.

When they had freed her, he lifted her, bore her down again. She cried out, expecting pain, but her body was yet heated to the point of combustion and all she felt was a momentary discomfort and a rush of pleasure. As he began thrusting inside of her, her body skated upward again toward crisis. Within moments, she was shaking, and then screaming as waves of excruciating pleasure washed through her.

Holding her impaled on his cock, he stood, moved to the altar, lay her down upon it and began thrusting into her, jolting her with each lunge, pounding into her until, at last, he went rigid all over, lifted his head and roared as his body pulsed with pleasure.

Mariel felt the jerking of his cock, felt his fiery, hot seed spilling inside of her and lost her grip on consciousness.

She came to when she was dipped into the bathing pool, looking around fearfully.

She felt little relief, however, when she saw no sign of the stone demon.

They would return her to him, she knew.

She began to think that she'd been wrong after all when they did not take her to the offering chamber. Instead, they took her to a room much like the one at the previous temple. She saw as they thrust her inside, however, and closed the door behind her, that Annomiz lay sprawled on the pillows, awaiting her.

"Come," he said in a low, growling voice.

Inside, Mariel quaked. Her legs seemed to lose all tone, but she managed to walk toward him. When she knelt at the edge of he pillows, he leaned toward her, grasped the chains attached to her rings, and pulled until she moved closer.

He examined her through narrowed, yellow eyes. "You are puny and weak... even for a human," he finally assessed her. "But your body pleases me. Your cries of pleasure please me even more."

He pushed her down onto the pillows and began to suck and lick and bite her--sometimes almost to the point of pain, sometimes past the point of pain. She was nearly delirious with the pounding demands of her body when he spread her legs and thrust his cock into her.

Her flesh yielded reluctantly, but his own body was more yielding now and the moisture of desire bathed her sex, allowing him to force his cock inside of her without the terrible pain she'd more than half expected.

He brought her to crisis over and over, tirelessly pounding into her. She was barely conscious when he roared out his own pleasure.

He allowed her to rest, a concession she would never have expected, but she sensed he feared he would break his plaything if he used her as he wished. She had no idea how much time passed, because she spent much of it in exhaustion or complete unconsciousness, but she thought he toyed with her for at least three days before he decided he was satisfied and allowed the priests to prepare her for the journey to the Temple of Efathziman, the man beast, the seventh and most powerful of the demons of Daeksould.

When the priests had draped her in a sheer, white robe, Behsart led her away and they rode from town. She studied him surreptitiously when they stopped to break their fast.

He did not seem angry and that worried her more than his anger had.

She did not once catch him staring at her with the hunger she'd grown accustomed to seeing in the demon's eyes and that worried her even more. After a few moments, when he seemed in no particular hurry to be on their way, Mariel settled on her side and began to play almost idly with one of the nipple rings through the sheer robe she wore--she hoped it looked unintentional anyway. "Do you think I have pleased the demons enough that they will allow me to keep my life?"

When he didn't answer at once, she glanced at him and caught him staring at her finger as it flicked the ring.

He looked away. "They are pleased. Annomiz was not happy that he couldn't fuck you more, but he concedes that, as a puny mortal, no more could be expected of you. You were wise to yield eagerly."

Mariel looked down, plucking at the ring. "I could not help myself. I knew nothing of the pleasures of the flesh when you took me from my home. I had always believed that people only excused their failings--that they did not try to control their baser urges. Perhaps I was right, because, knowing that my life depended upon yielding willingly, I did not really try not to feel pleasure. And now it is almost as if my body has a mind and will of its own. When they touch those places that give me the most pleasure, I burn with the need to find release until I can not think of anything else."

She heard him swallow convulsively.

"I do not want to die. If I had had a choice, I would never have chosen to become the possession of the seven demons. I would have chosen only to belong to one...."

She stopped herself before she said 'man', returning her attention to the ring. "I find the most pleasure when you possess me. I don't know why, only that I do."

He stood abruptly and dragged her to her feet. "We must go," he growled.

She helped him gather the few things he'd unpacked and followed him to the horse, standing quietly as he repacked the food, but leaning just close enough that his arm brushed her breast as he turned to lift her to the saddle. He stopped, watching the mound bounce.

Finally, he grasped her and lifted her onto the horse. Mounting behind her, he spurred the horse into a gallop.

She sat rigidly upright at first, but slowly began to lean back until she'd settled snugly against him. After a moment, his hand settled around her waist. She relaxed fully against him, satisfied that she'd made some progress, at least.

When they stopped to make camp for the night, he surprised her by removing the manacles. She had worn them so long her arms felt strangely light without them. She rubbed her chaffed wrists, smiling up at him. "Thank you."

His gaze flickered over her face, then dropped lower. After a moment, he rose and removed the bedroll, tossing it her. She untied it and spread it out next to the fire he'd built as he took the pack of food and the wine skin from the horse.

When she'd finished smoothing the bedding, she settled on it crossed legged.

Behsart stopped abruptly as she folded her legs, staring down at the clit ring that gleamed through the sheer fabric as it caught the light of the fire. After a moment, as if he was completely unaware of the lapse, he settled beside her and cut a portion of meat and bread and cheese for each of them. He stared at the fire while he ate.

Mariel fell into thought, wondering why he'd released her when he'd never done so before. She would've liked to think that he might be unbending, or offering her an opportunity to run, but she knew better. More likely, he was testing her and if she failed, she would deeply regret it.

When she'd finished eating, she brushed at the crumbs that had fallen into her lap and finally flapped the material of the robe, trying to shed them. Behsart was looking at her when she glanced toward him. She swallowed uneasily. "I need to relieve myself."

He studied her unblinkingly for several moments and finally nodded. "Do not make me come for you," he growled when she stood. "You will not like it."

She'd had no intention of trying anything. She wasn't stupid. It wouldn't take him ten minutes to run her down if he had been no more than a man. It was far less likely that she could escape a demon so easily.

The warning made her heart flutter uncomfortably, however.

She took care of her needs quickly and moved down to the stream, within his view, to bathe herself. Since she had nothing to dry herself, the robe stuck to her when she'd pulled it over her head once more.

It was a minor discomfort beside many others she'd endured since her journey had begun, however. She moved back toward the fire, drying herself and the thin fabric with the heat wafting up from it before she moved to the pallet. Behsart seized her wrist and jerked her toward him so that she fell across his lap. She stared at him wide eyed, her heart thundering in her ears.

After several unnerving moments, he released her. Rubbing her wrist, she moved meekly to the pallet and lay down, curling onto her side. He remained as he was, staring at the fire for some time. Finally, he rose and left.

She lay tensely after he'd gone, listening for sounds of movement that would tell her where he was, what he might be doing. Finally, she heard the splash of water and knew that he'd moved to the stream to bathe. The splashing stopped after a time and she listened for his approach. He halted nearby, merely standing for many minutes and she supposed he was drying himself at the fire as she had.

"Take it off."

Mariel rolled onto her back and discovered he'd come to stand over her. She stared up at him blankly.

"Now."

Without a word, she sat up, grasped the robe and pulled it over her head. When she had laid it aside, she saw that he had knelt at her feet. Grasping her ankles, he tipped her onto her back, pushed her thighs wide and buried his face against her pussy. She gasped at the ferocity of his assault on the tender flesh, feeling fire course through her. Within moments she was gasping for breath, quivering, jerking as bolts of pleasure stabbed through her. When her crisis caught her, he lifted her hips and thrust his tongue inside of her. She screamed at the keen sensations that tore through her.

Catching her arm, her dragged her upright and pulled her across his lap, thrusting into her. Heated delight surged through her still quaking channel at the invasion. She groaned, looping her arms around his neck as he guided her along the length of his shaft, thrusting upward and grinding against her clit each time she sheathed him to the hilt. Her muscles fisted tightly around him with each thrust until he began to groan, trembling as his body approached orgasm. Feeling his cock jerk as it neared ejaculation, Mariel's body shot toward the summit, erupting fierily even as he came.

He held her tightly as the tremors slowly dissipated, breathing harshly. Catching her hair, he dragged her head back and opened his mouth along her throat, sucking the tender flesh. After a few moments, she felt him growing hard inside of her once more. Twisting, he lay her down on her back and began the rhythm once more, moving slowly at first and then more quickly as his body began to reach toward the peak. As he began to shudder and jerk, he rolled onto his back, carrying her with him. Grasping her hips, he pushed her down on his cock, thrusting upward into her body until his seed spilled inside her once more.

She lay draped limply across him for a time, too sated to consider moving. When she finally gathered the energy to move off of him, however, he wrapped his arms tightly around her, holding her. She subsided and within moments passed into oblivion, his cock still firmly inside of her.

Chapter Nine

Mariel didn't quite know what to think of Behsart's behavior. Having resisted the temptation to possess her for so long, it began to seem as if he'd simply accepted the inevitability of it. Before, he'd been both angry and fearful when he'd lost the battle and yielded to his lust. This time, when they faced the worst demon of all, he behaved as if he did not care what the penalty of disobeying might be. Instead of trying to hide the fact that he'd fucked her, he spent the days of their journey taking her at every opportunity, sometimes stopping along the way only to do so.

She didn't object, even though, to her vast disappointment, she could see no sign of Cavan--and she didn't know what to think about that either.

She did begin to worry about the consequences, however.

If Efathziman was displeased with Behsart, would he not also be displeased with her? Would he destroy Behsart, freeing Cavan? Or would he destroy them both? Would he be displeased enough to demand her sacrifice after all, even though she had pleased the other demons and they were willing to allow her to keep her life?

She didn't try to question Behsart.

He remained so unconcerned she began to wonder if there was any chance that he'd decided he would not take her to the temple, if he'd made other plans.

She dismissed the thought almost as soon as it occurred to her, but it kept coming back as day after day passed and they did not reach the temple. After a time, she was able to put the fear from her mind for short periods of time, to simply enjoy his lovemaking, to allow herself to daydream about a future.

On the morning of the fifth day, her hopes were completely dashed. They topped a rise at the edge of the forest and, in the distance she saw the temple of the most dreaded demon, the Demon Efathziman, the man beast.

She glanced fearfully at Behsart. His face was grim, but otherwise she could tell nothing about his thoughts.

A shiver skated through her as he kneed the horse and set it into motion once more. Dread seemed to mount inside of her with every mile they covered until she began to feel cold and ill.

They reached the temple mid-morning. Again, Behsart left her with the priests and vanished. She was taken to the purifying pool and bathed, oiled, scraped and bathed again. When the priests had prepared her to receive, her hands were bound behind her back and a black hood lowered over her face.

The moment the thing fell over her face, blinding her, seeming almost to deafen her, as well, her blood ran cold with stark terror. She was only slightly reassured when she discovered that she could breathe without difficulty.

She'd been blindfolded when she was taken to Annomiz and she didn't want to know it the hood had been placed on her head for the same reason, or if this ordeal would be even worse.

It took an effort to keep from blubbering in terror when they lifted her and carried her to the chamber. The dread did not dissipate as she was set on her feet. Instead, her stomach tightened even more. Her hands were unbound. Gripping her wrists tightly, the priests led her a short distance and then turned her and pushed her back against something solid. Lifting her arms out to her sides, they clamped manacles around her wrists once more.

Despite her fear, puzzlement descended upon her when she realized that the 'wall' seemed to end somewhere along the middle of her back.

Hands gripped her legs just above her knees and her legs were lifted and spread wide. For many moments, she hung from her arms while something almost as wide as the length of her thighs was wrapped around them. It was tightened, lifting her thighs wider and higher. The pain in her shoulders eased, but she thought the pain in her thighs might have overshadowed it anyway. Fingers parted her nether lips. Something hot, moist, and faint rough penetrated the mouth of her sex, startling a reflexive jerk from her.

It was pushed slowly along her channel, almost as if it was exploring the cavity, until it touched her womb. After a few moments, it was withdrawn.

The tension went out of her as it was removed. A few moments passed and then she felt fingers parting her flesh once more. Again, something hot touched her. This time, however, it was smooth, rounded, large and solid. She gasped, panting as it was pushed inside of her, stopping a hair's breadth from her womb.

It was so hot that for the first few seconds after it was pushed inside of her, fear surged through her that it would begin to burn. To her relief, although it felt hot inside of her, still there was no discomfort from the heat of it. Neither was it so large as to cause her pain, although the rigidity of it did produce some discomfort.

She was not reassured, not when it was so reminiscent of her previous experience. She had thought her fears groundless, despite the mask, when they had taken her and pinioned her to the wall--or whatever it was that she was bound to. They had forced an object inside of her much like the priests had at the temple of the stone demon, however.

She knew the next would be bigger and the one after than larger still. She tried not to think about the possibility that she had angered the demons and that they might decide to sacrifice her by splitting her body on a stone cock.

Something hot, moist and faintly rough raked over the skin of her leg, sending a shock wave through her. It felt much like a tongue, except rougher, and longer. In an almost leisurely manner, it 'licked' her belly. Moving upward, it stroked first one breast and then the other, making her nipples pebble painfully and stand erect. Heat and moisture gathered in her sex as it continued to stroke her breasts, alternating between them. Within a few minutes, she was moaning and panting with pleasure instead of fear. The pleasure escalated rapidly until she began to squirm and shudder, the muscles of her passage tightening spasmodically around the stone cock. She struggled harder and harder to drag in enough air into her lungs as the tension inside of her approached its peak.

Abruptly, sharp teeth fastened over one breast, digging in almost painfully, and a mouth closed around her, sucking so hard it flung her over the precipice into scalding, mind drugging ecstasy. When she'd ceased to shudder and gasp hoarsely, the mouth was withdrawn.

Slowly, the shaft was pulled from her body.

The warm of her release vanished as abruptly as the shaft was pulled from her for she knew her ordeal had only just begun. She waited in tense dread for the next assault upon her senses.

When her body had cooled completely, she felt fingers tugging at the lips of her sex. A heated, round-tipped shaft spread the mouth of her channel. Her belly clenched in resistance as it was pushed deeply inside of her. After a few moments, the tongue began stroking her flesh again, bringing her to heat. This time, however, instead of feeling a mouth and sharp teeth on her breast as she began to tremble with release, fingers pulled her nether lips back and she felt the hot, rough stroke of the tongue on her clit. The fourth stroke brought her to a shattering orgasm.

Weak as she was after two hard climaxes, dread filled her when she felt the shaft removed. A few moments later, she was stretched wide to receive an even larger shaft. She panted as it was forced slowly inside of her, stretching her until her muscles quivered and cramped painfully around it. The rough stroking of the tongue began almost at once. Her body responded with reluctance, tense from the probing shaft. The caresses became more and more insistent, demanding a response. The stroking of the tongue ceased and her breasts were sucked into a hot mouth, teased unmercifully until her body began to quake in nearly painful spasms around the hard lance stretching her passage.

She was left to rest while her body cooled. All too soon, she felt the touch on her sex again. She fought the suffocating terror that filled her as she felt the size of the thing they wedged into her opening, telling herself it was no bigger than the stone demon's cock, that her body would adjust.

She didn't know whether it was or not, but she realized very quickly that if it wasn't, she'd forgotten more of the experience than she realized. She was weeping by the time they'd forced it inside of her.

Despite the pain, relief filled her as the manacles were removed from her wrists, for she knew, hoped, it meant that she would not have to endure having anything bigger forced inside of her. A moment later, her thighs were released and her legs lowered. As the weight of her body shoved the enormous thing more deeply inside of her, she uttered a choked gasp.

Her feet touched--nothing. Her whole body rested on the hard shaft as her arms were bent behind her back and her wrists bound together and for many moments her mind was so clouded with red hot pain that she could not even think. As the pain began to subside, she realized her buttocks were resting on something hot and covered with hair.

She was not even vaguely curious to know what it was, however. She could think of nothing but the huge, hot thing inside of her, stretching her to the point of pain until she could only pant for breath, couldn't seem to fill her lungs. So long as she remained perfectly still, her body merely pulsed and throbbed of the edge of pain. The slightest shifting dug the thing deeper and sent a new wave of agony through her.

When the stroking began, she fought to close her mind from it. After a few minutes, however, the tenor of the caresses changed to a demand. The sharp teeth clamped over her flesh, bearing down just hard enough to promise suffering if she resisted. Her nipples were stimulated with the heat and adhesion of a hot mouth, the abrasion of the rough tongue until she began to pant and moan with rising need and moisture flooded her passage.

The need rose and fell, climbing until she felt close to release, then dropping from under her when the muscles of her sex clamped painfully around the thing that yielded not at all.

The fondling moved down her belly. The fleshy lips of her sex were pulled back and the tongue began stroking her clit. She could not hold back the rising tide of fire inside of her then. Within moments, her body was scaling the heights, flying off the edge in a wracking orgasm that drew a sharp cry from her throat.

She'd barely caught her breath when the stroking began again, wringing a response from her, forcing her body to explode in ecstasy. Even as the last tremors of release shuttered through her, it began again.

She began to hope for unconsciousness as her body was wracked over and over by climactic seizures until she was exhausted, trembling all over. It did not come to her rescue, but weariness eventually did. When she'd reached the point where her body simply ceased to respond with more than a twitch, she was pulled from the hard shaft and borne away.

The hood was removed when she had been taken to a small cell. She was left to attend her needs and rest. She managed to choke down a few bites of the food that was left for her, but she felt no hunger, only complete and utter exhaustion. Her entire body throbbed. Her sex pounded harder, clenching each time her mind settled on the memory of that enormous thing that she'd been impaled on. Despite that, exhaustion held the upper hand and she slept. She was rested when they came for her again, but tired still.

The hood was placed over her head once more when she'd been prepared and she was taken to the offering chamber, bound as she had been the day before. She should have learned long since that the only thing that she could count on, ultimately, was that she couldn't count on anything. No matter how similar her ordeal began, it always differed from what she expected.

Dread instantly filled her when they placed the hood on her head, but so, too, did the half formed thought that tremendous, stone cock was something she would not have to face at once. She was bound just as she had been the day before.

She began to get her first inkling that it would not be the same when her sex was swathed with something slick... and still she expected they would allow her to gradually accept a larger and larger shaft. Instead, when her flesh was pulled back, the frighteningly huge thing was forced into the opening, the pressure relentless until she had been impaled on it to the root. The lubricant helped them force it inside of her. It did nothing to help her body adjust to the massive size of it.

She was sobbing by the time they ceased to push it into her, her body spasming painfully around it. The pain subsided after a few moments, because a numbing heat that seemed to radiate outward in every direction and finally began to leave her as the hot stroke of the tongue moved over her body.

Tortuous hours seemed to pass in a heated, mind numbing haze. She came to dread the touch of that rough tongue, the sharp teeth and hot mouth almost as much as the thing inside of her, for they forced her to climax over and over again and each time she did the pitch of rapture was excruciating.

When she passed the point of exhaustion, she was left pinioned on the shaft. All too soon, they began anew to torment her. She realized after a while that the hood itself seemed to prevent her from blacking out completely. Before, when she would begin to gasp air in really quickly, blackness would begin to crowd in around her. Now, no matter how desperately she gasped, oblivion eluded her.

That was enough in itself to make her want to rip it away.

In time, it filtered through the haze of her exhaustion that she had not summoned the demon Efathziman as she had Annomiz, if, in fact, she was impaled on the cock of Efathziman as she had been on that of Annomiz.

Had he simply decided not to take the offering? Had she failed to please him?

Fear tickled at the back of her mind, but she was in far too much distress for it to overtake her. When she had rested a second time, they began again and she felt like weeping. Her body was no longer her own, however. It responded with or without her consent, no matter how tired she grew, no matter how sated she was. Her body responded to the determined stimulus even when she thought she couldn't anymore.

At last she reached the point where her throat was so raw from screaming that she couldn't even make sound anymore, when her body had climaxed until it merely quivered. The torment stopped. The hood was removed. Slowly, as her bindings were released, her eyes adjusted to the light in the room.

Beneath her was the man beast, Efathziman, not a likeness wrought from stone, the beast himself. His lower body was that of a ram, his upper body that of a man.

His head was a lion's head.

He grinned at her and sat up. Wrapping his arms around her, he thrust his tongue from his mouth and dragged it along the side of her neck. A shiver went through her as she felt the roughness of it, her mind simply refusing to accept for many moments that she had been pinned astride him for nigh two days, that it had been his mouth, his tongue--his cock that had brought her to such ecstasy that she'd thought she would die of it.

After a moment, he lifted her from his cock, caught her against his chest and stood. She was too weak with exhaustion even to feel fear. She hung limply in his arms as he strode across the chamber. When he stopped, she glanced around vaguely, wondering why.

Behsart, she saw, was chained to the wall so that he could watch as Efathziman pleasured himself with her--as Efathziman dragged cries of pleasure from her. For an instant, she thought she saw a flicker of rage and hate in his eyes as he faced Efathziman, but it was gone so quickly she wasn't certain of it.

"Go to the Castle Valdamer and prepare for us. I will bring her when I am done with her," Efathziman growled.

To Mariel's relief, she fainted dead away.

She swam upward toward awareness after a time, but she fought it until she sank into exhausted slumber. When finally she awoke, she saw that she was staring up at a vaulted ceiling. She lay still, allowing her gaze to encompass the room she found herself in.

It looked like a cavernous bedchamber. She was lying upon a bed.

She felt a tug on her clit and nipple rings and glanced down to discover a chain had been treaded through them once more. Her gaze followed the chain to the hand that held it. Efathziman was studying her through narrowed, feline eyes. "Come here, my pretty, and mount me," he said in a rumbling growl.

Mariel swallowed convulsively, glancing at his erect cock and the gleaming wetness that coated it. Finally, she rolled over, crawling to him on her knees. Her heart was in her throat as she studied the monolith, trying to figure out how, and if, she could take it inside of her when it had been forced inside of her before. Finally, she simply straddled his belly. He lifted her, perching her on top of it.

She put her fingers between her legs, spreading herself so that he could push the head of his cock into the mouth of her passage. Her body objected, but the slickness coating his shaft, and the pressure as he bore down on her defied the resistance. She squeezed her eyes shut as he seemed to fill her beyond capacity, panting as she tried to catch her breath when he'd ceased at last to force her over his rigid member and she'd sank fully upon him.

Finally, as the discomfort eased, she opened her eyes. She saw that he was watching her expectantly. When she did not move at once, he tugged on the chain. Dragging in a shuddering breath, she lifted away from him and pushed down again. His eyes began to glaze with pleasure as she moved over him. After a moment, he sat up, flicking at one of her nipple rings. A shaft of pleasure arched through her at the touch and her muscles clenched around his hard shaft.

"These are pretty things," he murmured, flicking at the other ring. "How clever of Bileezal to adorn our pretties."

His mouth covered her entire breast. She jerked reflexively as she felt the prick of his sharp teeth, but as his mouth closed around her breast and he began to suck her, her entire focus became centered on the pleasure. She began to move up and down his shaft faster as her body heated toward culmination, spurred by his thorough attention to first one breast and then the other.

Suddenly, she felt his cock jerk. The movement sent her over the edge. He growled a long, rumbling growl as his body convulsed with ecstasy. He lay back when the shudders abated, studying her once more through narrowed eyes. Mariel held herself upright with an effort, struggling to catch her breath.

His hands moved from her hips to her thighs, stroking them for several moments before he skated his hands upward, following the curve of her hips and waist until he had cupped her breasts. He kneaded them for several moments before he moved his hands to her back. Slipping one down to her buttocks, he sat up, turned and laid her on the bed.

Gripping her hips, he began to pump his cock in and out of her, slowly at first, but quickly increasing the pace until he was slamming into her painfully. She came, uttering a hoarse cry. He did not. He continued to pump into her until her body convulsed yet again before he followed her.

To her relief, he pulled his cock from her.

"Rest," he growled. "I would not like to break my pretty so soon."

If she hadn't been so exhausted, the command would have terrorized her, but she was well beyond fear. Sometime later, as she drifted toward awareness once more, it was with the feel of his tongue in her cunt. Reflexively, she tried to close her legs. He placed his hands on her thighs, holding them against the bed, and continued to lap at the walls of her passage as if feeding off of her. Her belly clenched at the rough stroke of his tongue. It brought her to crisis within moments, but she discovered very quickly that that hadn't been the object. He continued to lap at her until she would've screamed if she'd been able to force the noise past her raw throat. She came again. Her body had already begun to quake in a third wracking climax when he withdrew his tongue from her passage and fastened his mouth over her clit, sucking and lathing it with his rough tongue. He lingered over it, feasting off of her until her body was convulsing almost endlessly and she blacked out from the overload to her senses.

She knew she could not have been unconscious more than a few moments, for when she became aware again, she felt his tongue lathing her thighs. Slowly, he worked his way up her body, over her belly and breasts and when he was satisfied, he worked his way down again.

Apparently, he liked the taste of her cunt best. He began lapping at it once more, lifting her hips off of the bed to give himself better access. After a while, when Mariel had begun to think she would die if he didn't stop, and to pray for it, he withdrew with obvious reluctance and allowed her to drift away again.

Days, she knew, passed. She had little conception of time when she spent almost every waking moment in a haze of desire, but she knew that it must be days. She didn't know whether to be glad or sorry that Efathziman was, very obviously, far more interested in tasting her than mounting her. Occasionally, he would sprawl out on his back, tug her over to him with the chain through her rings and command her to mount him and ride him until he came. Sometimes, he would press her into the bed and pound his huge cock into her until she thought he would split her in two.

Mostly, he was content to run his tongue inside of her cunt and lap her until she was mindless.

He showed no sign of tiring of playing with her.

Finally, however, he seemed to rouse himself to business and Mariel was prepared by the temple attendants to depart the temple.

Fear had been the constant companion of her dreams when she did not sleep the sleep of the deeply exhausted-- which she had most of the time. Her waking hours had been so filled with carnality that she'd had no mind for thought.

It wasn't until they bathed her and dressed her in a crystal blue robe that she was cognizant enough of her situation for real terror to set in. She only vaguely recalled that Efathziman had sent Behsart away, but it jolted through her with absolute clarity the instant she was escorted from the temple and saw that Efathziman was mounted on the horse that awaited her. Around him, six brawny priests, wearing hoods and loincloths and nothing else, sat on six black horses. They reminded her strongly of the six from the Temple of Demon Raezitath, but as she'd never seen their faces she had no idea if it was the same men or not.

Efathziman drew her up onto his lap when the priests lifted her up to him. Turning the horse, he kicked it into motion and they quickly left the small village behind.

The journey took three days. Mariel searched frantically for a possibility of escape now that she no longer had even a prayer of help from Behsart. None was presented to her. She was not bound, but Efathziman saw no reason not to enjoy her body. Each night when they made camp, he spread her on the pallet and lapped at her cunt until she was completely insensible. When she woke each morning, he was sprawled possessively over her body.

The Castle of Valdamer stood on a rocky crag. Built of the same stone as the mountain it topped, it was some time before she realized the regularity of the formations denoted a manmade structure. She felt ill with fear when the party turned their horses upon the winding road that led up to the castle.

The gates opened as they reached them, but as they road into the bailey, Mariel saw no sign of a living soul. The entire castle had the feel of a mausoleum, and that sense did not vanish as they entered the great hall.

She was led away by the six priests as they crossed the great hall, up a winding stone stair to a tower at the top of the keep. The room was sparsely furnished, but contained a huge bed, a chamber pot, a table with a pitcher and bowl.

Four narrow windows looked out at the view surrounding the tower, but each was covered with iron bars. The priests removed her gown, pushed her onto the bed and tied her spread eagle to the posts. When they were satisfied, they left again.

She could not fathom why she'd been bound. She couldn't possibly escape. If she'd wanted to fling herself from the tower, she couldn't... and she certainly had no desire to. Facing a knife could not be worse that falling so far and being crushed.

The stout door had been bolted from the outside.

When the sun sank low on the horizon and shadows began to crawl across the floor, the Demon Sheenigan appeared at the foot of the bed. She stared at the demon in horror for many moments, realizing belatedly why she'd been bound.

Climbing onto the bed with her, he pleasured himself on her until she was too weary to respond and then vanished.

When she woke, the room was filled with light and she found that she'd been freed. She spent most of the day pacing the room anxiously. As evening approached, the six priests returned and bound her once more, this time on her hands and knees. She wasn't aware that the Demon Trihern had appeared until she felt the bed dip. Her legs were pushed wider and he pushed his three pronged cock into her ass and her pussy. The third raked along her cleft as he fucked her, his appetite seemingly insatiable. Almost the moment he would come, he would begin all over again.

One by one, she was visited each night by one of the seven demons, who had gathered their power to appear in physical form.

On the seventh day, Efathziman came to her.

When two days passed and none of the demons appeared to take their pleasure again, she realized she had reached the time that she had dreaded since she had been taken from her home. She felt almost calm when the six priests came for her, bathed her and dressed her in a pale golden robe, for it had finally occurred to her that, with or without her mortal body, the demons had claimed her. They would not let her go.

She was led down the winding stairs, and then down a short corridor to another set of stairs that led from the main level of the castle, until she knew they must be in the bowels of the earth. Flickering torches lined the walls of the vast chamber they reached at the foot of the stone stairs. In the center was an altar. She was led to it and laid upon it on her back and bound hand and foot.

The six priests who had escorted her moved to positions at the edge of a circle paved into the floor with black stones. Behind them stood six robed, hooded priests. Each wore the color of the temple they represented.

Silence reigned for perhaps a minute. A few moments later, a High Priest, wearing a golden robe entered, moved to the side of the altar and lifted his arms. She saw when he lifted his arms that he was holding a dagger perhaps twelve inches long. The blade was jagged, like a thunder bolt, and had been carved from crystal.

At his signal, the drums began to beat. The priests began to chant, calling forth the demons by name. Slowly, one by one, the demons began to materialize. With the exception of Annomiz and Efathziman, they were faint and indistinct at first. As they became more solid in appearance, they crowded around the ends of the altar and the side facing the High Priest, though their gazes were trained upon her avidly.

Her calm slowly evaporated. Fear began to gather in her belly as Mariel stared up at them, meeting each gaze in turn, seeing nothing in their gazes beyond lust.

The drumming stopped. The chanting priests fell silent. The High Priest lifted the blade toward the ceiling. Fire and light flowed from it, as if it were a torch rather than a cold crystal.

"Most dreaded demons--Bileezal, Efathziman, Hezifath, Sheenigan, Annomiz Raezitath, Trihern--I, Behsart, who are we, give you your bride, Lady Mariel Champlain--NOW!"

Mariel squeezed her eyes closed as she saw the blade slamming down toward her body. The sound of shattering crystal sent a jolt through her and her eyes flew wide. Time seemed to have slowed to a crawl.

As she looked around the room, without comprehension she saw the robed priests slowly withdrawing the knives they held from the bodies of the six massive priests who had escorted her to the castle, saw bright red blood begin to flow down their chests from the gaping grin carved into their throats, watched blankly as they began to sink slowly toward the stone floor.

Turning her head, she looked up at the demons surrounding her. On their faces, she saw shocked disbelief and dawning rage. Finally, she glanced toward the priest, staring at the broken sacrificial knife for several moments before she looked up at him.

He had tossed the hood of his robe back, but it was not Behsart who stood above her... not the one that she had come to think of as Cavan, the man held hostage in his body by the demon Behsart.

Instead, she saw a horned demon, more man than beast, but most certainly not a mortal man. Hair, black as night, streamed around his broad, muscular chest and shoulders.

His face was Cavan's.

Abruptly, the howls and screams of the demons filled her ears until she thought she would be deafened, drawing her curious gaze from the demon priest. As she turned her head to look at them, she saw that they had grown faint, like wraiths, watched as their forms thinned to vapor and finally vanished.

She looked up at the High Priest as he dropped the shattered blade.

"I vanquish you!" he roared, lifting his arms in triumph.

When the echoes of his roar had died, he looked down at her for several moments, his eyes narrowed, speculative. "I, Demon Valdamer, claim Lady Mariel Champlain as my bride," Cavan growled.

Chapter Ten

Mariel was too stunned and confused, her mind too chaotic even to grasp what had happened. She stared at Cavan mutely as he released her. Scooping her into his arms, he turned, crossed the room and ascended the stairs with her. He did not stop when they reached the ground floor. Instead, he strode to the second set of stairs and ascended them to the second floor. Reaching the main corridor, he strode down the length of it and entered a vast, opulent bed chamber.

A huge four posted bed stood in the center of the room. He strode toward it and laid her gently on the mattress, then sprawled out beside her on his side, his head propped in his hand, a faint smile playing about his lips.

"Where are the demons?" Mariel asked hoarsely.

"I… you and I have banished them to their dark world. They will not trouble us again."

She didn't know whether to believe him or not, but they had certainly vanished. She frowned, studying him carefully, wondering if her eyes had played tricks on her before, for now he looked as he always had. "You said you were a demon."

"I am."

Mariel swallowed with an effort. "But… you said you were Lord Valdamer."

"I am." His eyes had begun to gleam with suppressed laughter.

As tempting as he looked, Mariel glared at him. She had spent months in terror, culminating in the near sacrifice of her body. She was too confused to rest easy, too afraid that it wasn't over to release her fear.

She saw no humor in the fact that she was so thoroughly confused.

Chuckling at the look on her face, he wrapped his arms around her and dragged her half across his chest, stroking her back soothingly. "It's over. I give you my word. I'm sorry I frightened you, but there was no other way."

He pulled away slightly, staring down at her. "Many years ago, I came to take Daeksould from Lord Belean. It wasn't until I had slain him, however, that I realized it was not he who ruled, but the seven dark demons he had summoned forth to give him power.

He frowned, then shrugged wryly. "Perhaps I would have been arrogant enough to have tried anyway, but I did not know, and I was caught off guard. They overpowered me and again took control of Daeksould--this time through me. For many years we have battled and I had begun to despair that I would find a way to vanquish them. For the most part, the best that I could do was to keep them from the sacrifices that made them stronger.

"When your father came to me to sell you, he brought your likeness to me and I sensed an interest in Behsart that led me to believe that you were the strength I needed to vanquish them."

"It was Behsart who held you then?"

He frowned. "It is hard to explain to a mortal. Behsart was a part of the others. Thus, the name and that is also why he was the weakest of them. I allowed them to believe that he kept me chained, because I knew that if they doubted it they would bind me more tightly."

"He told me you were Cavan, Lord of Reugal."

"I am--Lord of Reugal and also of Daeksould--now."

Mariel frowned. "I don't understand how you thought sacrificing me would weaken them if it didn't before."

"I never intended to sacrifice you. I could not have stopped them once they decided to take you. I did not have the power to do so."

"You said you'd stopped the others," she said accusingly.

He frowned at her, obviously striving for patience. "They did not lust for the others. It was not that difficult to pander to their arrogance and convince them they had no need for more virgin sacrifices. They had no use for the others, beyond consuming their spirits, drawing strength from it. You, they lusted for. They would have to expend energy to have you and once they had decided that they would have you, I could not prevent it. I had not expected that you would be as brave, clever and--lusty as you were."

Mariel reddened. "I...uh... I."

He smiled faintly, brushing the backs of his fingers over her cheek. "I am not complaining. Their lust for you consumed them. If you had not responded, they would not have been so enthralled with you that they did not even notice how weak they were growing. I am certainly not complaining on my own account."

His arrogance irritated her. She frowned. "You are assuming that I am yours."

His expression changed instantly. "Make no mistake, my love, you are."

Mariel felt a little prick of uneasiness, but the truth was she didn't really object. After a moment, she sighed. "I was not courted," she complained.

He chuckled. "I am more than willing to court you-- however you wish to be courted."

Mariel rolled her eyes. Men were never romantic. If you had to instruct them on courting you, there was little point in it.

He hooked his finger beneath her chin and forced her to look up at him. "Tell me--of all the things that you have experienced, which pleased you most?" he asked huskily.

Mariel reddened. That wasn't exactly what she'd had in mind, but she supposed since they'd honeymooned most of the way to the Castle Valdamer, there wasn't much point in weeping over the courtship she'd missed. In any case, she couldn't help but be intrigued by his claim. "You could... do that?" she asked hesitantly.

He gave her an arrogant look. Abruptly, he sat up, hooked his finger in the thin fabric of the robe and ripped it down the center from the neck to her crotch. "I am the benign Demon Valdamer. Anything a dark demon can do, I can do better."

The End

Printed in the United States
61661LVS00001B/84